Meet me in Tahiti

GEORGIA TOFFOLO

CANARY STREET PRESS

**CANARY
STREET
PRESS™**

Recycling programs
for this product may
not exist in your area.

ISBN-13: 978-1-335-45818-6

Meet Me in Tahiti

First published in 2021 by Mills & Boon, an imprint of HarperCollins Publishers Ltd. This edition published in 2024 with revised text.

Copyright © 2021 by Georgia Toffolo

With thanks to Avril Tremayne

Copyright © 2024 by Georgia Toffolo, revised text edition.

For questions and comments about the quality of this book, please contact us at CustomerService@Harlequin.com.

Canary Street Press
22 Adelaide St. West, 41st Floor
Toronto, Ontario M5H 4E3, Canada
CanaryStPress.com

Printed in U.S.A.

Also by Georgia Toffolo

Meet Me in London
Meet Me at the Wedding

To the risk takers and boundary breakers at Whizz-Kidz who constantly remind me anything is possible.

one

ZOE TAYLER'S MOBILE PHONE PINGED, ALERTING her to an incoming email.

Her fingers froze on her computer keyboard.

She knew that email would be from mum.dad@taylers.co.uk. Yes, Selena and Noel Tayler not only owned a domain name, they also had a dedicated address for corresponding with their only child. That was how serious they were about keeping a not-so-proverbial eye on her.

Whenever Zoe was on an international job her parents' email obsession ratcheted up to frenzy level—particularly on day one, which brought an avalanche. Only gradually did the frequency taper off in the ensuing days, easing fraction by fraction with each of Zoe's instantly returned *I'm fine no need to worry* replies.

Today—sigh—was day one. This would be their fourth email of the day, and the just-roll-with-it process of allaying their myriad concerns lay depressingly ahead of her.

It was noon in French Polynesia, which made it 11 p.m. in England. There should be time for only one more communique before her parents went to bed, so within the hour she should be free.

Unless...

Well, unless she decided not to answer this one. In which case she could be free immediately.

Her fingers twitched on the keyboard as the idea of going off-the-grid took hold.

And then she laughed.

Futile to hope her parents would shrug their shoulders, assume she was fine and go to bed. The more likely scenario was that they'd call Zoe's mobile, and keep calling, and when Zoe didn't answer (because answering would render her little rebellion redundant) they'd fret over what ills might have befallen her—everything from a fever-inducing cold caught during her plane trip to her lying unconscious on the floor with a cracked skull. Within twenty-four hours they'd be knocking on her bungalow door with an ambulance on standby.

Yeah, hard no to that!

She leaned back in her chair, rubbing her hands up and down her thighs to remind herself why her parents needed to know she was all right.

Of course she was going to reply.

"Fight your big battles to the death but don't sweat the scrappy skirmishes if you want to win the long war," she murmured, and her hands abruptly stopped moving as she realized what she'd said. Not that those words didn't suit the situation, but it shocked her that she could recite them—verbatim—after...what...twelve years?

Yes, it had been twelve years since Finn Doherty had said those words to her that idyllic summer they'd worked together at the Crab Shack in Hawke's Cove.

Her parents hadn't wanted her to take the job at the Shack;

hadn't seen the need for it given the generous allowance they gave her. But all of her friends had summer jobs lined up and she'd pleaded, and her BFFs had pleaded, and even Ewan, the owner of the Crab Shack, had pleaded (*such* a softie), and at last she'd been given the OK to be just like every other sixteen-year-old in the village.

Unfortunately, a week into the job she'd had a wisdom tooth out—typical that she'd get her wisdom teeth earlier than any other kid *and* that one of them would be impacted. (Seriously, it was like the universe had it in for her!) Her parents, true to form, had acted like she was about to be measured for her coffin and it had taken two days in bed and an extra day of frantic begging before Zoe was allowed to return to work.

But her parents' capitulation had come at a price: constant phone calls.

After their eighth call on her first day back, Zoe had decided that giving up the job was preferable to having every Shack employee lining up to throttle her. She'd hurried out to the storeroom, phone gripped in one hand, blinking tears away because she didn't cry, *ever*, when Finn had...well, materialized.

He'd looked at the phone, at her face, and understood the situation instantly. That was when he'd said those words to her. And then he'd told her that the big battle had been getting her parents to agree to the job, but the phone calls? Pfft, they were nothing.

And just like that, the phone calls had ceased to matter. So she'd called her parents, right there in front of Finn, and explained that if she didn't answer a call immediately it didn't mean she was being rushed to hospital, only that she was busy, and in such cases she'd call them back within half an hour, cross-her-heart-hope-not-to-die. Then she'd set the phone to vibrate, and whenever it had buzzed in the back pocket of her jeans, she'd smiled at Finn and he'd smiled back, sharing the secret. And over the next few days the calls had tapered off.

The way the emails she was currently dealing with always did eventually.

So deal with it, Zoe. The sooner you deal, the sooner you're free.

She switched windows on her computer. For long responses—and she was determined to compose a long one, knocking off every possible issue she could think of as a forestalling tactic—she preferred keyboard typing to tapping on her phone.

She couldn't imagine what there was left for them to warn her about but when she opened the message she saw they'd found something: Cristina, Zoe's regular travel companion.

The email was oh-so-carefully worded; this wasn't a hill her parents were prepared to die on lest Zoe decide no more travel companion *at all*, but nevertheless the dictates were clear: Zoe should remember Cristina was there to help. It was fine for Cristina to enjoy herself, and nobody expected her to hover over Zoe twenty-four hours a day, but Zoe shouldn't see it as an imposition to request Cristina's assistance whenever she needed it. Cristina was stronger than Zoe as well as being a trained nurse, so Zoe shouldn't insist on doing all those transfers to and from her chair herself all the time.

The easy way to head this particular concern off at the pass was to let her parents know that Cristina had become as tediously dedicated to Zoe's well-being as they were, to the point where Zoe had to send her on made-up errands to win herself some breathing space. Today, for example, Zoe had asked her to carry out a completely unnecessary accessibility check of the entire Poerava resort. Problem was, though, if she told her parents Cristina had been afflicted with the protect-Zoe-Tayler-at-all-costs disease they'd probably kick off a campaign to get Zoe to hire Cristina as a permanent live-in assistant.

Not! Happening!

Zoe wished she knew what she did that made people want to stand guard over her so she could stop doing it. It happened to everyone who came into her life sooner or later, and as for those who'd known her from her cradle?

Well, gah! Just…*gah!*

Yes, three miscarriages before Zoe was born had conferred "precious" status on Zoe. Yes, Zoe had suffered all the health issues associated with being premature. Yes, Zoe had been a sickly child, in and out of hospital with bronchiolitis. But—ginormous, important BUT—by the age of eleven she'd been as hardy as any kid in the village. Small, yes, but perfectly formed and perfectly fit. And yet a slight breeze sent half the village running for her coat. A yawn and the other half would urge her to rest. A scratch on her arm and she'd be fending off offers to drive her to the hospital. As though she were a piece of delicate porcelain teetering on the edge of a cliff and it was everyone's collective responsibility to stop her going over.

Thank God for her best friends, Victoria, Malie and Lily, who treated her like they treated each other: no fuss, no concessions, just love. Without them, Zoe would have spent the span of her life from primary school to coming-of-age peering through the windows of her parents' clifftop mansion—or as the girls called it "Palace de Prison"—at everyone else frolicking on the beach below.

Zoe smiled around a sigh, as she always did when thinking of her friends. She depended on the girls in a way she never let herself depend on anyone else. It didn't feel like a weakness to need them, to lean on them when the going got tough. They had each other's back, always. Knew each other's frailties and strengths. Knew each other's scars. Were always there for each other—whether it was a quick phone call between two of them or an all-in session via video conference.

Zoe's visit home last Christmas had come about after one of those video calls. It hadn't been easy, going back to Hawke's Cove. But Victoria had been struggling over a decision that might have torn her from the man she loved (her now-fiancé

Oliver Russell) and so Zoe had sucked it up and joined Lily and Malie on a surprise visit. They had a codename for those big deals—the scared-to-death and flying-high ones, the heartbreaks and exaltations, the ones that meant you dropped everything to be there: the Lost Hours.

Zoe was proud of the fact that she'd been the one to inspire that codename. They'd taken a trip to Ibiza to celebrate Victoria's birthday and because V was the last of them to turn eighteen it was all-out-for-freedom that week. So all-out Zoe had managed to get lost at a foam party. One moment they'd been dancing as a group, the next the foam had gone right over Zoe's head—she was the shortest, at just over five feet—and pandemonium had apparently ensued as Victoria, Malie and Lily had searched for her for the next three hours. They'd been scared out of their wits and checked her over as thoroughly as a doctor when she'd resurfaced, despite Zoe reassuring them that she hadn't been kidnapped or drugged or conked on the head. Eventually they'd let the matter rest—perhaps reading the gleam of mischief in Zoe's eyes that told them she was thrilled at having had a secret adventure.

It had been two months before the summer ball that would mark the end of school, and with the daring still racing through her blood Zoe had made the decision then and there that the ball would be a turning point, kick-starting a new life.

Careful what you wish for.

That night had certainly kick-started a new life. A new life for all of them. Just not in a way anyone could have anticipated.

Which she was not going to think about now. She was going to think only positive thoughts. As though by magic, her phone lit up.

Video call.

Lily.

Zoe smiled as she hit the button to accept. "Hey!" she said. "It's close to midnight over there! Do you miss me that much?"

Lily opened her mouth…then closed it.

"Lily?" Zoe said, alarmed at the distraught look on her friend's face.

Lily opened her mouth again…and burst into tears.

"Lily!" Zoe clutched the phone so tightly in her hand she was in danger of cracking the case. "Tell me, *tell* me what it is!"

"Sorry, *sorry!*" Lily wiped furiously at her eyes. "It's just… Blake." A sob escaped her, but Zoe could see her pulling it all together, the way she always did. "H-he's d-dead."

"Oh Lily! *Lils!* I'm so, so sorry. Do you need me to come? I will, you know I will."

Lily shook her head furiously. "You hate Hawke's Cove."

"This isn't about Hawke's Cove, it's about you."

"You're on a job."

"I'm a fill-in, nothing more. It's a *junket*. Like…blerrgh. You know I don't do those."

A ghost of a smile from Lily. "And yet there you are."

"Meh!" Zoe tossed in nonchalantly. "I like the guy who asked me to do it, that's the only reason."

"As in *like*?"

"As in *no!* Geez! Rolf lives in Germany. It's an online friendship, nothing more. Let's leave the romance to V and Devil, shall we? On the subject of which, this is Lost Hours business. They're joining us, right?"

And just like that, Lily was crying again. "I was going to dial them in but I…I mean, they're both…you know, all loved up with Oliver and Todd. But Mum's not here and I just…I feel kind of lost, and I knew you were in a time-friendly zone and…oh, I don't know what to do!"

OK, sound the alarm! Lily *lost*? Not knowing what to do? It. Did. Not. Com. Pute.

"Just hold on, I'll conference in V and Devil and we can all cry together."

"You never cry. And you wouldn't have to even if you did. You barely knew him."

"I'll cry for you like a professional mourner. And Malie will cry for real. You know she adored him almost as much as you." She started tapping at her phone.

"Not V!" Lily said suddenly. "I mean, the Hawkesbury Estate!"

"The estate? I don't see what that has to do with V. Unless it's a will thing? But how could that— OK, what am I not getting?"

"Not a will thing, a wedding venue thing. Not that there's going to be a problem, because I won't let anything go wrong, but she might worry."

"Er…if you think the death of the richest man in Hawke's Cove can be kept a secret for more than an hour you're dreaming. Or is Mrs. Whittaker dead too? 'Cause I'll bet she's already got the megaphone out."

"Oh. I just… I'm not thinking."

"Not thinking? You? You're scaring me with that kind of talk! Anyway, Victoria isn't going to give a damn about her wedding!"

"Victoria certainly is going to give a damn about her wedding," Victoria said, laughing as she joined the call.

At which point Lily burst into tears again.

"Or…maybe…not?" Victoria said. "What's going on?"

"Blake Hawkesbury's dead," Zoe explained.

"WHAT?" Malie said, announcing herself.

"Today," Lily said, and kept on crying. "It happened today."

"And Lily's mum's out of town," Zoe said, imbuing the phrase with as much meaning as she could. Subtext: *someone has to get there fast!*

"Right, I'm coming," Malie said, and actually jumped to her feet.

"What about Todd?" Lily sniffled.

"We're not joined at the hip, you know."

Lily shook her head, adamant. "No, you can't come, you've got that surf competition coming up."

"There'll be other competitions," Malie said, and then abruptly started crying too. "But there was only one B-B—" But she choked, and couldn't continue.

She didn't have to. Everyone knew Blake Hawkesbury had loaned Malie the money she'd needed to flee Hawke's Cove after the accident. Maybe he'd done that out of a sense of responsibility—it had been his only son Henry's girlfriend, Claudia, driving the car that night—but Zoe had always thought it was simply because he was kind. The deep down type of kind. To all of them. Especially Lily, though, to whom he'd become a mentor, almost like a father, after giving her a job in his hotel kitchen when she was sixteen.

Zoe may not have had much to do with him but the memories she had were good ones. "Hey," she said, overwhelmed by nostalgia, "remember how he always let us get away with sneaking onto his private beach for our barbecues, pretending he never knew we were doing it?"

"Yes!" Victoria agreed, smiling mistily. "And how he sent that case of his finest champagne to me and Oliver to celebrate our engagement? He was so happy to be hosting our wedding at the Hawkesbury Estate." Her smile dropped as the tears came to her too. "And now he won't even be there."

Silence, except for Lily, Malie and Victoria weeping.

And then Malie blew her nose. "Right. What do you need?"

Lily heaved in a shuddery breath, then let it out, making a visible effort to get back to her normal self. "I need *you* to go to that surfing competition and win it for Blake." Another heaved-in breath. "And Zoe, I need you to stay where you are and write me something poignant to say at the funeral. And Victoria—"

"Save your breath," Victoria said, cutting her off. "I'm coming to Hawke's Cove tomorrow and it's not to discuss wedding plans."

Lily gave a choked sob. "Of course you're coming. Of course you are, and I need you to come." Another hitching sob. "But right now, I'm going to get into bed and cry my eyes out."

Lily rang off, leaving Malie, Victoria and Zoe staring at each other.

"Will she be OK?" Zoe asked.

Malie blew a corkscrew curl out of her eyes. "She'll pretend she is, anyway."

"Maybe I should come over for the funeral?" Zoe said, tentative.

"Maybe you shouldn't," Victoria said. "You think we don't know how much you hated coming back for Christmas?"

"Yes, but—"

"But nothing. I'm not taking the risk that another visit so soon will have you vowing to stay away forever when I need you at my wedding in August."

"Not to mention *my* wedding when the time comes so don't let the Cove outstay its welcome. Or do I mean you outstay your welcome? Whatever, just don't pretend you don't loathe Hawke's Cove with a passion and would rather swim with the piranhas in the Zambezi than come home."

"I think you mean the Amazon—"

"Details!"

"But, OK!" Zoe huffed out a short-lived laugh. "Hey, do you think Henry might finally turn up?"

Malie rolled her eyes. "Who knows?"

"Who *cares*?" Victoria said, and then grimaced. "Sorry, I don't mean that, I take it back. Henry may have been a spoiled brat—"

"Not may have been, he was a spoiled brat, and probably still is a spoiled brat!" Malie threw in.

"*But*, if you'll shut up, Malie, for a few seconds—I think he suffered as much as the rest of us. Not physically, obviously, but emotionally. I mean, yes, it was an accident, but Claudia *died*, right next to him in that car. How do you even start to deal with that?"

"Claudia's parents still blame him," Zoe said, and then she sighed. "And so do mine." Another sigh. "Talking about my parents, if I don't email them within the next ten minutes they'll declare a state of emergency. So that's me, signing off."

"Measurements!" Victoria called out. "Remember, I need your measurements if I'm going to make your bridesmaid's dress not look like a sack on you!"

"They'll be the same as they were at Christmas—and incidentally I'm wearing that divine pink dress you made me to a cocktail party tonight—but yep, fine. Measurements. As soon as I locate a tape measure."

Zoe disconnected and returned to the email from her parents, rescanning the words and heaving another sigh.

She was going to have to refer to Blake Hawkesbury's death, and she really hoped that didn't have them harking back to the accident. She'd used up a lot of energy over the years putting that night behind her, leaving Hawke's Cove in the past.

Lately, though, fate seemed to be conspiring against her.

The Christmas visit.

Victoria's wedding, coming up in a few months.

Malie's decision to move back there and reopen her family's surf school in the near future, taking her entrepreneur fiancé with her—not that it was so much taking him with her as it was him being willing to follow her to the ends of the earth.

And on the subject of Malie, *damn* her for bringing up Finn Doherty during that visit to Hawaii in February, because ever since he'd been popping into her head at inopportune times. Damn her for all of her talk about how Finn used to look at Zoe like he wanted to strip her naked.

Damn her...but God, how Zoe loved her.

How she loved them all. They were her anchor and her safe harbor.

But they were also the tide, pulling her back to where she didn't want to go.

You hate Hawke's Cove. Lily.

You think we don't know how much you hated coming back for Christmas? Victoria.

Don't pretend you don't loathe Hawke's Cove with a passion. Malie.

She'd worked so hard to escape, she had escaped…but because of the precious friendships she'd forged there she was afraid she'd never truly leave it behind. In fact she felt a terrible, burning certainty that Hawke's Cove was waiting for her to return, daring her to remember it all—a feeling that had been growing stronger since Christmas.

Maybe it was tiredness getting to her; since December she'd done practically back-to-back trips—Mexico, England, the Caribbean, Hawaii, New Zealand. And yet she'd so easily shelved what she'd thought was a firm plan to chill at home in Sydney for a few months. She should have turned down this job—it was so last minute she hadn't been able to do her usual meticulous research, plus she really, truly hated junkets—but a nagging discontentedness had had her accepting.

And so here she was, replying to yet one more email, drowning in the…the suffocation of her life, the same suffocation she thought she'd fled ten years ago.

"And you think Henry Hawkesbury was a spoiled brat?" she asked herself out loud. "Get over yourself, Zoe Tayler. Blake Hawkesbury just died, Lily's mourning, Rolf's got pneumonia, and you're complaining? You're alive, you've got a job people dream about, you're in paradise—stop bitching about having to write an email."

Quickly, she typed:

I just heard Blake Hawkesbury died. Lily's mum's away at the moment so I hope you'll check on her—you know how close to him she was.

And then she switched to autopilot and kept typing. She'd been typing versions of the same email for so long she could just about write it in her sleep. Soothe, placate, deflect.

She reread her message, checking for typos, hit send, then returned to her interrupted article.

But stubbornly, the words wouldn't come. As she sat there watching the cursor blink, it struck her that when she'd checked for typos in that email she hadn't absorbed one word of the actual content.

She went back to the email she'd sent, read it again, and knew why the content hadn't pulled her in: it was tepid, it was practiced, it was *nothing*. Even the reference to staying in her room all day writing her story on Malie's godfather's surf school was a glib throwaway, nothing but a facile reassurance that they could go—to—bed—please!

Strictly speaking she *would* be working in her room all day. She was going to finish that article, then she was going to write a brief on the surf school for a documentary maker she'd met on a trip last year, then she was going to tackle the research on Poerava she ordinarily would have done a week before flying in. But she had oh-so-carefully "forgotten" to mention the cocktail party she'd be attending *in the evening*—an omission that suddenly troubled her.

She started to rub her hands up and down her thighs, then stopped herself. She didn't need to remind herself why her parents worried; they never stopped *telling* her they worried. And at almost twenty-eight years old she didn't need to confess every single thing she did or feel guilty about skipping an occasional detail that might cause them unnecessary anxiety.

Especially since she *knew* nothing was going to happen to her at the cocktail party. Nothing interesting, anyway. She'd been to so many of these events she could describe *exactly* how the evening would unfold. She'd dress up and do her hair and makeup. She'd drink champagne, eat canapés. Meet the resort manager if he/she was there, be schmoozed by the public relations executive who'd arranged her travel. She'd talk to as many people as she could, gathering information on the resort and the area's most interesting attractions. And at the end of the evening she'd return to her room with Cristina and go immediately to bed to rest up for the always busy first day of action.

Boring.

So boring maybe she should just skip it. After her recent travel-fest no one could blame her for preferring a quiet night in. Even when you were being flown business class (as she invariably was), air travel was exhausting, especially when you had to navigate airports in a wheelchair. And then, of course, she had jet lag to contend with, which could kick in at any moment, not to mention—

"Oh. My. God!" she exploded. "Listen to yourself. Sermonizing on the evils of travel. Who even *are* you?"

She sat up straighter. She wasn't going to lie to herself by pretending she was too tired to go to a party when what she was actually suffering from was a guilty conscience over not telling her parents she was going out. Nor was she going to send a follow-up email mentioning the party.

What she *was* going to do was remind herself—visually, since she couldn't trust the tortured inside of her head—that she was living the life she'd always dreamed of.

She pushed away from the desk and wheeled herself onto the sundeck of her bungalow, gazing at the endlessness of blue.

Blue was her favorite color, and it didn't get more beautiful than this, laid out in shades shifting seamlessly from crystal to powder to electric to azure to sapphire, all the way out to the horizon where the lagoon collided with a vivid cerulean sky. Her bungalow seemed to be suspended between two worlds—and in a way that was exactly what it was, perched on stilts over water, not earth. There were glass panels in the floor inside that allowed you to see the colorful fish darting freely below, but Zoe preferred this outdoor vantage point. In her soul she was soaring, skimming across the lagoon, rising into the air, flying straight up to the heavens.

This was why she'd fought so hard to not return home to Hawke's Cove with her parents. This beauty, this freedom.

It had been worth every trade-off she'd negotiated—the apartment that had been bought for her off-plan before construction so modifications could be made for her wheelchair, the physiotherapist who came twice a week, the cleaning service, the detailed itineraries provided to her parents whenever she was traveling, Cristina's assistance, the regular phone calls when she was at home, the barrage of emails when she was working, a hundred other inconsequential intrusions.

It had been a fight for her life…at the cost of her parents' hope for a cure.

"Fight your big battles to the death, but don't sweat the scrappy skirmishes if you want to win the long war," she said again, looking out across the lagoon.

Once more she heard Finn saying those words. But now she could *see* him, too. His crooked smile with the tiny chip in his front tooth as he'd tucked a hank of her hair behind her ear. She'd looked into his too-blue eyes that day and seen more than a color. She'd seen, so clearly, that Finn was mysteriously older than his eighteen years. His life had been nothing like her pampered existence—and yet he'd believed, he really had, that she was as strong as he was, capable of fighting for what she wanted, ready to do whatever she set her heart on.

What would he think of all those compromises she'd made to get where she was? Would he see her as a victor or would he say she was…

"Lost," she said, and closed her eyes, trying to unblock the memory of the very last time she'd seen him.

Impossible.

As usual, only a snippet or two resurfaced, just enough to tell her it had been traumatic; the rest stayed safely buried.

She opened her eyes, stared out at the horizon, and saw again his eyes, the same color as the French Polynesian sky.

She may not have the full memory of that night but she knew one thing: however Finn Doherty may have looked at her during that Crab Shack year, his opinion had gone through a dramatic metamorphosis in the two years that followed.

And it didn't matter. It really, truly didn't.

She hadn't seen him for ten years and she'd never see him again.

Which was just fine with her.

She had an article to finish, a party to go to, and a life to live.

two

FINN DOHERTY WALKED SLOWLY AROUND THE
hotel ballroom with Aiata, the resort's PR manager, looking
for flaws to be corrected before the guests arrived.

But there were no flaws. Everything was perfect. No, not
perfect.

He hated the word "perfect." "Magnificent" was a better
descriptor.

Yesterday this had been a moderate-sized room running the
length of the *fare pote*—the communal house—which was com-
prised of an airy lobby, Tāma'a restaurant, the Manuia bar, a
quiet library room and a ruthlessly modern but hidden com-
mercial kitchen. The floor was rich brown teak, fairy lights
were strung across the ceiling, and full-length glass doors replaced walls on three sides, opening onto a wraparound deck.
The doors offered uninhibited views onto a grass clearing that
was ideal for small soirees, which was bordered by stunning

gardens landscaped to merge with the island's natural rainforest beyond. Elegant and picturesque, but objectively speaking, not vastly different from any other expertly designed, well-positioned hotel ballroom.

Tonight, however, the roof had been retracted, the glass doors concertinaed all the way back to the communal house, and teak extensions had been attached to the deck, stretching across the grass clearing so that the gardens became the walls—and the result was enchanting. A secret bower nestled within a rainforest, accessible only via a broad teak ramp that led through a natural opening between two coconut palms and circled back to the main entrance of the resort.

Nothing was needed to beautify the space except for subtle lighting spiked among the plants. There were no bars set up, no food stations; instead, wait staff would circulate continuously, bringing refreshments through the swinging doors from the kitchen servery. No plinths with flowers—just a few high tables scattered with hibiscus petals for those wanting to put down their glass or napkin. And even those petals worked some strange magic, looking as though they'd drifted in from the riot of colorfully bold hibiscus plants dotted throughout the gardens—reds and yellows, oranges and pinks, whites and purples.

Finn moved to the edge of the teak extension, breathing in. Out. In. Out. Warmth. Tang. Green. He'd have sworn he could isolate the creamy lemony scent radiating from the small white blooms of his favorite flower, the Tahitian gardenia—*tiare mā'ohi*—the national flower of French Polynesia, whose shape of seven petals had inspired the name of the island. Fanciful to think he could smell that among the crowd of other plants that included equally fragrant frangipanis in the usual white, pink, and yellow as well as several ancient tree varieties bursting with rare red and orange flowers, plus a dazzling array of orchids, meter-tall spikes of football-sized red torch ginger blooms, and jasmine—which he preferred to call by its local name, *pitate*, when he was here.

When he was here...which wasn't as often as he would have liked.

He had other resorts to oversee. In the Daintree. Fiji. Langkawi. The health retreat in the Maldives. This place, though, was special. The first resort he and Gina—his ex-wife and business partner—hadn't bought as a going concern. As satisfying as it was to retrofit and refurbish a property, nothing compared to building a success from an idea, which was what they'd done with Poerava, his gem at the very center of the flower that was Tiare Island.

And OK, it was actually too soon to tell if Poerava could truly be counted a success, but the signs were there. The travel industry buzz, robust forward bookings, media interest. They'd got Poerava into every key luxury travel brochure and feedback was that people were clamoring not only for the outrageously popular overwater bungalows but also for the garden suites within the rainforest.

He'd been involved personally in every single part of this development and was proud of it. He'd overseen the design, by his favorite architect; he'd supervised the construction; he'd chosen the decor; he'd even named it, after the exquisite black pearls that Polynesians once upon a time dived for off one of the island's petal-shaped peninsulas. The only thing he hadn't seen through from start to finish was tonight's launch party—not by choice, but because a situation in the Maldives had needed his undivided attention for a full month.

Not that he could have done a better job. In fact, there was only one problem with tonight's launch, and it had nothing to do with Poerava. It was simply that he no longer had any excuse for stonewalling Doherty & Berne's next portfolio acquisition, which Gina, as the Berne half of the partnership, had been working on diligently for six months.

Gina had never made any secret of the fact that her dream was to expand into the UK. She'd joked that one of the reasons she married him was because she had a Brit obsession! It had been unwavering, that dream of hers, since they'd formed their company seven years ago and he owed her a shot at achieving it.

Problem was, her preferred property was a fortified manor in Devon, which Finn had pinpointed on the map in his head the minute he'd seen the photos. Way too close to Hawke's Cove. Which left property number two: a loch-side castle in the Scottish Highlands. But was it fair to Gina to sway the decision on the basis of his reluctance to go back to a place just because his memories were not fond? At thirty years old it was way past time to put those memories behind him.

"Boss!"

Finn, startled out of his thoughts by the sharpness with which that one word was uttered, saw that the usually strictly deferential Aiata was regarding him with an expression just shy of exasperation.

"Sorry, what?" he said, wincing because obviously she'd been trying to get his attention for a while.

"The first guests have arrived," she said.

Which was Aiata speak for *Step it up, put your game face on and get over there to meet and greet.*

He glanced round, surprised to note that the wait staff briefing he'd intended to join had happened without him, and that one of the staff was offering welcome drinks to a small group of guests. The band hired to provide background music had set up, the singer conferring quietly with the ukulele player.

He checked his watch. OK, there were still five minutes to go before the scheduled start time, but how had he not noticed everything happening around him?

In the time it took to raise his eyes from his watch the number of guests had increased from six to eight...ten...eleven. They were coming in early *and* fast.

At the first strum of the ukulele he examined the guests more carefully. Noted that a VIP—a director of the tourism board—was among the early arrivals, being charmed by Poerava's manager, the glamorous Nanihi.

"Right," he said to Aiata. "I'll join Nanihi and do the VIP schmoozing but I also want to meet all the international travel journos. How many do we have here tonight and how many are staying for the full week?"

"Fifteen tonight, ten are staying," Aiata said, and the almost-exasperation was back. "The document I emailed had names, publications, background information on each of them, sample articles, the personalized itineraries I've put together according to their individual preferences, plus—"

"Yes, yes I got it," Finn said, wincing again at having cut her off. It wasn't her fault he hadn't done his due diligence on the media. He devoutly hoped it would be the last winceworthy moment of the night. "Sorry, I didn't get a chance to go through it because of the Maldives issue. Maybe you could give me a rundown now of who they are." He shot another glance around the space, estimated that a third of their expected two hundred-plus guests were already here. It often happened like that. A trickle became a flood which eventually reverted to a trickle. But midflood there was no time to talk about which media wanted to do what activities. "Forget that. Just tell me if there's anyone who needs special attention."

"There's a last-minute stand-in for Rolf. You know, Rolf Vameer? You asked for him specifically after he did that piece about the Fiji resort but—"

"What? No Rolf?" Finn said, and winced again at having interrupted her once more. He blamed his impatience on that manor house in Devon. He accepted a glass of champagne from a passing server and took a sip, forcing himself to relax. "Is he going to be a problem?"

"He?" she asked, frowning.

"Rolf's replacement."

Her frown cleared. "She, not he. And no. She's a sweetie. Easygoing from what I could tell when she checked in. I was surprised because she normally won't do junkets and she's only doing this one because she's a friend of Rolf's."

"She doesn't do junkets?"

"No. She thinks junkets put pressure on writers to hide the downsides of a place. Plus she hates seeing everyone come out with the same basic article post trip."

"Sounds like trouble."

"That's not my impression. And I've taken pains with all of them to offer points of difference in their itineraries and plenty of free time, so the issue about everyone writing identical stories shouldn't arise. There are certain things they'll do as a group but each of them has a choice of other activities and I'm talking to them separately to craft individual story angles."

"OK, great." Another sip of champagne. "Then if there's no one who's a problem I'm happy to wing it and keep things with the media informal tonight. Anyone who needs a corporate perspective will want an in-depth interview which I can't do tonight anyway, so you can set up a time for them to talk to me on the phone once I'm in the UK. For the destination features I'll leave it to Nanihi to give them what they need during the week."

"You got it, boss," Aiata said.

"And, Aiata, thank you. For everything. I can tell it's going to be a great night."

She smiled at him with her more-usual warmth, murmured something about Nanihi heading his way, and glided quietly away.

The next forty-five minutes flew by. A blur of faces, chatter, music. Finn gave a brief, well-received speech, introducing his team. The band was perfect. The resort staff managed the flow of people brilliantly so that he met everyone he needed to meet. The flood of arrivals had eased. Everyone seemed happy and relaxed.

Figuring he'd earned some off-the-clock-time, Finn collared Kupe Kahale, owner of the Mama Papa'e restaurant on nearby Heia Island, with whom he'd formed a close bond over the past year. The bombastic Kupe always gave the impression that those to whom he deigned to speak were being granted an audience by royalty—a view with which Finn concurred: Kupe was a legend in these parts and Finn considered he *was* being granted an audience. If Finn hadn't been flying out in the morning he would have sailed across to Mama Papa'e and enticed Kupe and Kupe's wife, Chen, to share more raconteur-like reminiscences of "the good old days" in French Polynesia over an excellent meal and a bottle of wine.

It was in the middle of Kupe's story about the invention of his signature cocktail that Finn became aware of a disturbance—actually, it was more like a ripple of interest, an impression of people directing their attention to one point in the room. He was curious but not unduly so given there was no crash of glassware, no raised voices, no break in the general hum of conversation. It wasn't until Kupe himself briefly paused as something caught his eye beyond Finn's left shoulder that curiosity got the better of Finn; Kupe was not the type to pause midanecdote for anything less than a volcanic eruption.

Sure enough, Kupe picked up the thread of his tale almost immediately, but Finn's concentration was shot: he had to see what was so interesting.

He waited until Kupe had finished the cocktail story and was distracted by a passing tray of canapés, then shot a look backward, over his shoulder. All he could see was Aiata. No, Aiata wasn't the focal point; that was whoever Aiata was bending down to talk to. Someone in a wheelchair wearing a lacy, beaded rose pink skirt draped down to the chair's footplate, the sparkly toes of a pair of lilac shoes peeping from beneath the hem of the skirt.

The Rolf replacement.

Aiata's swing of long black hair obscured the woman's face and torso but no way was Finn going to do the stare-and-wait routine. Aside from the fact that it didn't matter what she looked like, it irritated him that the simple fact of being in a wheelchair could get people gawking.

He turned back to Kupe, who'd finished his canapé and was waxing lyrical about a special pork dish offered at the Mama Papa'e restaurant.

Finn tried to locate his enthusiasm but it appeared to be MIA. In his head, he was seeing the pink skirt and pretty spangled shoes of the woman Aiata was talking to and remembering that Aiata had described Rolf's replacement as a sweetie. The way she dressed fitted that description. The gauze and sparkle, the choice of those particular shades. He hoped that ripple of disturbance wasn't going to be repeated, that people weren't going to either look or deliberately *not* look at her all night, because that would get up his nose in a big way.

Oblivious to Finn's waning attention, Kupe reached for another canapé and engaged the server in a discussion about the dipping sauce. While Kupe was preoccupied Finn risked another look over his shoulder—not that he had any idea what he'd do if he found his guests ogling the poor woman. He smiled as he imagined himself striding across the floor, shoving people left and right as he raced to rescue the damsel in distress. Counterproductive behavior that would draw everyone's attention, which he was fairly sure the damsel would not appreciate.

He started to turn back to Kupe but just then the crowd shifted enough to give him clear line of sight to Aiata straightening and stepping aside.

His smile fell away, the sounds of the party fading until all he could hear was his heart thudding in his ears.

The woman in the wheelchair was Zoe.

three

POERAVA WAS RATING EXCEPTIONALLY WELL ON the Zoe Scale of Fabulousness.

So well, she'd already started framing a vignette about its philosophical aesthetic for her article. That sounded grandiose but it really did seem to her that accessibility for people with a disability had been integral to the design, not an afterthought. The essential modifications were not only all present and accounted for, they'd been thoughtfully and artistically integrated. A welcome change from suites that didn't let you forget you were different with their utilitarian stainless-steel grab bars, cheap plastic shower chairs and ugly nonslip mats that railroaded over the top of any charm.

The exaggeratedly wide entrance to her two-bedroom bungalow, for example, was a feature of *all* the overwater bungalows. As was the enormous bathroom, big enough for two people to move around in comfortably. The shower was a walk-in—or in her case, a roll-in—affair, with a seat that looked like it belonged in an ancient Roman garden. And OK, the grab bars and safety rails were there, but they were shaped in gorgeous wave-like curves and semicircles that blended delightfully with the mosaic wall tiles. Special care had been taken throughout the suite with the placement of light switches, height-adjustable tables and counters, and the positioning of furniture to make transferring to and from her chair easy, but the differences were subtle enough to make them unremarkable. All the materials looked top-shelf—even the nonslip floor tiles in the bathroom and on the balcony, which looked like natural timber.

Everything about the bungalow was effortlessly lovely. Well, perhaps the electric pool lift installed on her balcony wasn't exactly *lovely*—in fact, it was the one incongruity—but she wasn't going to complain. The views were glorious but it meant more to her to be able to get into the water directly from her balcony like all those other guests who could descend from their balconies via ladders.

Even the ingenious wide teak ramp that led from the communal house to this party space—which could have been specifically designed for wheelchair users—looked more like an ancient tree that had simply fallen over and been worn flat over the years. It was hard to believe Aiata's explanation that it was a temporary ramp designed to fit into the floor extensions. Then again, she couldn't believe this space was officially called something as basic as the Poerava Ballroom when it looked like it had emerged from the surrounding rainforest.

Something to talk to the resort manager about, she decided, as Aiata led her and Cristina in his direction. She liked to have a conversation starter in mind when meeting managers and the cunning design features that had turned a ballroom into a mystical arbor seemed a good choice.

"The big boss" was what Aiata called the manager. She'd said his name, too, but that had been drowned out by applause from the guests following the singer's introduction of a special song, "*Te Tama Mā'ohi*". No matter. She'd find out soon enough and in her experience the manager was never the one to provide the best quotable quotes for her stories anyway.

Looking around, Zoe understood why the applause had been almost deafening: there were *a lot* of guests. If she'd known the scale of the reception she'd have arrived early and spared Aiata the necessity of battling her way through the throng to get her where she needed to be.

At least she would have *tried* to arrive early. Problem was, the surf school article had been more difficult to write than she'd anticipated and she'd taken too long on the documentary brief; if she'd stopped to read through all the information Aiata had provided as well she would have missed the party altogether.

Thankfully Aiata was a smooth operator, wending a way for them across the floor with admirable discretion. No bumps, jostles, or cringeworthy calls to people to get out of the way. But perhaps Aiata was a little *too* discreet? Because from what Zoe could see their quarry had moved on.

"Oh, we missed him," Zoe said, stopping and gesturing toward the man's back. "I can find him on my own if you need to be somewhere else."

Aiata glanced in the direction of Zoe's waving hand. "Oh no, that's Kupe Kahale. We're visiting Kupe's restaurant, Mama Papa'e, on Heia Island on Saturday. Not that our chef Gaspard isn't world class, but we're all about solitude and seclusion at Poerava, and you might be ready for more excitement by the end of the week. The Mama Papa'e dinner show is famous. The best dancers in Polynesia will be on stage."

Zoe shuddered inside, remembering her recent New Zealand trip, being coerced onto the stage and handed a couple of pois to swing. "Oh. Dancers. Lovely." She looked up at Cristina, who'd been similarly dragged onto the stage that night. They'd both agreed that kitsch shows put on especially for tourists were on the never-again list after that experience. "What do you think, Cris?"

Clever Cristina launched into a request for as much information as Aiata could provide on the mode of transport offered to Heia Island and accessibility details pertaining specifically to the restaurant there. Zoe recognized this as a diversionary tactic—go, Cris!—and concentrated on locating Poerava's owner so she'd know in which direction to head—her own diversionary tactic—as soon as the interrogation was over, because she was not going to be talked into going to that dinner.

Where Kupe Kahale had been standing there was now only one man. He had to be the boss, although he looked younger than she would have expected. Not that she could see his face: only his back, but his back looked...well, young. Or maybe "fit" was a better word. Broad in that hard way that suggested plenty of muscle. Like he was a rugby player, or worked out very seriously in the gym. He was tall—over six feet. His hair was short, thick, blue-black. He was wearing black trousers and a blue shirt that fit him to perfection.

A tingle snaked across her skin and she suddenly wanted to see his face. Silly, to wonder if he was handsome. His looks were immaterial; in all her years as a travel writer she'd never met a resort manager—male or female—who'd done more than shake her hand and wish her a good time during her stay. There was no need—they had PR people to escort her, answer her questions, make sure she enjoyed the amenities. She wrote *travel* articles—factual, descriptive, personal, experiential—not corporate exposés.

And yet...whoa, there was that tingle again, she really did want to see what he—

"Shall we move on?" Aiata, calling her out of her thoughts. "I'm not sure how long the boss will be here tonight, best to grab him fast."

After her blunder with Kupe Kahale, Zoe thought it best

to confirm where she was heading and nodded in the direction of the man in the black trousers and blue shirt. "That's him, right?"

"That's him," Aiata confirmed.

"Let's go then," Zoe said, and wheeled herself in his direction.

"Careful!" Cristina warned. "It's crowded, Zoe, take it slowly."

Which of course made Zoe speed up.

Aiata shot Zoe a glimmering smile, and serenely increased her own pace to match, forging their path a little more energetically than she had hitherto. A weight Zoe hadn't known was lying across her shoulders lifted. Aiata understood. The odds of enjoying her week on Tiare Island had just increased exponentially.

The three women reached their quarry without creating any more disturbance than could be addressed by an occasional apology as they eased past people chatting and came to a stop behind him.

Aiata lightly tapped two fingertips on his shoulder. Half a second, no more.

He seemed to stiffen, but didn't turn around.

One more second. Two. Three. And then, "Boss?" Aiata said, tentative, maybe even confused—as well she should be; he had to have felt that touch, light though it was.

OK, he'd heard her. Zoe could tell from the unmistakable tensing of his broad shoulders. But he still didn't turn.

Zoe would have supposed him to be annoyed at being disturbed if not for the fact that he was standing on his own: they weren't invading a tête-à-tête. The only thing they were disturbing was his perusal of the gardens, which, yes, were fabulous, but surely very familiar to him. Unless it was his thoughts that were being interrupted, in which case Zoe would be quite happy to leave him to th—

He turned, and Zoe gasped.

That tingle became a shiver. Electric. Hot.

She blinked. Blinked again. No. It couldn't be him. He looked so different. And yet…the eyes, so deeply, outrageously blue.

"Finn," she said. Or maybe she'd merely mouthed the name; her heart was pounding so hard she couldn't hear anything else and so didn't know if she'd vocalized it.

The last time she'd seen him he'd been wearing his usual age-faded jeans, washed-to-death long-sleeved Henley T, coming-apart Converse. His hair had been down to his collar, disheveled as though he'd run his hands through it a thousand times. He'd always looked scruffy. Now he looked scrupulously neat. But something of the old Finn was there, something dangerous, warning her there was unfinished business between them.

"Zoe," he said, and the hot shiver raced through her at the sound of his voice. The voice that had seemed way too gruff and gravelly for a skinny eighteen-year-old twelve years ago and yet had nevertheless suited him perfectly. It suited him even better now.

Cristina reacted to the shiver by putting Zoe's wrap around her shoulders. Zoe shrugged her shoulders so it slid straight back off—what healthy woman needed a wrap when the air temperature was nudging thirty degrees?—but the damage was done. Finn's lip curled in the barest approximation of a smile and Zoe wished Cristina hadn't done it, wished she'd fade into the background so Zoe could pretend she was on her own.

"Oh! You know each other?" Aiata said, entering the fray warily. And well she might be wary: you'd have needed not a knife but a meat cleaver to cut through the tension in the air.

"Yes," Finn said, and left it at that, neither elaborating nor taking his eyes off Zoe. "No champagne. Not allowed?"

Zoe felt the usual flash of despairing rage at being treated like an invalid who didn't know what was good for her. No, not usual, worse than usual, because Finn *knew* how it was with her. He'd promised never to do that to her.

Which meant…what? That he'd done it deliberately?

Well, she wasn't going to give him the satisfaction of reacting. No matter how hostile he looked, how tough and cold and… and hot, oh God, cold *and* hot and so, so sexy, so *mouthwateringly* sexy, she was going to hold her own. "I turn twenty-eight in a week," she said. "So yes, I'm allowed to drink champagne."

He looked not at her but pointedly at Aiata, who murmured something about sending over a waiter and excused herself with telling alacrity. Now if only Cristina would make herself similarly scarce. But Cristina looked mulish.

"Cris," Zoe said, sweet but firm, "would you mind going back to the bungalow for my painkillers."

"But—"

"I'd go myself but I need to talk to Mr. Doherty for my article and this might be my only chance." Decode: *this is work*; Cristina knew when it was work she had to leave.

"Have you got your phone handy?" Cristina asked.

Oh, for the love of—! Slo-o-ow breath. "Yes, I have my phone," Zoe said. "And don't worry, Mr. Doherty and I are old…" she hesitated over the word "friends" and settled instead on "…acquaintances." Yes, that would do. "I'll be fine. I'll be safe."

Cristina shot Finn a glare that promised retribution should Zoe *not* be fine and safe, which made Zoe want to groan, but at last she left.

The countdown was now on. Even though Cristina would have to look high and low for the painkillers since they were actually in Zoe's purse, she'd be fast; Zoe only had a few minutes. She wanted to get through this necessary interaction with Finn in as businesslike a manner as she could manage and be out of his orbit before Cristina returned.

She launched in with: "You didn't know I was coming, did

you?" at the same moment Finn asked: "You didn't know I'd be at Poerava, did you?"

Zoe's "No" crossed midair with Finn's "No."

Silence. Frozen.

A flash of memory. The Crab Shack. Ewan asking what they thought would be the best way of announcing a change to the opening time for the dinner service, and Zoe and Finn simultaneously saying, "Tell Mrs. Whittaker!" And then crying "Jinx" and spending five minutes arguing over who'd said it first, by which time Ewan, laughing and shaking his head, had left them to it.

But now all they seemed able to do was stare at each other.

Zoe fought against a wave of melancholy. Ridiculous to feel nostalgic. Memories were meaningless, worthless. There was nothing between her and Finn—no, not Finn, Mr. Doherty—except the article she would write on his resort.

She took a little breath and pasted on a professional smile. "Actually, this—" waving an all-encompassing hand "—was a last-minute invitation. *Wanderlust Wheels* had a different writer lined up but he ended up in hospital with pneumonia. I didn't have time to do my usual research."

"I flew straight from my resort in the Maldives without having had a chance to read up on what journalists would be here," he offered in response, which seemed to indicate he was equally determined to keep things professional even if he couldn't actually manage a smile.

"Oh! A resort in the Maldives too?" she said and remembered that Aiata had called him the big boss. "Are you, like, the global manager?" She trailed off as his eyes went glacial.

There was a moment of absolute stillness, except for Finn's eyes, which raked her from her head to her toes and back up again, briefly snagging on the return at her chest so that she had to fight an impulse to cross her arms over her breasts, then stopping at her mouth. She had the absurd thought that if he kissed her at that moment it would scald her despite the chill emanating from his eyes, that he would *want* it to scald her, want it to…to brand her like a hot iron. *I won't let you forget me.* She thought of what Malie had said about the way Finn used to look at her, and that shiver rushed, hotter, through her blood. What would it be like to be kissed by him, kissed so hard it hurt?

His mouth quirked in a mocking semi-smile, as though he'd read her thoughts. His eyes raised to hers at last. "The owner," he said. "Half owner, strictly speaking. The company is Doherty & Berne."

A waiter carrying a tray of champagne arrived and Zoe took a flute, then a sip, floundering in another excruciating silence as she processed that information. Finn Doherty had a business partner? They owned two luxury resorts? Finn had never even finished high school. And despite running with that gang he'd always seemed so…so alone, not the type to be anyone's partner.

She wracked her brain for the best thing to say. Asking about the engineering and design the way she'd intended seemed suddenly insipid. Ditto commenting on the party, her bungalow, the amenities, the food she could expect, the weather. *Just pick a topic, Zoe, break the ice!*

She opened her mouth. Closed it.

Aiata could talk to her about all that. She'd be eating at Tāma'a, having a drink at Manuia, relying on her personal impressions of both. The weather…well, the weather was the weather. What could he say? It was warm and humid and they could expect some rain? Those were not things to waste the owner's time with.

The *owner*! What could she say?

OK, OK, she knew what to ask. Projections for guests with disabilities. Marketing activities targeting people like her.

She opened her mouth again, resolute, and out came:

"I'm not lost."

She felt her eyes go wide. Had she seriously just bowled that out, apropos of *absolutely nothing*?

A heartbeat of a moment. She could see that she'd startled him. But he recovered lightning fast, his lip recurling in that not-really-a-smile.

"I'm glad to hear it," he said, so dryly she wanted to scream that it was true.

"I can look after myself," she said, and swallowed a groan. What was *wrong* with her? People who could look after themselves didn't need to announce it to the world, they just did it! Finn Doherty certainly had never announced what he was doing, he'd always just done it and screw anyone who questioned him.

"Glad to hear that, too." This time it was an amused drawl.

How it rankled, that she amused him. She'd never amused him before, at least not in this…this *patronizing* way. But still, she found herself needing to explain, to make him see that appearances could be deceiving, just like he used to say about her at the Crab Shack. *You look fragile as a snowdrop but you're an oak tree on the inside.* Stop! Stop remembering that time! "What I mean is that Cristina—"

"Look, Zoe," he cut her off, which was both disheartening and probably a good thing considering the mess she was making of things. "I'm sorry for the crack about the champagne. I really am. You made it clear a long time ago you had nothing to prove to me. If you're happy with what you're doing, that's great. Now, I see your friend—carer, minder, whatever you want to call her—is coming back in, so if you'll excuse me I'm flying to London in the morning and there are a few more people I need to meet."

And at last pride came to her rescue and up went her chin. "That's a shame. If you're leaving in the morning, you won't see that I…I mean—"

"I won't see you looking after yourself?" Taking over again

as though he'd had a gutful now. "But I don't need to." Pause. Infinitesimal. And then, "Right?"

A hovering moment. As though he were waiting for her to contradict him. She wanted to insist that he stick around, let her show him that she *could* look after herself, that she was doing *just fine*, that she'd already proven she didn't need anyone and he should just…just acknowledge that he'd been right about her *twelve* years ago and so very wrong *ten* years ago.

She opened her mouth. She had to get this out. *Had* to. "Finn—" she began, a little desperately, but then Cristina was there, saying, "I couldn't find the pills," and the moment was gone.

Zoe wanted to scream, but so ingrained was her need to smooth troubled waters that she smiled at Cristina instead. "Oh! Oh, I'm so sorry, Cris." *Smile, smile, smile.* "I forgot I had them in my purse."

"Maybe the champagne isn't such a good idea if you're taking those pills, Zoe. How about I get us both some water?"

Cristina hurried off before Zoe could protest, leaving Zoe with more impenetrable silence.

And then Finn shrugged one shoulder as though twitching away an invisible hand, a gesture that was almost dismissive… and yet somehow not. "Goodbye, Zoe," he said, and walked away.

"I'm not lost," Zoe whispered to his disappearing back.

As if he'd heard her—which of course he could not have—Finn stopped.

Zoe held her breath, willing him to turn around and come back…but with a shake of his head, he continued on.

A minute later, when Cristina tried—unsuccessfully—to swap Zoe's champagne for water, Zoe saw that he'd joined a group of women who seemed to be hanging on his every word. Well, he was the owner of a luxury resort—no, *two* luxury resorts—and the bulk of the guests here tonight were in the travel business so of course they were hanging on his every word.

OK, that wasn't true. At least, it wasn't the whole truth. Women weren't only interested in him because of his job but because of...of *him*.

A bit of rough with a reputation—Malie's description. *On every girl's radar, the bad boy every female wanted to be ruined by.* Yep, true. She could only imagine how many were lining up for him now.

She shivered again.

Cristina clucked and tried to replace that stupid wrap around her shoulders. Zoe took it from her, scrunched it in a ball and shoved it behind her back. She wasn't cold, dammit, she was... sensitized. Although she couldn't feel her legs every other part of her had become almost excruciatingly sensitive since the accident.

She wondered what it would be like to let someone like Finn Doherty explore those parts of her with his hands. Wondered what Malie would say if she could see him now. Would she still think he wanted to strip Zoe naked and have his way with her?

No. No way. To think Finn Doherty had ever been interested in her was ludicrous. And anyway, bad boy he might have been, bad boy he still might be, but if Zoe did end up in bed with him—an option that didn't seem to be on the cards in this lifetime—she knew that with her he would *not* be a bit of rough! One of the fleeting portions of memory from that dreadful night in the hospital was her own horror that he'd done a 180-degree turnaround, seeming to think she was a snowdrop after all, needing to be saved from being crushed underfoot. And Cristina's presence tonight would have been all the proof he needed of Zoe's frailty—and not one of the daring females she'd seen lounging about the Cove with Finn all those years ago had been frail.

She forced herself to search out Finn with her eyes, girding her loins (and wasn't that an apt expression given the train of thought she'd just indulged?) to take a good, long, final look at him. She would remind herself that he was not for her, that he never had been and never would be, and then she would close that chapter of the book of her life and move on.

She found him in seconds. He'd moved on from that group of women and was talking only to one—an exquisitely beautiful Polynesian woman. A match for him if ever Zoe had seen one.

He was side on to Zoe and seemed to be concentrating unwaveringly on what his companion was saying...but then, abruptly, he tipped his head in Zoe's direction and she had the strangest feeling he could feel her watching him.

Another shiver shook her.

"Er... Zoe? Are you sure you're not cold?" Cristina asked.

"How could I be—" She stopped because Cristina's mouth had pursed and she was looking at Zoe's chest.

Oh. *Oh!* Zoe looked down, saw that her nipples seemed about to poke two holes through her bodice. She recalled the way Finn's eyes had snagged there and thought if she could drop dead right that second she would be quite happy to do so. She snatched the wrap from behind her back, draping it around herself.

"Perhaps I am a little chilled," she said.

four

HE WATCHED HER.

Couldn't seem to help himself.

At least he did it covertly. Always when he was with someone else—listening as the virtues of Poerava were extolled, answering questions, giving what he hoped appeared to be his full attention.

Zoe couldn't have guessed that he knew where she was every minute, who she was talking to, when she was smiling/ frowning/ laughing, that she had a slick of sauce from one of the canapés on her chin she wouldn't be able to feel because the nerves in that spot had never recovered from that wisdom tooth extraction.

The pretty red-haired gorgon with her, though? She knew. He didn't know *how* she knew but she sure did know. He'd felt her steely gaze on him at frequent intervals, making it clear that she was guarding her fragile ray of sunshine from the threatening darkness.

And she did look fragile, Zoe. She always had, though she'd never seen herself that way. Small and slender enough to be snapped in half by a too-rough touch. Otherworldly, with all that white-gold hair either falling in perfectly defined waves to her hips or tamed into a ponytail or plait or bun with a glittery clip or a comb somewhere (diamanté stars tonight), the fair skin so translucent you could almost see the blood flowing through her veins, the heart-shaped face dominated by huge eyes that were lime—mint green like the lightest shade in the curve of a cold breaking wave, lips the color of untouched reef coral.

A mermaid, forced to walk on a too-hard earth.

When they were teenagers working in the Crab Shack, Ewan, the boss, had warned Finn that Zoe Tayler was off-limits to him. Finn had taken that to heart; Ewan had given him the job out of sympathy for Finn's ailing mother so he was already primed to be on his best behavior. But Finn hadn't needed to be told: he'd always known Zoe was off-limits. He'd never spoken to her before that summer but he'd seen her around the village. He knew her history, knew she was a protected species, knew she was considered too good for the likes of him, knew she *was* too good for him. She'd been off-limits in every conceivable way. Rich to his poor, light to his dark, cool to his hot, angel to his devil, sweet to his bitter.

And yet for that one summer they'd soared above their differences and become…something that didn't have a descriptor. How that had happened was a mystery. All he knew was that the tremulously inviting smile she'd given him when they were refilling the salt shakers ahead of their first lunch shift together had grabbed his heart and twisted it. She was a sprinkle of fairy dust amid the mundane drudgery that was his life, and as each day passed, they'd grown closer. It was like they were the two puzzle pieces waiting for every other piece to fit into a predetermined pattern before they finally slotted together.

Oh, who was he kidding?

If that puzzle analogy was anything other than romanticized claptrap they would have been able to stay friends once autumn rolled around.

The truth was that Finn had deluded himself into thinking they belonged together because that's what he'd wanted. But within a week of leaving the Crab Shack she'd started dating Brad Ellersley: clean-cut, conventionally handsome, sports star, straight-A student, heir to a fortune. That had been the start of two years of torment, their meetings in the village stilted and awkward as Finn had fought to keep her at a safe distance for his own sanity.

Until that last time he'd seen her, three months after the accident, when they'd moved past stilted and awkward but not to anywhere good.

And OK, with ten years' hindsight he could accept it wasn't her fault that the way he'd felt about her hadn't been reciprocated, but he sure wasn't going to thank her for kicking him to the curb that night, regardless.

He wasn't going to thank her, either, for still smelling the way he remembered. Like lemon because she always rinsed her hair—the only thing she was vain about—in lemon juice. Only better than lemon. She smelled like the *tiare mā'ohi*. His favorite flower. How had he not made the connection before?

She's not for you, she never was, she never will be, let her go.

"Um… Finn?"

He snapped his attention back to the moment to find he was being regarded quizzically by the editor of *Travel in the Fast Lane*. He didn't know her name because when Aiata had introduced them Zoe had been smack-bang in his line of sight talking to Joe Hauata, known locally as Captain Joe, the captain of Poerava's luxury catamaran, *Pearl Finder*, and Joe had been all but salivating over her. He knew his current companion had been talking about the turtle sanctuary, though, so probably all he had to do was say that a visit could be arranged.

"Problem?" she asked.

"Problem?" he repeated, mystified. It was a turtle sanctuary, not the Pentagon.

"You said something about someone being not for you."

Ah. He'd said that out loud. He was losing his marbles. "A staff member," he said, improvising. "She's not working out." Improvising *badly* because that wasn't the best thing to say to a journalist who was going to write about his resort. "I mean, she's terrific, but she has family in Australia and wants to re-locate to Doherty & Berne's head office in Sydney and there's no role there." He turned slightly to raise "save me" eyebrows at Nanihi and when she picked up her cue without a hitch and headed over, returned his attention to his companion. "Small thing, but it's preying on my mind because I'm flying out in the morning so I need to talk to her tonight to see if our Daintree resort might suit her." He flashed his best smile. "Which is no excuse for being distracted, but yes, I agree the Bora Bora Turtle Center is worth a visit, even though it's quite a distance from here and you'll have to fly. I'll leave you with Nanihi…" another smile, this time for Nanihi who arrived like the champion she was, "…and ask her to organize it for you."

He kept right on smiling as he backed away and headed for the ramp that would take him back to the *fare pote.*

He thought about stopping at Manuia, knocking back a shot of the vanilla-infused rum he loved, but a quick time check had him vetoing that idea. The cocktail reception would finish within ten minutes. In his experience many guests made straight for the bar after such events. He had a sneaking suspicion Captain Joe would be doing his best to persuade Zoe to join him for a nightcap and if he succeeded… Well, Finn did *not* need to see that. Much better to raid the mini bar in his bungalow and have his rum in private.

There was a well-lit path to the garden bungalows skirting around the thickest section of rainforest, but Finn opted for the more direct, less-traveled route, which arrowed into the heart of the rainforest. To the untrained eye this path appeared impenetrable, but it was there—a narrow, dimly lit track for the intrepid. And Finn was in an Indiana Jones frame of mind.

The path diverged at a central point where the foliage was thickest, leading in one direction to the bungalows, and in the other to a lagoon that was reserved for the private use of guests staying in the garden bungalows—compensation for not having water views.

He opted for the lagoon and a few minutes later, a little scratched and dirtied up, he was standing on the sand. Finn preferred this part of the resort—the intense privacy of bungalows built in individually carved-out clearings and an almost secret lagoon suited him.

Zoe would be in a postcard-picturesque overwater bungalow. All the media were. He wondered what she thought of it.

"Yeah, well, you had the chance to ask her, moron," he said, the words sounding too harsh juxtaposed against the almost-silence of the night.

They *weren't* too harsh, though, those words. He *was* a moron to have blown her off instead of talking to her. She was a journalist and he had a resort to promote. He wanted her to write a good story the same way he wanted all the journalists at Poerava to write good stories. It was a business relationship, nothing personal.

Then again, she'd made it personal, hadn't she?

He bent down, picked up a handful of sand, let it sift through his fingers. Seeing the sand fall made him think of an old-fashioned hourglass. Time being measured, time passing a grain at a time.

I'm not lost... I can look after myself.

Ten years later she still remembered what he'd said to her in that cruel moment.

There'd been defiance in her words tonight but surely she knew how ridiculous they sounded with her carer standing beside her, keeping watch over her.

The carer. Young for a dragon. Cristina.

She had a nickname—Cris—which meant she had to be very familiar with Zoe, who only gave nicknames to those she cared about. V for Victoria, Lils for Lily, Devil for Malie.

For him, it had been a nickname reversal: she'd called him by his full given name—Finlay. His burly Irish father had named him after Finlay William Jackson hoping Finn would become a cricketer or a rugby union player like his namesake. His father had ended up disappointed that his son lacked the bulk to make a decent sportsman. Finn had hated the name, hated his father's disappointment. His mother—delicate, refined, bookish, adoring—had predicted (correctly, as it turned out) that Finn would be a late developer, but when he'd shown no sign of it by the age of fifteen and his father had died with his disappointment intact, she'd quietly dropped the "Finlay."

The real miracle was that he'd not only let Zoe call him that when he would have punched anyone else for doing so, but that he'd *liked* it.

He ran an agitated hand through his hair, annoyed at the memory. Tonight, to Zoe, he was Mr. Doherty. Finn, not Finlay. And that was just fine. What did it matter? What did any of it matter? The nicknames. The past.

The present *certainly* shouldn't matter. And yet all it took was the sight of Zoe across the room to mess up his head. Zoe, guarded and protected as usual. Not that he should care that Zoe had Cristina in tow. How disingenuous, when he would have killed to have been able to afford a personal nurse for his mother in those last terrible months.

And yet…he *did* care. He was honest enough to admit it, if only to himself. He cared because Zoe had told him that night in the hospital that the position of caring about her, caring *for* her, wasn't available to him. She'd told him to go and look after his mother because she, Zoe, didn't need or want him, she could look after herself. So to see her tonight, letting herself be fussed over in a way he never would have fussed over her because he knew how much she hated it… Well, it rankled.

He sucked in a breath at the sudden realization that her attitude tonight was a direct result of that last meeting of theirs. How else to explain her…her desperation, almost, to be seen as independent.

I can look after myself… If you're leaving in the morning you won't see…

What she should have done was tell him it was none of his business how she lived her life. It *wasn't* his business. Tomorrow morning he'd be on his way to Pape'ete to catch his flight to London while Zoe, according to Aiata, would be one of three journalists cruising around Tiare Island on *Pearl Finder*, visiting the best snorkeling spots in the vicinity, and that would be that. Her living her life, him not seeing how she did it.

Although there was one thing he *could* see, at least in his head. Zoe on the boat, Captain Joe oozing his Polynesian charm all over her, giving her special attention because she was in a wheelchair. Or maybe just because everyone always gave special attention to the earth-imprisoned mermaid whether she asked for it or not.

They'd talked a lot about mermaids back in the day. Zoe had been obsessed with "The Mermaid of Zennor," an old Cornish legend. He'd seen her as that mermaid. Himself as the mortal who followed her off a cliff to live in her world.

Sentimental teenage drivel.

Although he *was* living in her world now. He never would have thought of going to Australia and applying for the job at

Travel in the Rough, his first real job, his stepping-stone to success, if Zoe hadn't filled his head that out-of-time summer with her dreams of traversing the globe one day. He'd borrowed her dream. He was traversing the globe.

And so was she.

Not that the fact they were living two halves of the one dream made them any more compatible than they'd been all those years ago. The saint, and the sinner who'd wanted to believe she could be his because under their skins they had the same burn for a life in a world that was different, bigger, wilder than where they were.

He'd wanted to believe…yet he'd known in his soul she could never be his.

And very suddenly, Finn felt like an imposter in his designer clothes and his Italian leather shoes, with his hundred-dollar haircut and his penthouse apartment with its view of Sydney Harbour. It was as though seeing Zoe had transported him back to the wrong side of the tracks, to that tiny, crumbling cottage just outside the village, the high school dropout who'd never amount to anything except a prison sentence.

That night, in the hospital, Zoe had called him a thug. Putting him in his place. She'd done it deliberately. Had meant to hurt him.

He'd said goodbye to her that night, in a way he hadn't quite managed to say in the preceding two years despite his best efforts.

He'd said goodbye again, in his head, the day she left Hawke's Cove. He'd been furious at her for going off to see the world without him, for doing it like *that*, holidaying with her parents when fleeing the village had always been about her escaping the prison they kept her in. So furious, he'd deleted every selfie of the two of them and then gone half-crazy with remorse at having not one image of her. He'd rehearsed what he'd say to her when she got back from her holiday. Vicious, biting, awful words. He knew he'd never get close enough to her to say them but he'd enjoyed forming them in his head anyway.

Then, three months after Zoe had left, Finn had had a more final goodbye to say, to his mother. And when she died there'd been no reason to stay in Hawke's Cove, so he'd left too. He'd stopped thinking about Zoe on the flight to Sydney. Just... stopped. Cold turkey. A bit like the way he'd given up smoking on his eighteenth birthday.

And now this. Tonight.

How could it be that after ten years of not thinking about her all it took was five minutes in her company for his head to be crowded with memories?

He didn't know, and he definitely didn't know what to do with those memories.

Block them all over again, he supposed. Go to his bungalow, drink his rum, read Aiata's briefing notes on every journalist *except* Zoe, and block them.

Sounded like a plan.

"Goodbye again, Zoe," he said, and headed back along the path.

five

SO MUCH FOR PLANS AND GOODBYES, FINN THOUGHT
as he stood under the shade of a palm tree well back from the
pier, waiting for Zoe to arrive for the snorkeling cruise.

If he had half a brain he would have set fire to Aiata's briefing note on Zoe the minute he'd got back to his bungalow
last night.

Instead, *just a peek*, he'd told himself, and only after he'd finished reading everyone else's.

Kiss of death, because page one had revealed that Zoe lived
in Sydney—*Sydney*, where *he* lived. Of course he had to read
everything in the file then, plus every one of her blog posts,
because that felt too much like fate.

And so here he was, *not* on a plane to Pape'ete, determined
to see for himself just how well Zoe could look after herself.
Not that it mattered, but she'd tossed that challenge at him last
night so why not at least—

He jerked so suddenly he hit his head against the trunk of the palm tree.

He swallowed a harsh curse—not only from the pain in his head but at the kick in the guts caused by seeing Zoe on approach in full sunlight.

No, not in the guts—the kick was higher, in the region of his heart, which ached the way it always had when he'd looked at her and wanted his hands all over her and known he wasn't allowed to touch her.

She was wearing white. A dress as long as the evening gown she'd worn last night, but this one was beach casual. It had long sleeves and a high neck and looked demure with the row of prim buttons fastening all the way down the front. But that demureness was an illusion; the dress was made out of something so flimsy and filmy he could practically see through it. He felt that old tremor of helpless, hopeless longing suffuse him. He'd felt like a lecher back in the day, salivating at the outline of her body through her oh-so-innocent attire, knowing it was sun protection that dictated what she wore and she was oblivious of what it revealed to his not-innocent-at-all eyes. She'd always been covered up, slathered in Factor 60, wearing sunglasses and a hat.

Her hat today was a broad-brimmed straw number with a band in her favorite color. *Blue ocean*, she called that shade, *like the Celtic Sea off the coast of Devon*.

And damn, he shouldn't have been able to remember something as inconsequential as how she'd once described that color. He wished that hat was on her head instead of on her lap because seeing her platinum-gold hair in the sunshine, bright as a beacon, drawn forward over her right shoulder in a braid threaded with a string of glittery green stones, made him remember the feel of it that one and only time he'd touched her.

She looked…ah, she looked beautiful.

No. Not that. "Beautiful" was like "perfect." What did

"beautiful" really mean? A symmetrical arrangement of facial features all in proportion. Gina was beautiful. Zoe was... more. A ray of light, more dazzling than the sun but gleaming fresh and cool.

How he'd wished she'd put her cool hands on him, once upon a time, and take the angry, shameful, lustful heat out of him. But she never had. And after that one time he'd touched her, when she'd been almost-crying over one too many phone calls from her parents, he'd never dared touch her again. Too risky, because that simple tuck of her hair behind her ear had made him want more than he was allowed to have. Ewan would have sacked him if he'd found out that what Finn really wanted to do was tangle both his hands in Zoe's hair, tilt her head back, take her mouth with his, and then take the rest of her too.

Oh boy.

What had happened to blocking those memories?

OK, seeing her was a bad idea. He needed to go back to his bungalow, rebook his flight, get away from Poerava.

But as he pushed away from the tree her laugh floated through the air to him, and his heart jumped and his breath stuck in his throat. Zoe's oversize sunglasses hid half her face but he knew her eyes would be glowing; they'd always glowed when she laughed, *she'd* always glowed when she laughed. She used to laugh all the time—carefree, joyous, as though it was a type of freedom for her.

He wondered now—for the first time since he'd stormed out of her hospital room ten years ago—if she still laughed all the time. Wondered if she still did that thing when her words got jumbled up and she covered her face with her hands and laughed into them, which had always made him want to grab those hands and kiss them and promise to make her laugh for the rest of her life. Wondered...what her day-to-day life was like.

He'd never seen Zoe in a wheelchair until last night. It jolted him now to realize that even during that scene at the hospital he hadn't imagined her being so...so restricted. She'd always longed for complete liberty to do and be whatever she wanted, and now...well, what was it like for her?

She'd reached the ramp that connected the boat to the pier. Finn took an automatic step toward her, his first impulse to help.

But then he saw Cristina was leaving Zoe to it, and he forced himself to stop. If Cristina wasn't rushing to assist that meant Zoe didn't need help. In any case, not only was the catamaran custom-made with full wheelchair accessibility but so was the ramp to get on and off.

Captain Joe called out to the two women from *Pearl Finder's* deck and Zoe called something back before wheeling herself onto the ramp with barely a pause.

There. Done. That was him told *and* shown: she really could look after herself.

Great. Wonderful. Time for him to leave.

Except that suddenly he knew he wasn't going to leave.

Suddenly he knew he was going on a cruise around Tiare Island.

On board *Pearl Finder*, Aiata gave Zoe a personal familiarization tour of the features and facilities on the main deck before directing her to the lift that would take her up to flybridge, where the other guests were already gathered.

But Zoe came to an abrupt stop when she was halfway toward the group.

Was she hallucinating or was that Finn Doherty standing in profile beside Captain Joe at the helm? As in Finn *flying out in the morning and won't see you being independent and I don't care anyway* Doherty?

Except he wasn't the well-dressed, polished resort owner she'd met last night. This man looked more like Crab Shack Finn—and yet not quite. He was wearing well-washed (but not disintegrating) jeans, a rumpled (but not faded) Henley T, worn-in (but not wrecked) trainers, and sunglasses (which he never used to wear). His hair, while a lot shorter than it once was, looked as though his hands had torn through it a time or two like they had in the old days. And he had proper adult stubble on his jaw instead of a sparse scattering of teenage facial hair. Small but telling differences.

A hybrid, that's what he was. Half familiar. Half stranger. Entirely disturbing.

As though he'd known she was there, he turned and smiled at her—an actual, real smile—and she saw that he hadn't had the goofy chip in his front tooth repaired and somehow that seemed so *Finn*, to not bother getting it fixed, she found herself smiling back at him. She wished he'd take off his sunglasses so she could see if his smile crinkled the corners of his eyes the way that used to make her want to trace the radiating lines with her fingertips.

He said something to Joe, then started toward her without waiting for Joe's response. Her lungs squeezed and her pulse raced and that inconvenient shiver was coursing through her and she knew, she just knew, her nipples would be sticking out, and she dared not look down because that might make him look down too and if he saw the reaction her body was having to him she would wheel herself overboard.

She had to get control of herself or she'd start babbling the way she had last night. But how, when just the sight of him wreaked such havoc on her body? *How?*

Her mother! She would channel her mother. Give him that regal keep-your-distance look her mother had always given him when she'd seen him on the high street and—

"We'd better make sure we get a spot in the shade," Cristina said, reaching her side just as Finn stopped in front of her—presumably in response to the heat Zoe could feel suffusing her face.

Cristina wasn't looking at her, though; she was regarding Finn in a decidedly Selena Tayler-ish way, and Finn was giving Cristina look for look.

Don't be fooled, was what she read in the expression on Finn's face: *I am not Crab Shack Finn.* He was still smiling, but somehow that chip in his tooth now looked far from harmless, it seemed almost…predatory.

Her imagination?

No, not her imagination. No matter how he dressed or how he smiled, he was not her old friend. She'd known that last night when she'd been so desperate to prove to him that she could look after herself despite Cristina's presence and he'd said she had nothing to prove, and she'd said…she'd said it was a shame he was leaving in the morning.

Ah. Of course. That was why he was here. To test the truth of her claim that she could look after herself. It seemed ridiculous—why would he care?—and yet she was positive the reason he wasn't on his way to London was because he'd decided to throw down the gauntlet: *go ahead and prove it to me, Zoe.*

Well, she was going to pick up that gauntlet by not proving a damn thing. She wasn't going to explain herself. She wasn't going to apologize for the way she lived. She wasn't going to chase Cristina off as though it was shameful to need assistance. If she decided to let Cristina push her chair, or lift her, or…or feed her grapes while she reclined on a chaise longue, it was none of Finn Doherty's business.

Decision made, she beamed her best smile at Cristina. "Yes, you're right, shade would be nice."

"If you want shade, Zoe," Finn said, "why don't you join the Q&A session I'm having with the other two journalists on board down in the cabin. The Americans, Matilda and Daniel. Did you meet them last night?"

"Yes, I met them, but no thanks, I'm not really into group briefings," she responded, quite regally she thought.

He raised his eyebrows. "It's only thirty minutes, nothing too arduous."

"In any case, I thought up here was the place to be," she went on despite the obvious dare in that "arduous" comment—as though she wasn't up to thirty minutes sitting around a table! She wasn't an invalid!

"Up here?" he said, slowly taking off his sunglasses, his smile unfreezing as though he was reading everything in her head correctly and was choosing to be amused by it. And yes, his eyes did still crinkle at the corners, and her fingers still twitched with the need to trace those lines. The cruise, she knew then, was going to be torture.

"The panoramic views…the…um…ambience." Ugh. Shades of last night's blithering idiotism! He needed to put the sunglasses back on so she could concentrate on something other than his eyes.

Finn shoved one arm of those sunglasses down the neck of his T-shirt. Like, seriously. It was sunny, he should be putting them on his face!

"You'll have lots of opportunities to enjoy the ambience up here, but it's up to you. Although—" transferring his attention to Cristina, his smile cooling "—of course you'd be welcome at the briefing if Zoe needs you."

Oh! *Oh!* "*Zoe* does not *need* anyone," Zoe said through her teeth. "*Zoe* can attend a media Q&A perfectly well on her own because it's her *job*."

Finn brought his eyes back to her. "So you're coming?"

"I'm coming." Double ugh. Zoe had the feeling she'd just been hooked like a mackerel.

"Great," Finn said. "I'll come down with you in the lift. I've been meaning to try it out for myself and haven't had a chance."

Zoe eyed Finn, thinking about the size of the lift. A briefing with other people around a table she could manage. Being alone with Finn in a tight, confined space was another story.

"I'm not sure there's room for the two of us in there," she said. "You're...well...big."

Finn's lips twisted, Cristina choked back a laugh, and Zoe—realizing how her words could be interpreted—slapped a hand over her mouth.

"Er...yes, I can confirm the rumors are true," Finn said, deadpan.

"Oh!" Zoe gasped, a giggle burbling up even as her face went furnace hot and her eyes...oh no, her treacherous eyes went to the front of his jeans for a flying second before she found the willpower to jerk them straight back up to find his eyebrows raised. "I mean..."

"That I'm six feet two inches tall and weigh fifteen stone?" he asked. "The weight's mostly muscle which takes up less room, I promise. Or are you telling me I need to get to the gym more often?"

"You...you... Oh, let's just go!"

"So you're coming to the briefing *and* I can join you in the lift?"

Zoe's answer was to start wheeling herself toward the lift.

And as Finn laughed, she knew she'd been hooked, reeled in and landed.

six

FINN DIDN'T MISS THE FACT THAT ZOE'S CHIN WAS
jutting out the way it used to when she was facing a challenge
as she propelled the wheels of her chair forward with revealingly jerky hands.

They reached the lift and he hit the button.

"What are you doing, Finn?" she asked, and although the
directness of that question shouldn't have taken him by surprise knowing that jut of her chin, somehow it did, because it
made him realize he had no idea what the hell he was hoping
to get out of this cruise.

Which was why his response was inadequate: "What do you
mean, what am I doing?"

"You can't be *that* interested in the article I'm going to write,
so why is it so important to you that I attend this briefing?"

Finn stood aside to let her enter the lift.

"Of course I'm interested in what you write," he said, stepping in after her and hitting the down button. That was one hundred percent true, even if there were other, darker truths in the mix that he wasn't willing to confront. "I read a lot of your articles last night. I particularly liked the one about the floor show in New Zealand. Pois, wasn't it? Very funny."

"Not so funny at the time," she said, and then a laugh burst out of her, and his heart kicked a rib because it felt so right. As right as the scent of her, like flowers made of lemon and sunlight.

And in that blinding moment, why he was on the cruise, what he wanted, became clear.

Time.

He wanted time with her.

Time to deal with the memories seeing her had unblocked. To know her life, to be reminded that she was not for him. To say that final goodbye so he could move on. What he wanted, what he *needed*, was closure. So that if he should happen to run into her in Sydney one day it wouldn't feel like fate, it would be just a coincidence.

"Well, I hope nobody coaxes you onto any stage this week," he said, keeping it as light as he could.

"You and me both," she said, and laughed again. He wished she'd stop laughing...and also, perversely, that she wouldn't ever stop.

"In fact, based on what I read last night I know you could do justice to a more personal story," he said, wondering at what moment since seeing her last night that startling notion had taken root in the secret recesses of his brain.

"What kind of personal?"

They came to a stop. The door opened. He exited. Stopped. Waited for her to clear the elevator. "I'll give you an exclusive if you have dinner with me tonight. Eight o'clock. Bungalow G11."

"But—"

"Are we ready?" he said, raising his voice and directing it into the cabin where the other two journalists were waiting with Aiata, phones already on the table ready to record.

"Any other questions?" Finn asked as the promised half hour drew to a close.

"Yes." It was the writer from *Hot Destinations*—Matilda. "I've heard Poerava has a management program to encourage local youth to pursue careers in hospitality. I'd love to hear more about that."

Finn turned to Aiata. "That's your baby, over to you."

He breathed a silent sigh of relief as Aiata started talking, happy to be out of Matilda's direct line of fire. She'd been interspersing questions with come-and-get-it looks and he was trying to subtly get the "nope, not happening" message out there and it was tiring.

Matilda was smart, she was also gorgeous, but Finn never had holiday flings with hotel guests. When the guest was a journalist the line was doubly uncrossable out of respect for his ex-wife. He and Gina had accepted that their marriage had failed but she didn't need to see him getting cozy in photos on a travel writer's Instagram. As far as he was concerned the obligatory handshake he'd exchanged with each of the journalists last night was the sole physical contact allowed.

He pulled himself up there, uncomfortable at the exception he was making for Zoe; she was a guest and a journalist, yet not only had he *not* shaken her hand last night but he'd made a date to have dinner with her that he hadn't extended to anyone else.

Well, not a *date*. It was work. He really was going to give her a story. He was going to give her *his* story.

It was with a sense of inevitability that his eyes locked on to Zoe at that moment. She was scribbling in her notepad and a glance at the page showed him her handwriting was as atrocious as ever.

A sudden laugh caught in his throat, only just audible and yet Zoe stopped writing and looked at him. He gave a half nod at the page. She looked at the page, then at him again. She smiled as though she knew exactly what he was thinking—and he was transported back twelve years to the time he'd teased her about how such a tiny girl could make such a big mess with a pen. His heart gave one of those rib-aching kicks, and one of the dark truths he didn't want to confront bloomed in his head like a flower: he still wanted, quite desperately, to touch her. *You should have done it last night*, he silently accused himself, furious that he'd missed the opportunity. *A handshake and you would have escaped purgatory. Now she's off-limits again.*

Zoe's smile faltered as though she'd felt his self-directed fury, or maybe she'd seen it in his face. She dropped her eyes to her notepad, and Finn realized he'd used the exact same phrase Ewan had spoken at the Crab Shack when he'd warned Finn away from her: *She's off-limits, and I mean it, Doherty.* His gang of bad brothers had all at one point or another used that phrase when they'd seen him looking at her. Mrs. Whittaker, once: *Finn Doherty, don't get any ideas, stick to your own kind, that girl is off-limits.* Even his mother: *Oh, Finn, my darling, I want you to have whatever you want, but Zoe Tayler is off-limits, you know that.*

Off-limits.

Of course he wasn't going to shake her damn hand last night. He still felt ripples of the rage that had exploded in him at how she'd been unable to mask her disbelief that he wasn't the manager but the owner of what she thought was two luxury resorts. He'd almost burst with the need to tell her that in fact he owned five, soon to be six resorts—and what's more he'd *self-made* his success, unlike Brad Ellersley who'd stayed in that village Zoe had been desperate to escape, content to *inherit* a career, not build one out of nothing.

Look at me, Zoe! See me as something more than the no-hoper who

*barged uninvited into your hospital room full of your dreams and how
I could help you get them.*

Idiot. Had been, still was.

Look at *him*?

Look at *her*!

A writer, a world traveler, a good journalist. Poised and professional throughout the Q&A, asking intelligent questions, listening carefully to the answers, jotting down notes and checking
them. As if she'd ever needed his help to achieve her dreams!
She'd fulfilled them for herself, despite her parents, despite her
wheelchair, despite Brad, despite *him*.

She had nothing to prove to him.

He was the one with something to prove: that he had *nothing*
to prove, not to her, not to her parents, not to any of those busy-
bodies in Hawke's Cove who'd tut-tutted at him for daring to go
near Princess Perfect. And OK, it was counterintuitive to have
the thing you needed to prove be that you didn't have anything
to prove, but it was nevertheless true.

Wasn't that really why he hadn't caught the flight to Pape'ete?
Wasn't that why he was on this cruise? Why he'd arranged this
media briefing with her as a spectator?

Time with her, yes. Closure, absolutely. But also to show
her who he'd become?

Wasn't that why he was offering to tell her, and only her,
his story?

Now *that* deserved a wince.

What had he done that was so special? If not for his mother's
life insurance money he'd never have been able to afford to
leave Hawke's Cove. If not for Gina half staking their business they'd never have got their first bank loan and he'd still
be working for someone else.

Nothing to prove? Nothing *worth* proving!

He'd have to rescind the story offer. It was too pathetic.
He'd cancel dinner.

No, not cancel. Not...that. But he'd find a different story for Zoe. He'd talk to Aiata. She'd said she was working with each journalist to craft individual story angles so it wouldn't seem weird to ask her to help.

But if he was going to do that he had to get onto it fast. Now. Immediately.

"Right!" he said, agitated, only to realize that Matilda had just asked another question.

They all looked at him, startled.

"Sorry," he said, and winced. "But we'll be reaching our first snorkeling destination in fifteen minutes so you guys might like to get changed and go out to the aft deck to gear up."

He kept his eyes carefully off Zoe as everyone on board made their way out to the deck. Listened to the safety briefing, then to Tiare Island's resident marine biologist Gaz giving a rundown of what they'd see. Next came demonstrations of the gear. Dividing into two groups, each with an assigned instructor to monitor them in the water.

Zoe laughed, and he reacted like a Pavlovian dog, wanting to see her, to know what she was thinking, feeling.

Funny, she'd always looked so delicate, so ethereal, you expected her to be the type to sit gazing out of a window reading a novel and eating macarons. In reality she was up for any mischief going. Criminal-in-training, he'd called her once, and she'd been thrilled, confessing that her life was so boringly *safe*, that she'd been trying to break through barriers, vault over hurdles, leap over fences, drive through roadblocks erected by her parents forever, and she *loved* the idea of *not* playing it safe.

Now he wondered what it was like for her living in Sydney, away from those overprotective parents he knew still lived in Hawke's Cove. He wondered if she lived alone—Google had failed him on that one point, but he felt she would have mentioned a boyfriend in a blog post. Unless the guy liked his privacy?

No rings, so he didn't think she was engaged or married.

OK, that was confronting. That he knew there weren't any rings when he hadn't even been conscious of checking her fingers.

But *was* it confronting? Really? He wasn't going to marry her. Wasn't going to sleep with her. Was determined not to touch her. All he was going to do was face his past with her and put it in perspective. See it for what it really was: a juvenile unrequited love story.

Anyway, what did the absence of such rings actually mean?

Maybe she had them tucked away for safekeeping. Maybe she didn't wear *any* rings anymore; all the glitter he'd seen on her last night and today was in her hair and on her feet. He and Gina had never worn wedding rings and he hadn't given Gina an engagement ring because she'd said if he wasn't wearing rings neither was she. And Gina was still a Berne, so the fact that Zoe was still a Tayler similarly meant nothing.

Uh-oh.

Gina.

He hadn't told her he'd been delayed.

Time zone calculation. It was 6 a.m. tomorrow morning in Sydney and Gina's flight was at 7 a.m. She'd be at the airport, thinking he was already in Pape'ete, wanting a report on how last night had gone.

He went into the cabin and pulled out the phone he'd had on silent during the Q&A. Two missed calls. Automatically, he hit the return-call button and Gina answered before the first ring had finished.

"Finn!" she cried, sounding frantic. "Are you on your way?"

"I'm still at Poerava. On the snorkeling cruise. There are media on board *Pearl Finder* so I… Well, I decided to do it."

He felt the chill wafting over the Pacific Ocean. "We had a deal, Finn. Poerava for the UK," she said.

He winced—he really wished he could stop doing that. "It's just a delay."

"A delay?" She sounded incredulous.

"A postponement."

"What's the issue? And don't tell me you're playing tour guide for the media—unless Aiata's quit between last night and this morning?"

"Something's come up that I need to…investigate."

"Again I ask, what's the issue? Maybe I can help. Two heads, you know?" Pregnant pause. And then, impatient, "Well?"

"I can't explain," he said. Wince.

"Usually the phrase is 'I *can* explain,'" she said dryly. And then she laughed, exasperated but throwing in the towel. "Promise me you'll go through the updated information I emailed on the two properties."

"Promise." Stoic, because he didn't want to do it.

"Go through it *carefully*."

"Yep."

"Look at the photos, assess the locations, get comfortable with the financials. I've included Jed's 3D architectural renderings to give you a sense of how the internal layouts could look. Just… I don't know…do your precious SWOT analysis, OK?"

"SWOT analysis, photos, locations, financials, renderings. Roger that. Anything else?"

Finn knew he sounded flippant and half hoped Gina would laugh again, but the pause that followed his words didn't feel amused. He could sense Gina's reticence. And he knew what it meant.

She cleared her throat. "This new delay—"

"It's just one day."

"Is it about your mother?"

"Ah no, Gina, not that, not now."

"You always say that: not now. But however many times

you put off this decision it'll still be waiting for you. She's been gone a long time, Finn."

His heart squeezed. Guilt. Regret. Grief. "I know."

"Don't you think it's time to talk to someone about it?"

"I did. I talked to you."

"And look how that turned out, right?" She sighed. "I get it, I forced the issue. And in retrospect I'm glad that discussion brought everything to a head. Divorce isn't the end of the world, and we... Well, you know how we were. But I still care about you, Finn, not just about the business. Which is why I can say that even though *I'm* not the right one you have to find *someone*. A professional? Or perhaps just someone who knew her, who knew what you were going through. Someone who knows you in a way I never did, a way I never could. A way you never—" She broke off.

Finn finished the sentence for her: "A way I never let you."

Another sigh. "It's OK, Finn. Water under the bridge."

"I'll think about talking to someone, OK? Pinky swear."

"Idiot!" she said, and this time he was rewarded with the laugh. "Gotta go. Boarding."

She disconnected and Finn, feeling pressured purely because Gina *hadn't* pressured him, pulled up Gina's newest email about the two properties. He should open it. He really should.

"Hey, Finn!" Ms. *Hot Destinations*, dangling a snorkel from one hand as she entered the cabin. "You coming in?"

He smiled—a perfunctory effort he knew she'd accept as genuine; people always did, because of that babyish chipped tooth—and shook his head. "Work to do, I'm afraid."

She shot him a sultry moue. "I was hoping you'd answer a question for me."

He looked down at the email that was waiting for him and shoved his phone in his pocket. "Fire away."

seven

"HMM?" ZOE MURMURED, DISTRACTED BY THE sight of Matilda, the American journalist from *Hot Destinations*, hanging with Finn inside the cabin.

"I asked if you were going on the…"

Matilda had flawlessly tanned skin. Chestnut hair cropped close to her head in a don't-mess-with-me style. She looked strong and fit and bold. No one would dare tell *her* to put a wrap around her shoulders! And that bikini was a knockout. Fire engine red. A color that would make Zoe look like every drop of her blood had been sucked out by a vampire.

A splash penetrated her abstraction. The first group was jumping into the water one person at a time. She returned her attention to Daniel, who was exactly the buff-tough type of guy who'd appeal to *Xtreme Travel* magazine's sporty readership—no wonder they'd sent him. "Sorry. I missed that. What?"

"I asked if you were going on the fishing trip tomorrow.

Apparently, in the old days fishermen would beat the surface of the lagoon using ropes with stones attached to them, driving the fish toward the shore to be speared."

Zoe grimaced at the thought of spearing a helpless, corralled fish. "It's not exactly my style."

Daniel laughed. "Don't worry, tomorrow we'll be using fishing rods. You can catch blue marlin, yellowfin, wahoo, bonefish, trevally, tuna, mahi-mahi, bonito and skipjack."

"How about mackerel?" she asked, laughing to herself. She detested mackerel, but she'd consumed more than her fair share during those beach barbecues with the girls in Hawke's Cove, not wanting to let the side down on those Girls' Own Adventures: *Four Go Off in a Stolen Rowboat and Fish.*

Except it wasn't really stolen. Did that make it a true adventure?

And why was she still thinking about Hawke's Cove?

"I think there's a kind of mackerel tuna you can catch," Daniel said earnestly, which made Zoe feel bad that she wasn't taking the fishing expedition seriously.

"Oh, really?" she said politely. "How interesting."

"So how about it?"

This time she suppressed the grimace, knowing it was at best idiosyncratic to enjoy eating fish while being unable to kill one herself. "That trip starts way too early for me," she said, a good enough excuse. "Cris and I are having a lazy day on the beach tomorrow."

"Is she, like, your minder or something? Does she go with you everywhere?"

Zoe made a concerted effort not to bristle, but it was beyond her at that moment to reply in her usual appeasing manner so she settled for: "No." One discouraging, repressive word.

But it didn't discourage or repress Daniel. "Then how about we grab dinner tonight, just you and me?"

What? Where had that come fr— Oh. She got it. He was *interested*.

She had a few seconds' internal debate on whether she could be interested back, but a laugh from Matilda drew her eyes to Finn and out came: "Sorry, I'm catching up with Finn tonight."

Daniel looked at Finn, then at Zoe, then at Finn again, and nodded as though he'd just figured something out.

Zoe bit down on a vehement denial of what he thought he'd figured out and said instead, "It's a work dinner," which nevertheless sounded way too defensive.

She wished she'd just said she was busy. She didn't owe Daniel an explanation of who she was having dinner with or why. It would be like her expecting Finn to explain why he was so absorbed by the questions Matilda was asking him. Mind you, she didn't understand what there was left to ask. He'd already answered a thousand of Matilda's questions during the Q&A. OK, slight exaggeration, more like ten. But ten questions was a lot in that environment. Especially when you combined those questions with the ones she and Daniel had asked…and…

And *ugh*, Daniel was talking again. "Huh?" she said, dragging her recalcitrant eyes back to him.

"I said it might be work but play isn't out of bounds on these junkets." He jerked his head in Finn and Matilda's direction. "Exhibit A."

She allowed herself another glance at Finn and Matilda. Finn looked so…so Finn. And Matilda looked so sexy. Her bikini was so…well, red! And tiny. It was almost indecent for her to stand so nonchalantly in that bikini next to a fully clothed man.

Finn's eyes flicked toward Zoe and she quickly returned her attention to Daniel, who was in the process of stripping off his T-shirt. Daniel's body really was fabulous. And if play wasn't out of bounds?

"Our group's going in, let's gear up," Daniel said, his smile a little too knowing. He was well aware of his attractions. "We're going to be the last two off the boat if we don't move fast and we don't want to limit our time in the water. Here, let me help you get out of your wheelch—"

"No!" she cried, and was instantly aware of Cristina taking a step toward her. She held up a hand to stop Cris, giving the subtle royal wave they'd agreed long ago would be Zoe's *I'm OK, as you were* signal. Zoe didn't want any drama. Nothing that would draw Finn's attention. That would draw *anyone's* attention, she corrected. "It's a bit of a production for me to get into the water but I have to do it myself. If you don't want to cut into your time, go ahead without me. We've only got an hour until lunch."

He stood. "If you're sure?"

She ordered her eyes not to roll. "I'm sure."

"It's just that I know how much it must suck getting out of the chair and if it'll save time I can just pick you up and take you in with me."

Oh, he knew how it must suck? No, he did not. "Thanks, but I've got this," she said as calmly as she could. "I do it all the time, you know."

"OK then," he said, and put on his goggles. A cocky thumbs-up signal, and he was diving off the boat. He surfaced, called out something about coming back to help her in a few minutes, and she actually groaned. He'd already pushed her in her wheelchair, against her protestations, from the cabin onto the deck, and if his chair technique was anything to go by he'd likely drown her if he got anywhere near her in the water. Or maybe she'd have a crack at drowning him.

If she were going to rely on anyone it would be Cristina, who was already in her swimsuit and talking with Captain Joe, presumably asking him about the submersible hydraulic stern platform—one of the *Diver's* special features Aiata had already explained to her—which would lower Zoe into the—

Oh. Revelation! Cristina wasn't *talking* to Captain Joe so

much as *flirting* with him, flicking her glossy red–gold hair and shifting her weight from foot to foot, her hips swaying toward him. Well, well, well. This was a first. Cristina romancing on the job.

Zoe smiled to herself. The swim platform wasn't that urgent. Especially since Zoe had to wait for Matilda to get into the water ahead of her and Matilda was still deep in conversation with Finn. Finn, who was still fully dressed so clearly wasn't snorkeling with them.

No, of course he wasn't snorkeling. This wasn't a pleasure trip for him, it was work. He probably had a million things to take care of.

She was embarrassed that she'd queried his motives for involving her in the Q&A. That had *obviously* been work. As dinner tonight would be. How could she possibly have imagined even for a minute that his missing his flight today could have anything to do with her? For all she knew Matilda would be joining them at dinner. Which would be fine with Zoe.

Well, no, not "fine," given Finn had pitched that story he was giving her as an exclusive.

But hey, if he wanted to invite Matilda, Zoe wasn't going to make a fuss. He might think she was…was jealous. Which she wasn't.

Nope.

In those two years after the Crab Shack she'd become immune to jealousy. Immune to *him*. It had been ten whole years since she'd thought about him, and she was only thinking of him now because of that trip to Hawaii two months ago when Malie had gone on about Finn and the way he *looked* at her.

"Get out of my head, Malie," she muttered and instantly regretted it because Finn's eyes were drawn straight to her, and her eyes locked with his, the way they had in the cabin when he'd been trying not to laugh at her handwriting. Malie was hammering the point in Zoe's head—*Finn was the bad boy every female wanted to be ruined by*—and she wanted to scream that he'd never made any attempt to ruin *her* so what was the point of all these shivers she was experiencing every time he looked at her?

Determinedly, she looked to the water where the instructor was waiting for the last three stragglers. She needed the swim platform deployed. Now. Immediately. Deshivering required. And if she was lucky a giant clam would swallow her.

"Hey, Zoe!" Daniel, calling out to her from the water. "There's a pontoon, so no need to freak out if you get tired. I can help you get onto it!"

Well, that got everyone's attention.

Zoe wanted to throw her snorkel at him even though his offer acted like the starting gun she needed: Captain Joe moving immediately to deploy the swim platform; Cris hurrying over to her; Matilda stepping away from Finn. Major downside? It also made Finn's eyes zero in on Zoe, sending those unwanted shivers into overdrive.

When Cristina asked if she needed help Zoe fought a brief, hard battle with herself. She could transfer from her chair to the deck on her own but it wasn't the most graceful process. Then again, hadn't she decided at the beginning of the cruise that she wouldn't be ashamed of needing assistance? All she had to do was say the word and—

No!

No, no, no.

She knew very well that if she accepted Cristina's help it wouldn't be because she needed it but because she wanted to look perfect in front of Finn. It was tantamount to hiding her disability and she'd made a pact with herself to never do that. Her disability was part of her, her wheelchair was part of her. She *should not care* that Finn Doherty would see that she had limitations.

"No, I'll be fine," she told Cristina and then she smiled at Matilda, who'd finally come out of the cabin. "If you're snorkeling you might want to get in the water ahead of me. It'll take me a few minutes. I'm not exactly agile."

Everyone except Cristina and Zoe was in the sea, their designated instructor treading water waiting for them.

Finn's natural inclination was to offer to help but he clamped down on the impulse because once again Cristina was standing back.

He'd already provided assistance by ensuring anything Zoe might need was available. A wet suit because some paraplegics had trouble with temperature regulation (which she rejected); webbed swimming gloves to make it easier for her to move through the water (rejected); a lifejacket (rejected); a pool noodle (hallelujah, she'd accepted that). But it wasn't easy to be reduced to spectator status, nor to be subtle about it so Zoe didn't catch him at it. An occasional darting look as he stood talking to Joe was all he allowed himself.

OK, he wasn't so much talking to Joe as pretend-listening to him. But his professional patter was so practiced he threw out the right lines almost by reflex. A comment about lunch… mention of the next snorkeling spot…reference to one of the journalists who'd booked a tour tomorrow being of the *don't you know who I am* variety.

But he stopped responding altogether as Zoe unbuttoned her dress because there wasn't enough breath in his body for an intelligible word to escape.

She slid her arms out of the sleeves, wriggled the dress past her hips, under her bottom, down her legs, tugged it free of her feet…then she sat up and that caught breath of his rushed out. She was wearing a dark blue bikini, not brief like Matilda's red number—more like a gym top and a pair of tiny shorts—but it made his mouth go dry in a way Matilda's did not, mainly because Zoe's nipples were hard. He was sure they'd never looked like that in the old days. Then again, he'd felt so guilty for his constant state of arousal around her back then, when she was so obviously innocent and he just as obviously was not, he'd tried not to look too hard or too long. Sixteen, only two years younger than him, but in experience terms it was more like a twenty-year age gap.

And he was *not* going to think about those days.

She yanked a rash vest over her head—an eye-popping pink that had absolutely nothing going for it—then laughed up at Cristina as she pointed to the circular logo on the front of it. His mouth got inexplicably drier. He saw that her braid was caught down the back of her vest and wanted to go over there and pull it free, go over there and just…just touch her hair, touch her *somewhere*.

No touching! Don't even think about touching her!

Fine thoughts, but so strong was the urge he had to turn his back and count to ten.

He'd got to eight by the time he realized Captain Joe had stopped talking and was giving him a weird smile.

"What?" he challenged.

"Nothing," Joe said too quickly.

Finn narrowed his eyes but let it go because he suspected he didn't want to know what was so amusing. "Are we done here?"

"We're done," Joe said, and waved to someone behind Finn's back, which had to be Zoe since she and Cristina were the only two left on the boat.

He turned around, because that wave had annoyed him, and saw that not only had Zoe liberated her braid but she'd liberated herself from the chair.

She was now on the bench seat that bordered the deck, the height of which was lower than her wheelchair, and was applying Factor 60 to her legs. A minute later, Factor 60 passed on to Cristina, Zoe's chest rose and fell—a deep breath, oh God, he was going to explode out of his jeans if she took another one—and then she did some quick repositioning, using her hands to place her feet on top of a spongy mat Cristina had laid on the deck.

Zoe gripped the edge of the bench and Cristina tensed as though preparing to step in at any moment. One—two—three, and Zoe reached a fisted hand down to brace her knuckles on the mat. Pause, then she swung her bottom off the bench and lowered herself onto the mat. That had to take some strength! Another pause, then she adjusted her legs and reached for the mask and snorkel Cristina was holding out to her. She put them on, then scooted forward.

Cristina swung around to where Finn was standing with Joe. "Ready!" she called.

The portion of deck where Zoe was sitting began to lower. Zoe was laughing again as she hooked her arm over the noodle, and almost the instant the platform had finished moving she was off, Cristina beside her in an instant, swimming away from the boat toward the instructor.

Finn turned to Joe, caught him gazing after Zoe.

"What?" Joe asked, sounding pretty much exactly the same as Finn had sounded a moment ago.

"Hands off. She's a journalist."

"No she's not, she's a nurse."

A nur— "Oh, if it's Cristina you're interested in, go for it," Finn said, only to find Joe regarding him with that weird smile again. "What's so amusing?"

"Just wondering what's going to be happening with your own hands tonight."

"What are you talking about?"

"I heard there was a *hands off the journalist* coming to your bungalow for dinner. Bungalow G11. Not sure why you bothered changing rooms when you're leaving in the morning."

"How did you…?" He gave up on that question. Everyone at Poerava always knew everything that was going on. "To try it out, that's why."

"Aha."

"And dinner tonight is business. Zoe's writing a story."

"They're all *writing a story* but they're not all coming to your bungalow for dinner."

"A different kind of story."

"What story?"

"I need Aiata to tell me that."

"A story you have no idea about and yet it requires dinner. Makes sense."

"Oh, shut up," Finn mumbled, fully disgruntled now, and stalked off, even though Joe's ill-concealed laugh made him want to punch the guy.

eight

IT TOOK FINN ALMOST AN HOUR TO SORT OUT THE
story for Zoe—an hour in which he resolutely ignored Aiata's
attempts to hide a smile that seemed to be a carbon copy of Joe's.

When the snorkelers started returning to the boat he was in
the cabin pretending to look at messages on his phone but with
a clear view of the deck.

Zoe was the last out of the water, hauling herself onto the
platform where Cristina was waiting for her, then positioning
her legs. Everyone else—with the exception of Matilda—had
made their way up to the flydeck for prelunch drinks. Even the
eager Daniel had disappeared, spurred on by Cristina's glare
when he'd offered to boost Zoe onto the platform.

"Hey, Zo, how about I wait with you while Cris sorts out
the platform?" Matilda asked.

Cris? Zo?

"Sure, Tilly," was Zoe's easy reply—nicknames all around

then. Almost as interesting as the knowledge that an offer of assistance wasn't always scorned.

A sound. Hydraulics. The swim platform rising.

Mermaid rising. *His* mermaid.

Finn looked down at his phone again, because in his head he heard her calling him Finlay as they talked about mermaids and myths and legends. His heart was aching and he didn't want it to. She was not his mermaid. That was just his own personal myth. She'd never been *his* anything.

He was going to get himself under the strictest control before he went out there or he wasn't going to go out there at all.

As Zoe settled herself on the bench, Matilda handed her a towel and asked: "Are you going in at the next spot?"

Zoe blotted her dripping plait with the towel. "The only thing that could keep me out is a great white."

Matilda made a silent-scream face. "Please! I'm freaked out enough out there without imagining lurking great whites."

"The water's so clear I don't think 'lurking' applies," Zoe said with a laugh as Matilda sat beside her. "You'll see them coming a mile away."

"Thank you for that!"

"You Americans. Scared off by a little old shark!"

"You Australians. Dealing with great whites on a daily basis!"

"I'm not Australian, I just live there. And I'd sacrifice my pride and let you tow me back to the boat in a heartbeat if I saw a great white." She peeled off her rash vest. "But Gaz said there aren't any great whites in French Polynesia."

"He also said we'll be seeing black-tipped sharks at the next spot."

"There's never been a fatality related to a black-tip attack."

"There have been attacks, though!"

"*Occasional* attacks."

"I'm quaking with fear! Can you see me quaking?"

"I'd bet good money you don't know how to quake."

"I quaked when you almost took my head off when I offered to tow you in."

"I warned you what she was like," Cristina said, coming back out onto the deck and taking a seat on the bench on Zoe's other side.

Matilda huffed out a laugh. "Luckily I handle rejection well. I still like her. *Despite* the way she glared at me when I was trying it on with the scrumptious Mr. Doherty."

"I wasn't glaring at you," Zoe insisted, a little too emphatically she had to admit.

"Oh, you most definitely were," Matilda said, "but so you know, in my book girl power trumps boy trouble."

"Wh-what?" Zoe sputtered.

"I said—"

"No! I heard… That was a 'what' of disbelief because… I mean, it's not like… Me and Finn, I mean, we're not—gah!" She covered her face with her hands, laughed into them, then let her hands drop. "Let me start that again: I don't have boy trouble, and it's not like that between me and Finn. And anyway, you can say what you like about girl power but I have two friends who've just found true love and I know who they'd be saving first in a great white attack. Hint: not me!"

"Oh, I'm not interested in true love," Matilda airily dismissed. "True *lust* is more my style, and under that scenario I'd be towing you back to the boat and leaving him to Jaws." She turned to Cristina. "What say you, Cris?"

"I'm all for girl power," Cristina said, "but I can't tell you how many times Zoe's mentioned needing some 'boy trouble' since she got back from Hawaii, so I think we know where her head's at!"

"Traitor," Zoe said, blushing but laughing.

"Yeah, I don't think that's her head!" Matilda said, expertly dodging an admonitory flick of Zoe's towel. "That man is one crazy-hot hunk so if you need boy T.R.O.U.B.L.E. he'd be choice number one. Choice number two is mighty fine too, though. And don't look all *oh-I-am-mystified*! I heard you and Daniel talking on the pontoon."

"That was Daniel talking and me trying to shut him up so I could hear what Gaz was saying about giant clams and— Oh." Because out of the corner of one eye she saw Finn emerging from the cabin.

Matilda, with the benefit of being able to direct both of her eyes—unabashed and admiring—toward Finn, thrust out her impressive chest. Zoe thought in that moment that girl power might well trump boy trouble—but nobody could call Matilda a girl; she was *definitely* a woman. And Finn Doherty wasn't a boy. In fact, he'd *never* been a boy. *Aaaand* she had no idea where she'd been heading with that train of thought because Finn had come to a stop beside where Matilda was sitting.

"Giant clams?" Finn said, and Zoe prayed he hadn't heard their entire conversation. "Did you see any?"

A general question, addressed to nobody in particular.

Zoe could have said an enthusiastic yes, she could have launched into a fabulous description of the colors she'd seen, the frilled rainbow of blues and greens and aquas and turquoises, she could have asked questions based on what Gaz had told them about the need to monitor numbers and protect the clam population for future generations.

Instead, what she said was: *"Tridacna Maxima."*

Ugh!

"Well, look at you, Miss Marine Biologist!" Matilda said. "Getting all scientific while all I was thinking about as Gaz was talking was that one of the damn things better not try to eat me."

Finn laughed. "Zoe could probably come up with a romantic story about that, of the Jules Verne variety. She always had a story half written in her head."

"Hey!" Matilda again. "You two know each other?"

"We grew up in the same village," Zoe said, keeping her voice as nonchalant as she could.

Matilda patted the space on the bench beside her. "Well, I hope one of you is going to tell us the story!"

"It isn't a *story* as such," Zoe said, as Finn sat beside Matilda. "We worked together one summer at a beachside café when we were…well, kids, really. But we didn't hang in the same circles or…or anything like that."

A heartbeat. Two. Zoe waited for Finn to say something, but he simply kept those too-blue eyes unwaveringly on her.

There was the shiver, on cue. "B-but I'll tell you a more interesting story," Zoe said, uncomfortable with the silence. "One Finn and I used to talk about, called 'The Mermaid of Zennor.'"

"Lay it on me," Matilda said, hanging her towel around her neck as though settling in for the long haul.

"It starts—of course—with a beautiful young woman—they're always beautiful, aren't they?—who occasionally visited the local church at Zennor. Which, incidentally, is a real place, not make-believe. Nobody knew who she was. They knew only that when she sang the hymns it was the most magical sound in the world.

"One fateful day a local man, Mathey Trewella, beguiled by her voice, followed her after the service, all the way to the cliff overlooking a notoriously treacherous cove. He was never seen again and neither was the mysterious woman. Everyone in the village presumed Mathey had fallen off the cliff and drowned, and that the woman had moved away. And in the absence of any news or any sightings, as time moved on and life in the village continued, both of them were forgotten.

"But one day, during a fierce storm, a ship cast anchor in the sea off that very cove below the cliff where Mathey was last seen. The captain heard a voice calling to him from the tempestuous waves. A siren's voice. Lyrical and luring, mesmerizing, bewitching. It coiled around the captain's heart like a rope and tugged him, helpless, to the side of his boat, unable to resist the pull despite the fear that clawed at him because he didn't know what he'd find. When he looked into the water he saw a beautiful face surrounded by white-gold hair floating and twisting in the turbulent swell.

"She rose from the waves, to her waist. Beneath the green of the sea he could see a tail of iridescent scales in blues and greens and purples and pinks—and yet her face, her arms, her bare breasts were undeniably, exquisitely human. She was, of course, a mermaid.

"But not just any mermaid. Her name was Morveren, and she was a daughter of Llyr, the king of the sea. She was also the beautiful stranger from the church.

"Morveren begged the sailor to raise his anchor, which was blocking the doorway of her house where her husband—the human who'd jumped off that cliff into the tumultuous sea to be with her—waited for her.

"The wildness in her eyes scared the captain and he quickly raised his anchor and sailed away as fast as he could, fearing Morveren would wreck his ship. But Morveren was interested only in getting back to Mathey. The wildness the captain had seen in her face was nothing to do with destruction; it was the agony of being parted from her love for even a moment."

Silence. A hear-a-pin-drop moment.

Into which Finn, at last, spoke: "We found a silver chain once, Zoe and I, with a single white pearl dangling from it. We told ourselves it was a gift from Mathey to Morveren. Remember that, Zoe?"

She laughed. "On Sir Gaden L. Baxter's private beach! We were returning the dinghy you…you'd borrowed, and we went to the police station to hand in the pearl but you wouldn't go in with me because…" Oops. Not finishing that sentence.

"Because a) I was 'known to the police'—I think that's the

phrase you're looking for," Finn said, unabashed. "And b) I wanted you to keep the pearl." He grinned. "I was the real criminal, you were just an apprentice. And don't try and pretend you didn't get a kick out of being in that motorized dinghy, which I didn't 'borrow,' I regularly *stole* whenever Sir GLB didn't come down from London for the weekend. I know it was much more your style than the rowboat old Mr. Michaels used for rock fishing, which you and your friends thought you were so daring for stealing when everyone knew he let you get away with it. *And* you were bona fide trespassing with me, unlike your secret fishing barbecues with the girls on the Hawkesbury Estate because Mr. Hawkesbury knew very well what you lot were up to and let you do it."

"Hmm," Matilda said. "Stealing boats, trespassing, finding treasure, private beaches, visiting police stations. All that just because you worked at the same place for one summer? Did you really not hang in the same circles? Because you seem to know all the same people."

Finn shot Zoe an inscrutable look. "We really did not," he said. And then he gave the almost dismissive shrug of one shoulder he'd given her last night. "That's life in a small English village, everyone knows everyone and what everyone else is doing." Another of those shrugs. "Anyway, that was a long time ago. I'm respectable now."

"Well, that's a shame!" Matilda said, winking at him.

"I'm respectable *most* of the time," he corrected. "So, Matilda, Cristina, why don't you two go on up for lunch? No giant clams on the menu, mind. Even though they're considered a delicacy and are eaten by locals, we don't serve them at Poerava for reasons of sustainability—and there's definitely a story in that if you want to grab Gaz, Matilda."

"I'd be delighted to grab Gaz!" Matilda said cheekily.

Finn laughed before turning to Zoe and asking, "Can you spare me a few minutes?"

No! was what Zoe wanted to say, because his laughter had faded, and the look on his face was unreadable, and he was so *not* her old friend Finn, yet those memories he was dredging up were so painfully good to hear they made her wish he *could* be the old Finn.

Cristina was hesitating, and Zoe experienced another of those moments of detestable cowardice: she could ask Cristina to stay with her, help her transfer to her chair once she'd dried off, even though she didn't need assistance. Flickering at the edge of her consciousness was the insight that what she wanted from Finn was more complicated than a moment or two of nostalgia. More complicated, more…physical. T.R.O.U.B.L.E.

Matilda clapped her hands together as she stood. "Let's go, Cris, and leave these two to reminisce while we snaffle all the shrimp."

And what could Zoe do but give Cristina the royal wave and wait until the girls had disappeared. She forced herself to smile as she asked Finn, "Are we still on for tonight?"

Finn edged into Matilda's vacated spot, which brought him closer to Zoe, and the scent of him—she recognized that just-showered smell even without taking a deep breath, which was beyond her at the moment—made her pulse thrum. Soap. He'd always smelled like soap. Some people had thought he looked dirty, but she knew that he'd always been scrupulously clean. His mother would have made sure of that even if his own pride hadn't demanded it. In a twisted way he'd loved it when people were surprised that he smelled like soap instead of sweat and grime.

She wished he smelled of expensive cologne, something that would make him completely new to her, because this melding of past and present was confusing, disturbing. He smelled the same as he used to but he was not the same. He was edgier, darker. As though he'd grown out of the gang and into his very own dangerous reputation, embodying it completely at last. And her reaction to him was not innocent as it had been once upon a time. Not because of the trauma of that night, which had changed everything between them, but because of something else, something that made her intensely conscious of his legs so close to hers. If he moved a mere inch his knees would touch hers, and even though she wouldn't feel it she thought she would *feel* it. In her blood and bone and soul.

"Yes," he said, the deep timbre of his voice imbuing the simple word with a sense of just-us-two intimacy that had the shiver whispering through her, making her skin prickle.

"Then what?" She licked her lips nervously, feeling an undercurrent, like a rip that would drag her out of range, out of her depth, forcing her to fight her way back to the shore, to safety. "I mean, is there a problem?"

"No problem. I just wondered if you'd heard the news about Blake Hawkesbury."

"Oh." It made sense that he'd want to talk to her alone about that. If only she could stop overreacting to his nearness. "Yes. I spoke to Lily yesterday. Do you remember Lily?"

"Of course. One of the awesome foursome."

Zoe blinked at him. "Is that what we were called?"

"The Hawkesbury set called you that. Henry. His friends."

"I...I like that. I think?"

"I'd definitely take it as a compliment. More poetic than the village riffraff."

"I never called you that, Finn."

"No, but you once called me a thug. And your parents had a few choice epithets for me."

Thug! A brief flash of his face in her hospital room. Yes, she had called him that because he'd said he was going to beat Brad to a pulp.

She attempted a laugh, wanting to deflect from the memory. "Not as choice as they had for Henry Hawkesbury."

"I guess I'll take *that* as a compliment since he was all that and I...was all wrong." Pause. He seemed to be choosing words. "I don't know when the funeral is but if it's this week and you want to go back for it Doherty & Berne will give you a rain check."

"Thank you but no. Not that I don't want to be there for Lily but…well, just no."

She saw that Finn was looking at her thighs, realized he was watching her rub them, and immediately shifted her hands to the bench either side of her.

The shrug again. "I'm flying to the UK myself tomorrow," he said.

"Tomorrow? Oh. So it was just one… I mean…you…here…not…not there… I mean…gah!" She covered her face with her hands, embarrassed. "Sorry, sorry."

"Er…yes, one day, yes, I'm here not there, but I will be there, and there's no need to apologize. Did I get all that right?" he said.

She laugh-groaned into her hands before dropping them, and found Finn smiling the way he'd always smiled when she did that stupid face-covering thing, and she remembered the way he'd always interpreted her babble perfectly, which made her unutterably sad because he wasn't actually smiling at her, he was smiling at a memory. "Yes, you got all that right," she said.

"So, you're definitely staying on here."

"Lily insisted."

"And do you always do what Lily tells you?"

"She doesn't usually tell me what to do. No one does. But this time… I mean, the Cove… It's…difficult."

"Because of the accident?" he asked softly.

She sucked in a sharp breath as a memory came at her like a hot dart. A sound, a screech. Then gone. She shook her head, as much to clear it as to deny. "It's just that I didn't know Mr. Hawkesbury the way Lily did. If I were to go back it would only be for her and she wanted me to stay here because she knows." Stop. Enough. "It doesn't matter. I'm staying but I'll be writing her eulogy for the funeral."

"A eulogy, travel stories, a blog." He considered her, head tilted to one side. "But no novel?"

She sucked in a breath at the unexpectedness of that. It was a valid question; they'd talked many times about her becoming a novelist one day. Of course he'd be curious, there was no harm in it—but she nevertheless found it surprisingly difficult to confess: "Not yet."

There was a drawn-out pause as Finn continued to regard her. And then he said: "You were going to reset 'The Mermaid of Zennor' in Hawke's Cove on Sir Gaden's beach."

"Oh, I'd forgotten."

"I went to that beach a time or two after you told me your version, imagining your mermaid rising from the waves at midnight, the moment of enchantment, when two worlds would become one."

She stared at him, picturing him alone on that perilous beach at midnight, watching the waves, waiting for magic. One of her hands came up, hovered over his thigh. She wanted to touch him, to comfort him, console him, and she didn't even know why.

He looked at her raised hand and swallowed, his throat working as though maneuvering around a rock. And then those blue, blue eyes went to her face, so fiercely intent she read a warning in them: *keep your distance.*

"Just kids, hey, Zoe?" he said. "Dreaming about traveling the world, telling stories that never got written."

"Yes," she said, bringing her hand back to her own thigh, smoothing up and down, unstoppable.

"You know, I've heard a version of 'The Mermaid of Zennor' that I like better than the version you told today. One where Morveren goes to the church to hear Mathey sing and she's so enraptured by him she waits for him outside. She leads him away deliberately, unable to breathe without him, either in his world or her own." Another of those shrugs. "Makes a nice change from the man chasing the poor mermaid off a cliff!"

"He might have chased her in my version but at least he jumped in after her."

"It was a bold move, I'll give him that, going after her with all guns blazing." He stood. "Myths, huh? I guess we were always meant to outgrow the magic." He smiled at her, no chipped tooth, no eye crinkles, unreadable. "See you at eight o'clock. Bring your notepad."

nine

ZOE POSITIONED HERSELF IN FRONT OF HER BED-
room mirror, checking her makeup and pondering whether Finn
expected her to come to dinner on her own or with Cristina.

She should have asked him.

No, she shouldn't have *had* to ask.

If it was work—and it *was*: seriously, his last words to her
on the boat had been to bring her notepad—her default position was to go alone.

Work. Definitely. The dinner angle was nothing but a time
management byproduct. He'd hopped into a dinghy and zoomed
away at their second snorkeling spot to deal with an emergency,
apparently, *plus* he was flying out in the morning, so it made
sense for him to combine dinner (he had to eat, right?) with
business. Ergo, how embarrassing if she turned up with Cristina
only to find the table set for two, not three.

She peered at her reflection, noted the potential mixed message attached to wearing six extravagantly embellished hair clips to an interview, and ripped all the clips out. Time to be as restrained, as self-controlled, as Finn. Seeing her last night had to have been as much a shock to him as it was to her, but he'd kept it together masterfully compared to her unhinged babble-a-thon—which she'd compounded by treating him to a second babble-a-thon on the boat today.

She really hoped she didn't babble over dinner, but she had to admit the possibility was there because the idea of being alone with all-grown-up Finn Doherty was unnerving. As unnerving as the sense of urgency racing through her veins, an urgency telling her that time was running out, that part of her was missing and if she didn't find it fast she never would, and she needed that part or she'd never be whole.

The memory of that night in the hospital, perhaps...

No, it was more than that.

She'd felt the same despairing urgency before the accident. She'd felt it every time she'd seen Finn in the village after that summer, every time she'd gone across to him tripping over her words in that way that had made him laugh in the Crab Shack days but no longer did. Every time he'd waited her out with barely veiled impatience, the formidable bad boy who was too cool to associate with her now she was back at school.

The first time—a week after she'd stopped working at the Crab Shack—she'd dragged a reluctant Brad with her, only belatedly noticing that Finn's hands were all over Shona Tucker. But there'd been no turning back—no *reason* to turn back, despite the sickening swoosh in her stomach. She'd introduced them, and Finn had looked at Brad over Shona's head, then looked at Zoe, and with a jolt Zoe had realized Finn had moved on, that he had other pursuits, adult pursuits, that she was barred from.

That should have been the end, but she hadn't been able to stop herself from going over every time she saw him. She'd been through Ava and Dora and Jen and Sally and Maeve and so many other girls. And as Finn had scrupulously, insolently, introduced her to them she'd seesawed between hope and anguish, certain she could salvage something from their old relationship even as she felt the connection between them fraying... fraying...fraying.

Until that last time, when she didn't go over to him.

A Saturday night. She'd just got back from Ibiza and was out with her mother. They'd been planning "The Great Surprise 50th Birthday Bash of Noel Tayler" over dinner. They'd talked about the guest list and Zoe had found the intestinal fortitude to ask that Mrs. Doherty be invited. Her mother had agreed because Margaret Doherty, just home from another stint in hospital, could do with some cheering up. She only hoped the "dreadful son" wouldn't have to accompany her—although he was so busy "gallivanting around the village with one girl after another" there was little chance of that. What a trial that boy was to his poor mother!

Finn wasn't a trial to her, Zoe had piped up, he was a *comfort* to her. He was working *at least* three jobs because his mother couldn't work and he wanted her to have everything she needed.

And how did Zoe know what he was doing? She hadn't been *seeing* him, surely?

She'd heard it from Lily. Lily's mother spent a lot of time with Mrs. Doherty.

Mothers often saw their children through rose-colored glasses, had been Selena Tayler's response. Zoe had almost rolled her eyes because what color glasses did her mother think she herself was wearing?

But she hadn't felt like rolling her eyes as they'd exited the restaurant and seen Finn standing on the opposite side of the street with his back to the wall and a girl—Jess Trewes; beautiful, smart and kind—plastered against his chest. What she'd *felt* like doing was scouring her eyes out of her head before scurrying away in the opposite direction because why would he want to talk to any other girl when he was with Jess Trewes? Especially a girl who was out on date night with her own mother.

Finn had caught Zoe's eye and moved his hands to cup Jess's bottom. Zoe had shivered just like she was doing now, and it was like a veil lifting—she knew what he'd be doing with Jess later, knew it was the same thing he'd done with *all* those girls only she hadn't allowed herself to imagine it.

Her mother had said, with stinging irony, that yes, Finn Doherty was clearly a *great* comfort to his mother, and smoothly segued to a comparison with the far more admirable Brad Ellersley.

The thought of having sex with Brad hadn't ever entered Zoe's head but she'd decided on the spot that she'd lose her virginity to Brad the night of the summer ball—the night she'd already chosen to mark her liberation. Not because it was time, not because she even wanted to, but as an act of mutiny. She was going to prove to Finn, even if he'd never know what she'd done, that she was every bit the adult he was, so he could stop giving her those sneering you're-just-a-little-girl looks.

But she hadn't had sex with Brad.

She'd given up her virginity in an unmemorable one-night stand four years later, during which she hadn't thought about Brad at all; all she'd thought about was how she wanted it to be over.

Would she have wanted it to be over if the man had been Finn?

Stop! *Stop!*

She should not be staring into a mirror like some lifeless store mannequin remembering things it was too late to change and worrying about hair clips.

Back to the here and now, if she took Finn at face value dinner tonight was just business.

If she took him at face value...

"Why *shouldn't* you take him at face value?" she asked her reflection.

But almost before the question was out she had the answer: because he'd told his version of the mermaid story, with the mermaid chasing the mortal, and he'd told her about his lonely vigil on that private beach, the one he'd once called *their* beach.

Her heart started to pound, the shivering taking over as every receptive nerve in her body zinged with an almost unbearable intensity. And oh God, just look at her chest! She covered her breasts with her hands but her nipples stabbed her palms and she didn't know what to do except put on a coat so he couldn't see what he did to her when he looked at her the way he'd looked at her last night, the way he'd looked at...

The way he'd looked at all those other girls.

Slowly she dropped her hands. Stared hard at herself. Re-called the almost insolent way his eyes had traveled over her last night...

And that sense of urgency, of time running out, was swoop-ing, swirling inside her, goading her, daring her. Finn was fly-ing to the UK tomorrow, and tonight would be the last time she saw him. And she didn't care if the way he looked at her was insolent as long as he *looked* at her, looked at her and saw she wasn't a child.

There would be no coat. But by God there would be hair clips. She shoved back in all the glittery hairpins she'd removed and then opened the clip case she brought on every trip, re-moved an eye-popping blue and purple hair clip in the shape of a seashell and shoved that sucker in as well.

One night was all she had.

She was going to chase Finn off the cliff.

Finn opened the door at eight o'clock, letting room service out as Zoe arrived.

He murmured a welcome and took a lightning-fast inven-tory as she wheeled herself over the threshold. Ankle-length dress in sky blue; crystal-studded silver sandals on her slender feet; a profusion of spangled clips in the tousle of her hair that made her look like a sea princess…and that mutinously jutting chin, which gave him a premonition of disaster. She'd always been at her most adorable when she looked mutinous and he'd be damned if he was going to adore her again.

He led her out to the poolside deck where he'd had the table set for dinner, reminding himself that he was no longer that twenty-year-old Sir Galahad idiot who'd barged into her hospital room begging her to need him. He could manage this… this *thing* between them—whatever it was—for a single night.

Surprise flitted across her face as she took in the three place settings, the two chairs waiting to be occupied in addition to the space for her wheelchair.

"I thought you'd bring Cristina," he explained.

Her chin rejutted. "Did you?"

Ah, so that was the battle. He'd tossed a dare at Zoe on *Pearl Finder* when he said Cristina could attend the briefing if Zoe needed her, so no way was Zoe going to "need" Cristina's protection tonight. *So there, Finn Doherty!*

Finn shrugged, take-it-or-leave-it, nothing to see here. "It's not an accusation, Zoe."

"She's having dinner with Captain Joe, if you must know," she replied, clearly wanting to underscore the point she was making.

"Good for her," Finn said, calmly retrieving a bottle from the ice bucket in its stand beside the table. "Wine?"

"I'd *love* a glass of wine," Zoe said, still in obvious point-making mode.

Finn poured her a glass, then took his seat and poured his own.

"How long has Cristina been with you?" he asked, as Zoe served herself from the selection of canapés on the table.

"I'm not sure what you mean by 'with' me, but five years."

Finn picked up a set of tongs and concentrated on transferring food. "She's a nurse, right?" he said, just because he had to say *something* and that was the most innocuous thing he could think of off the top of his head. "I developed a huge respect for nurses when I was in hospital a couple of years ago."

"Oh, you...you were in hospital? I didn't know."

"No reason you should," Finn said. "No life-threatening injuries. Nothing like what you went through."

She drew in an audible breath, like she had on the boat when he'd raised the subject of her accident; a prawn she'd impaled on her fork stopped halfway to her mouth. A moment only, and then she shoved the prawn in her mouth, chewed it furiously but without any obvious pleasure in the taste.

"Mine was a motorbike accident," he said.

She swallowed. "I remember you always wanted a motorbike. When you were...were..."

"Eighteen? Yeah, well, I wanted a lot of things I shouldn't have when I was eighteen." Pause. "I gave the bike up after the accident. I learn from my mistakes, especially the painful ones." He wondered if she understood the inference.

Apparently not, because with an air of preoccupation she speared another prawn and ate it.

Fair enough. How could she possibly understand what he was saying? She'd always been oblivious to his ridiculous crush on her.

"So Cristina travels with you everywhere?" he asked. If he wanted to know more about Zoe's drastically altered life that seemed a safe place to start; she clearly wasn't going to volunteer anything herself.

He got a prickly "No," for his trouble, and then: "But since you're so interested I can tell you she's twenty-nine, single, and she likes fishing and cooking and watching sunrises."

He laughed, couldn't help himself. "I don't want to date her, Zoe."

"She also loves to travel but she *didn't* come with me to...to

Hawaii, for example, in February." Now that was definitely a *so there, Finn Doherty!*

Another apparently tasteless prawn went the way of the first two, and Finn laughed again, imagining the look on Gaspard's face should he see Zoe shoveling down his delicacies.

"What's so funny?" Zoe asked, still in prickle mode.

"The way you're holding your fork, like you're going to skewer me. I was just making conversation, not trying to re-enact the Spanish Inquisition."

She looked at her fork, closed tightly in her fisted hand. "Oh."

"How about you tell me what you'd like to talk about, Zoe?"

She laid down her fork, swallowed despite having no food in her mouth, took a deep breath as though gearing up to make an important announcement as the bright pink of a savage blush burned across her cheeks...and then the doorbell rang.

She closed her eyes and let the breath out, her shoulders slumping.

Dammit.

Finn got to his feet. "That'll be room service to set up for the main course," he said.

How about you tell me what you'd like to talk about, Zoe?

I'll tell you what I want to talk about, Finn. Sex. With you. Tonight.

Maybe it was just as well they'd been interrupted. He seemed to be more interested in Cristina than in her.

Getting brutal about it, all she had to go on for making such an outrageous sexual proposition was an old story about a mermaid and a throwaway line from Malie about how Finn used to look at her. And really what would Malie know? Malie was confident, bold, daring, and even *she'd* been in awe of Finn Doherty. The baddest, hottest guy in the village, who could have had any girl he wanted—and he'd certainly given the *having* of them a red hot go!

But not her. She was good enough to have lunch with when they were working in the same place, good enough to have tag along like a little sister on an occasional adventure, but not the type of girl to ask out on a date or even to *see* once she left the Crab Shack job.

Had she really thought she could waltz in here tonight and Finn Doherty—*Finn Doherty!*—all grown up and a hundred times more potent than he used to be—would say, *Sure, Zoe, I'm your man, how do you want it?*

She covered her breasts with her hands, ordering her nipples to deflate...and a new truth hit home. He'd checked her out as she'd entered the bungalow so he'd no doubt seen the state she was in, but after that he hadn't let his eyes stray from her face. He had to be the most sexually experienced man on the planet; he would have known exactly what she wanted, he would have known he could have her, but clearly he *did not want her that way.* He never had, never would.

But if she'd got up the nerve to ask him he probably would have said yes. "Yes" had always been his default setting when it came to sex, from what she'd heard. It wouldn't have been lust driving him in her case, though, it would have been pity, or kindness—or whatever it was that had propelled him into her hospital room ten years ago trying to make up for the fact that her boyfriend had dumped her because she was in a wheelchair.

Zoe reached for her wine, took a large sip, then rolled the cool glass against one hot cheek. She was such an idiot. She had to stop thinking about what Malie had said, forget about sex, get through dinner, do the interview, and leave.

"Out on the deck," she heard Finn say. She smoothed her dress across her thighs despite her dress being perfectly smooth already. The only thing about her that wasn't smooth was the inside of her head.

Silence reigned as the server cleared and reset the table, now for two people, and laid out an array of dishes. A silence so impenetrable all she could do was stare at her plate.

"Well?" Finn asked, once the server had left.

"Well?" she repeated, forcing herself to look him in the eye.

He gave one of those careless one-shoulder shrugs she decided she hated. "*Well*, what do you want to talk about?"

And didn't it say everything about their relationship—or lack thereof—that he'd picked up their conversation seamlessly while she'd had no idea where they were up to?

"The food," she said because it was there in front of her and she couldn't think of anything else except sex and that was not going to happen, *so get over it, Zoe*. "I want to talk about food."

"Food," he repeated slowly.

"Yes." She placed her table napkin across her lap. "It looks delicious!"

"It is delicious. But I don't think that's what you were going to say."

And oh God, his eyes were dipping, eyebrows rising, and she had to say something, get his eyes up, *up*. "I...you... I was thinking...that is...tonight I was...gah!" Up came her hands, covering her face, and *whew* her elbows covered her breasts in this position.

"For once I don't know what you mean," Finn said. "So how about you tell me?"

She shook her head, keeping her hands firmly in place.

Long moment, and then she heard Finn sigh. Heard the sound of more wine being poured. "Food it is, then," he said. "I ordered French Polynesian specialities. Scallops soaked in lime juice. *Mahi-mahi* served with vanilla sauce. *Fafaru*—marinated parrot-fish with crushed shrimps and crab. *Pouletfafa*, which is chicken and taro leaves." Pause. "Just one thing—sorry, but there's no mackerel."

What the…? Oh! She snorted out a laugh and dropped her hands. He was regarding her with his old crooked Crab Shack smile and the tension drained out of her as if by magic. "I can't believe you remembered."

"That you hate it? Yes. That you used to pretend to love it because that's what the awesome foursome cooked on the Hawkesbury beach? Yes. I remember a lot of things." Again the one-shoulder shrug. "That night, for example. If it's about that night, what you were going to say when the doorbell rang, my advice is to get it out so we can clear the air." Another shrug. "Tonight is a little like the end of that summer at the Shack. Lives diverging. There won't be another chance."

Time running out. Oh God. How could she grab it, hold on? And suddenly the words were there, not an inarticulate babble. "Did we ever have one, Finn? A chance?"

In the air-crackling pause that followed those questions she was intensely conscious of Finn's stillness, the scent of his soap reaching her like a bittersweet memory of what she'd wanted but never had. "I don't know how to answer that, Zoe," he said at last, so serious. "I thought we did, or at least we could have had, but that night… Well, you know what happened that night."

She swallowed against an unexpected lump in her throat. "But that's just it. I don't. I…I barely remember that night."

He blinked at her in disbelief, his mouth tightening. "That's the way you want to play it?"

"I'm not playing."

"That's the way you want to *keep* it, then? Because if you really can't remember and you want to, I'll help you locate the memory. You're not the only one who could do with some closure."

"I don't… I mean… I can't… It's just…"

"Do not!" he said. "Do *not* cover your face. You look at me and tell me you want to forget that night happened. That's all you need to do."

"You don't...don't understand."

"I think you'll find I do, Zoe. I was *there*."

She shook her head. "I mean I don't want it *told* to me. I don't want *any* of it told to me. Not the accident, not anything t-to d-do with the accident. I want the memories to already be in my head because they're *meant* to be there." She raised one hand, rubbed the palm across her forehead. "But all that's in here are fragments and...things I've been told that somehow don't seem to...belong to me, they're not really *there*. And there has to be a *reason* for that, a reason I can't remember."

"Or a reason you won't."

"Or a reason I won't," she conceded.

His turn to lay his napkin across his lap. He looked down at it for a long moment, and then his head came up. "You know, Zoe, one of the things I remember about the old days is how you always managed tense situations by detouring around them. Playing nice. Keeping the peace. Making everyone's road smooth even if the destination you wanted to reach threatened a bump or two along the route. Little white lies to your girlfriends, like how you felt about fishing. Pleading with your parents for space but never all-out fighting to take it for yourself. Letting everyone in the village smother you rather than insisting they leave you alone." He laughed, a short, harsh sound. "I never heard you raise your voice until that night, with me."

"*Please*, Finn!"

Another long impenetrable silence which she could not fill with anything except her thudding heartbeat.

And then Finn leaned back in his chair. "So be it, Zoe. Consider that night expunged from the record." He looked at the table. "Food, right? That's all we're talking about? Well, for dessert we'll be having *po'e*, which is a pudding made from papaya, mango and banana, Tahitian coconut cake, and a fruit platter that's heavy on the pineapple because the pineapple in French Polynesia is the best in the world. So save some room."

ten

AT LEAST HE COULD LEAVE IN THE MORNING KNOW-
ing he'd tried to get his precious closure.

Tried and *failed*, but still.

He hoped Gina didn't push him for an explanation for his staying an extra night at Poerava because he had no idea what he could say. Well, it was a long flight to London, he'd think of something.

Something that did *not* involve food, because there Zoe went again "—I saw this scallop dish on the room service menu, not that I ever order room service, oh, I don't mean *tonight* because this is an interview—" her tenth, twentieth, thirtieth bridge-over-troubled-water comment across the table.

Maybe inane food talk was his penance for forgetting the lesson he'd learned that night at the hospital: to stop rushing into situations with all guns blazing. It hadn't been an easy lesson because he'd been more impatient than ever after that night.

Restless, edgy. Ravenous—not for food, although he'd often been hungry for that too, but for an unnamed *more* from his endlessly hopeless life.

During that one summer with Zoe, as she'd shared her frustrations and dreams, he'd envisaged a different future. The hope of that had calmed him, somehow. Remembering now how she'd snatched all hope from him that fateful night, knowing she *chose* not to remember that he'd offered his heart to her—ripped it out, beating like a suddenly freed wild thing, only for her to tell him to stuff it back in his chest, aching and bleeding, and keep it to himself—made him want to grab the table and throw it in the pool.

Now *that* would be all guns blazing. She'd be out the door in a nanosecond, rushing to safety.

But it would still be more satisfying than the way he'd handled tonight's fraught moment, the oh-so-diffident invitation to talk about that searing memory.

He should have just spat it out: *Hey, Zoe, remember when I told you I'd do anything for you and you sicced your parents onto me?*

"Remember that scallop pie they used to serve at the Crab Shack?" she asked. "I never understood why people ordered that instead of the grilled scallops with the—"

"You've got coconut milk on your chin," he interrupted because he could not take any more inconsequential talk about food when they were supposed to be talking about *them*, dammit!

Down went her fork, up came her hand, scrubbing at the exact spot, the spot where the sauce always landed. "Why didn't you tell me?"

"I just did."

"You know what I mean."

She stared at him. He stared back.

And they burst out laughing at the same time, and he thought, *I give up, let this be how I remember you when I leave tomorrow.*

She picked up her fork again, speared a piece of chicken, shoved it in her mouth and deliberately let the sauce dribble onto her chin.

"You still eat like a pirate," he said.

"Hey, my appetite is tiny! You know I've never been very interested in food."

"For someone with a tiny appetite who's not interested in food you've been talking about it a lot tonight. And my pirate comment still stands. I don't think you've tasted one thing, you've been so busy shoving it down."

"And you've hardly *eaten* a thing. But then, you were always into self-denial."

"Self-denial? Me?"

"Hmm, maybe I mean self-sacrifice. Kind of…monk-like."

He was speechless. He'd slept with half the girls in the village by the time he was eighteen and a good portion of the other half by the time he was twenty and she called that monk-like?

"In a way," she said, and blushed. "Not *that* way. Obviously."

Not *that* way. Heat crawled up the back of his neck, even though he didn't know what he had to be embarrassed about. He'd wanted her to know he was sleeping his way around Hawke's Cove in those two years after that summer; had made *sure* she knew, hoping she'd take the hint and steer clear. Why feel chastened now?

And hang on, not in *that* way? Then in *what* way? He certainly wasn't going to ask.

"You know," she went on, intent on telling him what way even though he didn't want to know. "Abstemious."

Abstemious?

"Like the way you made sure you didn't eat all of the food from the free meals we were given at the Crab Shack. Only half your portion. Sometimes not even that. You always said you weren't hungry."

"Because I wasn't," he said, as the heat crept around from the back of his neck and across his face.

She gave him the tremulously inviting smile she'd given him once upon a time across the salt shakers, and just like that he was back in Devon. Eighteen years old and hungry, always hungry. And there was Zoe, insisting the two of them combine those on-the-house lunches, claiming she was full after only a bite or two, packing what was left in takeaway containers because Ewan would be offended if they didn't eat it all and would blast them if they threw it away, and although her parents had been invited out to dinner that night/they were throwing a party/she was on a diet, or some other made-up excuse, maybe Finn would find his appetite later?

The memory was so sweet it stole his breath, but it was only a moment before he was shoving it aside, ruthless. If she could pick and choose what to remember, so could he. "It had nothing to do with being abstemious or self-denying."

Her smile faded. "No, it didn't. It was just you, looking after your mother, because that's the kind of son you were."

He hoped she couldn't see what that insight did to him.

He hadn't thought about those hungry days for ten years but he'd known, of course he had, that it hadn't been a game they were playing back then—him pretending he wasn't hungry, her pretending to believe him, stealing those takeaway containers like naughty children and hiding the leftovers at the back of the fridge in the kitchen, even though Ewan wouldn't have cared, would himself have packed whatever meals Margaret Doherty needed if Finn's pride had allowed him to ask for them.

Finn tried to swallow whatever it was that was stuck in his throat. How could she do it still? Reach inside him and see him, understand him, make him yearn for what he didn't have?

"It's amazing, really," she went blithely on, as though she hadn't just grabbed his heart and squeezed it, "how much you've…well, grown, I guess is the word. *Good* amazing. You were too skinny back then."

Skinny. Yes, he'd been skinny enough for his ribs to show through his skin. Quite a contrast to Brad Ellersley who—although not as tall as Finn—had weighed a lot more, all of it hard muscle, bursting with outdoorsy health. Prince Perfect.

"Enough that you don't have to give me half your meal anymore," he said.

She looked at the plates on the table, then reached for the serving utensils. "OK then, even though I'm already full I'm going to eat exactly half of everything while you tell me this mysterious, exclusive, personal story. Does it start, perhaps, in Devon and end in French Polynesia, with a stop at the Maldives along the way? It must be satisfying. I mean, I know travel was my dream, not yours, but two resorts in ten years? Wow!"

Five resorts in seven years. The words trembled on his tongue, but no. No! *You have nothing to prove, remember?* It would be pathetic. *He* would be pathetic. A rescue dog begging for a pat on the head: *good boy, look how far you've come from that old horrible life, now someone can love you.*

Still, he brooded over the word "satisfying" and came up… *un*satisfied.

Owning a business had never occurred to him before he'd met Zoe. Even when he'd visited her in hospital his head had been full of fulfilling *her* dreams. The "how" of it had been only a vague notion of working to support her in whatever job came along because that's what his life had been. Odd jobs, all jobs, any job, supporting his mother.

He *should* be satisfied with what he'd achieved, proud even.

It came as a shock therefore to realize that the same discontent that had gnawed at him all through his teenage years was still gnawing at him. That it had gnawed at him all through his marriage. Through every deal he'd done. That it was gnawing at him as he sat in his jewel-in-the-crown resort with the one person he thought he'd never see again, the person he'd deliberately not thought about, been careful not to ask after, for ten years.

No, he wouldn't tell Zoe his story. Not ever. If she wanted his story let her do what he'd done to learn hers—look it up.

"It's not my story you're getting, it's Kupe Kahale's," he said. "You know that prince you always wanted to plonk in a story? Well, Kupe swears he's a descendant of the royal family of the Kingdom of Ra'iātea."

She leaned forward eagerly, eyes gleaming. "Royal family?"

"French Polynesia was once divided into four kingdoms, each with its own flag, laws, government, and royal family. But it's Ra'iātea that's considered the spiritual heart of Polynesia."

eleven

"WHAT DO YOU THINK?" FINN ASKED AS HE CAME
to the end of the story, but Zoe could see his lips twitching
with the effort not to smile.

"Oh, you *know* what I think!" she accused. Kupe Kahale's
life story had everything she'd told Finn she wanted to write
about in those once-upon-a-time days. Drama, adventure, history, romance. An impoverished hero in love with the only
child of a wealthy Chinese merchant couple who thought he
couldn't keep their daughter in the style to which she was ac-
customed. An elopement, family reconciliation, a rags-to-
riches story as Kupe went on to amass his own fortune. "Will
he talk to me?"

"Sure." Finn poured coffee into two cups. "But since you're
not interested in going to Kupe's restaurant on Saturday night
it'll have to be over the phone."

"How do you know I'm not going?" she asked as he passed

one of the cups to her, and then answered her own question because *duh!* "Aiata told you."

He raised his coffee cup as though toasting her perspicacity. "You're not going because you don't do junkets, you think dinner shows are touristy and you prefer to write about more authentic dining options—markets, street food, out-of-the-way places where only the locals go."

She gave a half laugh, a little impressed, a lot disconcerted. "Wow, she's thorough."

"I know you live in Sydney, that your parents still live in Hawke's Cove, that you've traveled to every continent, that your favorite flavor is raspberry, that you go to the gym every morning at seven o'clock, that your hair clip collection is out of control—"

"Stop, stop!" she begged, with another half laugh. "Are you sure Aiata doesn't work for MI6?"

"Aiata told me about your junket-aversion and that you weren't going to Mama Papa'e." He paused there, kept his eyes on her in a way that was somehow assessing, then squared his shoulders as though it was time to face the music. "The rest was down to Google."

Her jaw dropped. "You *googled* me?"

"I did."

Zoe didn't know why that should shock her so much…and yet it did.

"I found your blog, read your posts," he went on. "Read a broader selection of your articles than Aiata provided in her briefing pack. So…" He looked away from her, toward the rainforest, letting silence linger so that she was squaring *her* shoulders, bracing for impact, before he brought his eyes back to her. "You know I live in Sydney."

Automatically, her hands went to her thighs—up, down, up. "Yes."

"What else do you know about me?"

Her hands stopped as her mind blanked. What did she know about him? "Motorbike accident," she ventured.

"I told you that an hour ago. What else?"

Nothing came to mind.

Her parents had never mentioned him. Nor had her friends. No, that wasn't strictly true. There was that one time Lily told her about the death of his mother and that Finn had moved to Australia, but that had been on her birthday call, nine months after the accident. It had been the first all-in girl-call since Zoe had left England; she'd been too dazed and confused during that soul-destroying find-a-miracle tour to pretend everything was fine so she'd withdrawn from contact with everyone she knew, even Victoria, Malie and Lily. And when Lily had started talking about Finn on that call she'd rushed past the topic because the disorientated, half-buried impressions of that night with Finn caused her too much anguish. Which meant the only conversation she'd had with anyone about Finn Doherty in the past ten years had been the one with Malie two months ago in Hawaii, and she was hardly going to repeat *that*.

"I know you own two resorts?" Was that the right thing to say? Oh. Maybe not, because he stood abruptly, his face shuttering.

"Which reminds me," he said, all business now, no hesitation. "During the Q&A on the boat today you didn't ask about the accessibility features of Poerava."

"I didn't have to," she said, feeling like she'd just been whirled around and repositioned exactly where he wanted her: at an emotional if not a physical distance.

"You're writing for *Wanderlust Wheels* and you don't have to ask about wheelchair access?"

"Aiata provided me with a comprehensive accessibility fact sheet but it's more important that I live the access. I'm in a wheelchair-accessible room, today I was on a wheelchair-accessible boat. During the week I'm going to use those wheelchair-friendly ramps that take me across the sand to the beach lounger that's been set aside specifically for me as a wheelchair user. I'll dine at Tāma'a, have a drink at Manuia, take a book to the quiet room and read. I'll definitely describe the differences between my overwater bungalow and the equivalent garden suite. But all those things are a sidebar to the main story, which will focus on the destination."

Silence.

Zoe didn't know how to proceed, how to recapture that hopeful feeling of nascent camaraderie of only a few minutes ago. All she could think to say was: "How about I ask you some questions about those differences? My bungalow...yours?"

He sat again, picked up the notepad she'd left on the table, looked at it as though he could x-ray through the cover. And then he raised his eyes. "How about you live that, too, Zoe? Take a tour at your own pace, go through the place. I have some emails to deal with so no rush."

She couldn't quite believe he was going to let her roam around his private space when he'd so emphatically closed himself off from her. "You mean now, alone?"

"Now, alone," he said, and held out her notepad. "Or, sure, ask questions instead if that's too...what...personal, for you? I can get Aiata to give you a garden bungalow inspection tomorrow or any other day you choose."

Personal. Hadn't it always been personal? The truth was she was desperate to know what his room looked like, what it smelled like, what it would reveal about him. She looked at the notepad, at his strong fingers. What if she took that notepad and let her fingers brush his?

She reached for the notepad before she could stop herself, but he pulled back just before their fingers could connect. Even so, one of those now-familiar shivers ran through her and she didn't have to look down to know how her body was reacting.

"I'll do the tour now," she said, and fled.

★ ★ ★

Finn waited for Zoe to go inside before releasing a long, slow breath.

Enough.

It was done.

Or as done as it was ever going to be. She'd be gone soon and he'd get on that flight in the morning and start working on forgetting her all over again.

Definitely time to read the email from Gina about the UK properties.

He pulled out his phone, opened the email, started reading, and knew immediately that he was wasting his time. He couldn't take anything in with Zoe roaming through his bungalow.

He closed his eyes, concentrating on the air around him. Letting the warmth suffuse him, the air caress him, the sounds calm him. The garden bungalows were so called because of the vine-covered trellises that delineated each one's specific territory but they could as easily have been named for the rainforest that was so densely packed beyond those trellises it always seemed on the verge of encroaching into the humans' space. It made him think of nature barely kept at bay so it always surprised him how quiet it was, although his attuned ear could make out an infinitesimal rustle of foliage, an almost imperceptible whisper of breeze. He felt his aloneness more keenly here, but it had always been a peaceful aloneness. Strange, now, to not feel at peace…and yet to still feel alone.

He had no idea how long he stayed like that, drinking in the loneliness, until he smelled a hint of lemon, heard Zoe coming out.

He tried not to tense his muscles as he opened his eyes but his body went right ahead and locked itself up anyway as she reached the table. He pantomime-glared at his phone and tapped out some gobbledygook with a harsh finger so she'd think he was dealing with something important. Only then did he look up, turning his phone facedown on the table.

"Questions?" he asked, wanting them over and done with so she could leave.

"Yes," she said, frowning. "How did you get it all so right?"

"I didn't, Jed did. Jed Grierson. He's an architect."

"He's good. People without a disability can't always imagine all the things that make people like me...well, anxious. It's virtually impossible to foresee all the obstacles we have to navigate on a daily basis. What you've achieved here is—"

"Jed's a genius," he said, cutting her off because something akin to admiration had crossed her face and the idea of her admiring him was intensely irritating. "He's also a quadriplegic."

"So you...you hire him specifically for the accessibility stuff?"

"No, I hire him for *all* our stuff. I like his style."

She stared at him, apparently thunderstruck. "This bungalow..." she started, but seemed to be having trouble finding the words she was looking for. "I mean... Are all the garden bungalows designed for people with disabilities?"

"There's one overwater bungalow and there's this one, that's it."

"So...are all the other bungalows booked out? I presume no one else needed this room. People without a disability are usually only given these rooms if there's no other room available."

"All the overwater bungalows are booked but two other garden bungalows are free."

"Then you being in this one...is it a test, the way you tested out the lift on *Pearl Finder*?"

"No," he said.

"Then I guess..." She licked her lips, then shook her head. "I guess I don't know why you're..."

He imagined telling her that he knew the effect he was having on her, knew what the shivers meant, knew why her nipples were hardening whenever he was close. Imagined telling her he wanted to take her to bed and show her exactly what he'd been doing for those two excruciating years, what she'd been missing while she'd tortured him by practicing those anemic boyfriend-girlfriend touches with Brad Ellersley—the hand-holding, the how-does-this-work laying of her head on his shoulder, the awkwardly inexperienced kisses and stupidly childlike arm bumps.

Imagined…but he knew he wasn't going to say any of that, which would smack of all guns blazing, and *he had learned that lesson.* So, "My guess is you do know," was as far as he allowed himself to go.

He heard the uptick in her breathing. Saw the longing flit across her face. Awareness. Desire. She could be his. *Say it, say you want me, say you want to know what it's like with me, say it and I'm yours, touch me and I'm yours, make the move.*

He leaned across the table, edging his hands to within touching distance. "But if you really, truly, honestly have no idea?"

He saw the swallow she took as she looked at his hands, he could almost feel the tremble in her. "It was for me," she said. "You're in this room because of me."

And there was that tremulous smile, the one she'd given him across the salt shakers, and dammit, the memory *hurt*, turning him back into good old Crab Shack Finn, so full of yearning and restraint he was an aching blob of misery. God, he couldn't do this. Not to her, not to himself. A one-night stand wasn't going to bridge all the years between then and now and he damn well knew it.

"It's no big deal," he said, and pulled back his hands.

"Isn't it?" she asked softly.

God, he hated that softness, he didn't want *softness*. "Is it?"

"I think…yes, actually. That you'd go to that trouble to make sure I was comfortable tonight."

Comfortable. That hadn't exactly been top of mind for him. "Yeah, well don't tell anyone, you'll ruin my reputation."

She laughed, a little breathlessly. "As if you ever cared what anyone thought of you."

"Proving that you didn't know me as well as you thought you did. Or any other teenage boy for that matter. We all care, Zoe."

"Teenage girls too," she said, her smile slipping. "But you always knew that. You knew me. Better than anyone."

"I thought I did, once upon a time," he said. "Like a fairy tale. It *was* a bit like a fairy tale, wasn't it, that summer?"

"Yes," she said, and the forlorn wistfulness in her voice had him reaching for a memory that would make her laugh again, edge them back from the intensity that was saturating the air, the dark chasm she'd opened between them that couldn't be bridged in one night no matter what he wanted, and imbue this last fragile interaction with the light they'd once shared, not the darkness that had ended it.

"Talking about fairy tales, remember the time you decided you needed to write a reverse take on 'Rapunzel,' with the princess breaking herself out of the tower?"

She laughed, as he'd wanted her to, but he knew she'd forced it out. Smoothing the road, as usual. "She traveled the world searching for her prince, only to discover that just after her escape he'd ridden to her rescue—too late!—and ended up locked in that old tower of hers," she said.

"And she had to go on a quest to find the key to release him because his hair wasn't long enough for her to use it to climb up."

"And we kept taking turns to add to the story."

"There were dragons—"

"And witches—"

"And goblins—"

"And a time travel machine, with Rapunzel zipping between

the past, present and future, looking for her prince through space and time."

"No, she was zipping between the present and the future, but she couldn't get back to the past where the idiot prince was imprisoned," he said, and wanted to laugh but he didn't have that skill of hers, to smooth the path, and it jammed in his chest.

Here they were reminiscing about one part of their past, the safe part—that one naive summer—so tangible he felt as though they could reach back and touch it and yet he—could—not— laugh! All he could think was that it was no wonder she'd always looked so confused, so hurt, when she'd come up to him in the village after that summer. And seriously, after those two years of his calculated, feigned indifference to her, how could he possibly have thought it was a good idea to explode into her hospital room, not asking her what she wanted but telling her what she needed? Riding to the rescue too late, just like Rapunzel's prince.

They'd *need* a time machine to fix that. To go back and re-write that part of the story. They could have him *not* play the sneering villain every time she'd ventured near him, and then he could visit her in hospital as the friend she'd believed him to be, *wanted* him to be, tried to make him into, nothing more.

"If you had a time machine, Zoe, would you go back to the past or into the future?" he asked.

She looked down at her legs, considering that, and he thought he knew the answer.

But no, he didn't, because she shook her head and said: "I'd break the machine, and stay in the present, and dream about the future."

"I'd go back," he said, too fierce.

Up came her eyes. "But...but your life. I mean, then, and... and now. Your *life*!"

He understood what she was trying to say—and also trying not to say. His life used to be pulling beers at the local pub on his side of the bar for people like her to drink on the other side, going hungry, wearing charity shop clothes, loitering with intent on the streets of Hawke's Cove with the villagers giving him the widest possible berth. *Now* he was the half owner of an array of boutique luxury resorts; he lived in a penthouse apartment; he led a glamorous international life; he could eat at the best restaurants; he sat on the "right" side of the bar; he had enough money not to flinch at the cost of a new shirt; he'd finally got that motorbike; he'd even found love, although it had been a bit like the motorbike—fun while it lasted but ultimately a mistake. He'd lived all right, hard and fast.

And yet…he wasn't happy.

The hunger was still inside him, a yearning for that elusive more. He didn't know what the more was, but he knew where: buried in his past. He just hadn't found the key to the map that would take him to where "X" marked the spot, and Zoe had told him tonight she couldn't help him with that.

"My life is good, I know that, but it…" He shrugged, restless, impatient, frustrated. "It doesn't feel like my life."

"I don't understand."

"That's because you were always certain of what you wanted. Your dreams were all about travel and adventure. Even when you were stuck in Hawke's Cove you knew what you wanted. Knew you wanted to see everything and do everything and write everything. And I…well, when I finally left the Cove I still didn't know what my d—"

He broke off, hearing footsteps on the path to the bungalow, then a loud laugh.

"I think the cavalry's arrived," he said.

"The cavalry?"

"That's Joe's booming laugh and my guess is Cristina is with him."

He didn't mean anything by that, but Zoe looked upset out of all proportion. "I didn't arrange this, Finn."

"You don't have to explain yourself, Zoe."

"But I didn't, I *didn't* ask her to come."

"OK."

"I mean it. I would have stayed. If you…you wanted me to. Did you want me to? I mean…*do* you? Want me to stay? I mean for a while. Or…"

Doorbell.

Dammit! Damn! It!

Ah well. It was probably for the best. Somewhere during tonight's reminiscing he'd lost the bitterness that would have made a one-night stand a victory. He was fairly certain the only thing a one-night stand would achieve was him having to spend another ten years getting over Zoe and he was done with that. "It's OK, really," he said. "It's for the best. The story's told, dinner's over…and you're looking forward not back."

And as he went to answer the door, he breathed a sigh that was almost relief. But not quite.

twelve

FINN RETURNED TO THE DECK AFTER HE'D SEEN Zoe, Cristina and Joe out.

What a mess of a night. A seesawing mix of nostalgia, awkwardness, laughter, fear, anger, hope, longing, yearning, wanting, caution…and disappointment.

His brain was tired from the onslaught.

He wanted to stop thinking for a while. Stop regressing to Finn Doherty the lowlife high school dropout who could land all the odd jobs but not move past them, run himself ragged caring for his mother but not save her, get any girl in the village except the only one he despairingly wanted.

He wanted, especially, to strangle the feeling that had slithered out of its dark hiding place in his soul the moment Zoe had left the bungalow: the helpless, painful certainty that had taken root that long-ago summer that the two of them were meant to *be* somehow, if only he could find a way.

He knew the moment for that was past, that he was deluding himself if he thought it could be recaptured in a new place and time. She knew nothing about who he was today. Had never, not once, done an online search of Finn Doherty. Didn't that tell him there was no way to find for the two of them to be together?

The past ten years' obliteration of him he could understand; it would be hypocritical to think she'd be hunched over a computer dredging the internet for mentions of his name given how comprehensively he'd quashed any curiosity about her from the moment he'd boarded his flight to Australia.

But last night, having seen him again, when he'd been jolted into madly researching her at last, she hadn't spared him even one thought? This afternoon, after the cruise, knowing she'd be interviewing him for a story she thought was *his* story, she'd looked up not one fact about him?

It hurt, but he had no choice but to accept it. He *wanted* to accept it. Wanted to not dream about her the way he'd dreamed about her last night, even if he had no idea how he was supposed to manage that with her scent threading through the air he was breathing all alone.

He wanted to not want to see her again.

He wanted to not regret that he hadn't let their fingers touch when he'd handed her that notepad.

But he *did* want to see her again.

And he *did* regret not touching her so that he would know, at last, if her skin on his would be as cooling, as calming, as he'd always thought it would be...or if it would do nothing at all, which would be even better, because the spell would be broken.

No. Not quite right. What he was yearning for was for *her* to touch *him*, not the other way around.

But he was leaving in the morning and he'd blown his chance. He'd have to get on with life as it was and not how he wished it could have been because his life was good.

And if he really wanted to put the past behind him, the best place to start was with Gina's email, which he *still* hadn't managed to read.

He pulled out his phone again, stared at the screen...and heard Zoe saying, *I would have stayed if you wanted me to...*

And he knew—dammit, he knew very well—he wasn't leaving in the morning.

So instead of reopening that still-unread email he pulled up Gina's number, his finger suspended over the call button.

He and Gina had never had what either of them would call a grand passion but they'd been faithful to each other, caring of each other, attuned to each other in business and friendship. How was he supposed to explain this thing, this bond with Zoe, when he'd never so much as mentioned Zoe's name?

He'd have to wing it, see what came out of his mouth.

He hit the call button, and almost before she'd uttered his name, he said: "I need a week here. Please don't ask why, just let me explain it when I see you."

He waited, every muscle straining. *Please.*

And then she said: "One week, explanation due on arrival, and I will expect it in full and unabridged."

He closed his eyes in relief.

"Finn, if you've found someone..." He tensed all over again as she hesitated, but then she laughed softly. "Just know that it would be OK with me. In fact, I think it'd make it easier. To move on, you know?"

"That's not... I mean, it is about moving on but..." Nope. No idea how to explain it, not yet. "Look, so *you* know, it'd be OK with me, too, if you found someone. Someone better than me."

"Define better."

"Someone less...rough around the edges."

Gina sighed. "Now you see, that was always your problem, Finn, thinking a rough edge was a bad thing. It's not. Pleasantries and compliments aside, however, if you're not on a plane next Monday I'll fly over and drag you bodily off that island in handcuffs."

"Oh, so *now* you get brutal with me!" he said. "Who knows what might have been if you'd found your inner cavewoman three years ago?" And as she laughed—as he knew she would—he rang off and stared at his phone, too wired to think of going to bed, too restless for answers.

Hell, he still didn't know if Zoe had a husband, a boyfriend, someone she lived with. He hoped she did. That really would be the end. Was there someone in Hawke's Cove he could call? Not without word getting back to the eerily omnipotent Mrs. Whittaker and spreading like wildfire that Finn Doherty *still* had a crush on Zoe Tayler, which would find its way to Lily's mother, and then Lily, and then Zoe. Perish the thought. But he scrolled aimlessly through his contact list for want of anything better to do.

He stopped at the Ks. *Kupe.* He had to tell him how the story had gone down. He hit the call button.

"It's late, Finn," Kupe said when he answered. "Is something wrong?"

"No! No. Just… Zoe Tayler, that journalist we talked about, she loved your story and I wanted you to know she'll likely call you in the next day or so." Finn paused as he realized he knew exactly why he'd called so late and it wasn't about the article. It was to gather his tools, his weapons, for the siege. The big battle had begun. "And I need a favor. That associate of yours, the one with MS—he has that pontoon boat…"

thirteen

"NOT FEELING IT TODAY, ZOE?" CRISTINA ASKED. "How about we call it quits?"

Zoe checked the time. Ugh! Only 7:45. Fifteen minutes to go.

She endured rather than enjoyed her morning workouts but never had she cut a session short. This morning, though, she didn't know how she was going to make it to the end. She was curiously deflated at the prospect of the week ahead. Not to mention exhausted, courtesy of last night's mishmash of dreams and half-formed memories that had broken her sleep into fragments.

"OK," she said to Cristina. And then she caught a tiny twitch at the corner of Cristina's mouth, which told her Cristina knew very well what—or more specifically *who*—was responsible for Zoe's frame of mind, and in the spirit of rebellion added: "You go back to the bungalow, I'll stay and finish."

"If you stay, I stay, you know the rules," Cristina said, but nevertheless emitted a teeny-tiny moan when Zoe doggedly grabbed a set of dumbbells.

As Zoe started her biceps curls another memory popped into her head. Ewan telling her the reason Finn started half an hour late at the Shack was because he also did odd jobs at the gym in exchange for using their equipment. Ewan had thought he was wasting his time: what Finn needed to do if he wanted more bulk was to eat more. Which of course was why Zoe was always pushing her food on him.

He'd certainly put that bulk on. And not just by eating more. You could tell by the muscles straining at his clothes that he'd worked out *a lot* over the years. She could easily picture him in workout gear—a loose singlet and shorts sticking to his sweaty body—his face hard with concentration—muscles tensing as he worked...

Uh-oh, the shiver was back!

Do not *think about Finn's muscles, think about Poerava's state-of-the-art adapted fitness equipment, think about...*

Nope. No use. Muscles. That was all she could think about. She checked the time again. Five minutes to go.

She looked at the suffering Cristina and had to laugh. "I know a better way to exercise my arms, Cris. Let's go fishing."

"But you hate fishing!"

"I do, but Captain Joe is skippering the boat and while you're flirting with him—uh-uh, don't even think about pretending otherwise—I can flirt with Daniel."

"Daniel? But you said—"

"That was yesterday. Today I have a whole new perspective on...on muscles. And Daniel's are impressive. I'm opening my mind to the possibility, anyway."

Scrubbed, primped and hair clipped, Zoe sallied forth, certain that being away from Poerava with a different man in her sights would distract her from unproductive thoughts of Finn.

And yet she found herself searching for him the moment she was aboard a charter boat that was so much smaller than *Pearl Finder*, Finn's absence was immediately obvious.

It was undeniable at that point: she had secretly harbored a hope that Finn had missed his flight again *and* learned she was going fishing (which he knew she never did) *and* decided to come along.

Confirmation that she was an idiot!

After the way he'd ushered her out of his bungalow oh so easily last night when she'd all but insisted he take her to bed, she knew she should be *glad* he wasn't on board, distracting her with his muscles, his guarded eyes, his waiting stillness, his dismissive shrug, his chipped tooth, and…and any other part of him. In fact, she *would* be glad. Glad he'd left Tiare Island. Maybe now that disturbing jangle of half memories would dissipate and give her some peace.

But as the fishing rods came out, an intact memory emerged from the jangle. That time she'd confessed to Finn that she didn't bait her hook because killing the fish she was going to eat made her feel like an executioner. He'd laughed so hard he'd got a stitch in his side. And the next day he'd taken her out on Sir Gaden's stolen dinghy after work, with two borrowed fishing rods and no hooks at all, and they'd pretended to fish. That was when she'd told him about her biggest life goal: to travel the world and write books.

How much of herself she'd revealed to him that summer. Everything she wanted, everything she needed, everything she liked and loved and hated. All her dreams.

How had she never realized that he hadn't shared a dream of his own?

She could have asked him. She *should* have asked him. And if he'd said he didn't know they would have talked about it, and she would have intuitively known what he was trying to say even if the right words weren't there—the way he always knew what she was trying to say when she couldn't find the words—and they would have found the perfect dream for him. But now the only clue she had to go on was an unfinished one.

When I finally left the Cove I still didn't know...

She could no longer find the words for him. He'd become opaque. She'd never know how that sentence ended because Finn had gone, back to his life, and she would be going back to...what, exactly?

"Zoe? Zoe!" Daniel snatched her fishing rod out of her hands. "Let me bait your hook for you."

An offer that was the beginning of a truly hideous day.

Daniel was a nice guy, he meant well, he was Hollywood-handsome with a spectacular body—but he was as annoying as hell in a heat wave.

Not content with baiting Zoe's hook, he tried to take over when Zoe's line went horrifyingly tight and everyone could see she'd caught a fish. Ordinarily Zoe would have handed over the rod with immense gratitude and averted her eyes when the poor fish was pulled into the boat, but on principle she clung tenaciously to her rod.

Thank goodness Captain Joe, reading the mood—and perhaps Zoe's disgust when the fish was reeled in—insisted the defenseless tuna was too small to keep and threw it straight back into the water.

Joe and Cristina ran interference from that moment, but despite their good intentions Zoe was so frazzled by the time the fishing expedition ended she took to her room for what was left of the day, opting for—shock, horror!—a room service dinner. Not even Matilda's laughingly made offer to monopolize Daniel for the evening if Zoe joined the media group at Tāma'a could get Zoe to change her mind. Because the truth was Daniel wasn't the problem; he was a symptom, not the disease.

The *disease* was hidden inside her. An endless need to be "on." Smiling and cheery and never angry and always understanding, even when people trampled over her need to demonstrate her strength and independence. Finn had called it detouring but she thought of it as containment. Keeping her aggravations wrapped tightly inside because if she didn't she might start screaming. And strong, independent people didn't scream and wail and feel sorry for themselves.

It was exhausting. *She* was exhausted. And she was sure she looked it when Cristina didn't demur at Zoe's insistence that she take Joe up on his offer to take her out to dinner again so she could rest.

Peace. Quiet. No one waiting for her or grabbing her chair or nagging her or worrying over her.

It should have been blissful. Instead, the feeling washing over her was melancholy. And with nothing to do her thoughts returned to Finn, to dinner last night.

Princes and princesses.

Time machines and fairy tales.

The past.

Those things he'd said.

I remember a lot of things…that night for example… I'll help you locate that memory…the story's told, dinner is over…and you're looking forward not back.

Yes, she was looking forward, but she knew there was something she had to go back for, knew she wouldn't be able to… to *breathe* until she did.

She closed her eyes and focused, trying to force her mind to open to the past, but what emerged wasn't a memory but a vision of Finn at midnight, waiting on that beach, and her heart swelled with grief, and tears that she *would not shed* pricked at the back of her eyes. It wasn't real, that image. The real image, the real memories, were skulking in the shadows daring her to find them, claim them, own them. Like that tide that kept pulling her back to the girls. But she knew those memories would be no gentle tide sweeping her toward the truth, they'd be a tsunami and she'd need all of her strength to swim through them if she wasn't to drown. Drown…

Crash…

Shattering glass, lights, shouting. It was there, it was *there*! *Show me*, show *me, let me feel it.*

But as quickly as the flash had come, it was gone.

She opened her eyes. Her heart was thudding, her breaths coming in pants.

She had to do something. Anything.

Write. She had to write.

Lily's eulogy for Blake. She'd write that. Those memories, at least, had no power to hurt her.

Some scenes came fast as she typed—the fishing expeditions to the Hawkesbury beach, Malie leaving for Hawaii with Blake Hawkesbury's support, Lily's joy at getting the job at the Hawkesbury Estate. Some came more slowly as she tried to delve into what made Blake the man he was—the accident was part of that, Blake's son Henry, the aftermath. How strange to know the experience of the accident because people at the hospital had talked about it but not to see it in her head, not to *feel* it.

Like her, Victoria, Malie and Lily never really talked about the accident; they'd left it in the past—three of them had left it geographically as well. Now Zoe wondered what it was like for Lily, the only one of them to stay in the Cove. Had she been able to move on? Had she felt abandoned? What was it like for her now that Victoria and Malie were engaged to be married—V so close in London, Malie planning to return to the Cove with a fiancé.

It seemed to Zoe that V and Malie had both come alive. Was that what happened when you belonged to someone?

Lily had belonged to someone once. Zoe never had, and yet she thought she understood what it was like to feel more alive, more *yourself*, when you were with a special someone.

It was how she'd felt last night. Not comfortable but certainly alive, in a way she couldn't remember feeling for so, so long.

Her anxious second-guessing as she was getting ready. Her aborted plan to seduce Finn. The nerves, the laughter at shared memories, the longing for a look that would recapture the magic, even the disappointment at how the night had ended. For the first time in ten years she hadn't known what was going to happen, she'd known only that because it was Finn something *could*. The prospect that something might happen, because she was with him, was what had made that summer fun, exciting, thrilling.

"And tonight is neither alive, nor fun, nor exciting, nor thrilling," she said out loud. "Just like the countless other nights you've spent all over the world."

Ugh. She was whining again.

There was nothing wrong with her life. She had everything she'd ever wanted.

Except that she didn't.

She didn't have the ability to walk.

And she didn't have Finn.

If you had a time machine, Zoe, would you go back to the past or into the future?

I'd break the machine, and stay in the present, and dream about the future.

But what if she *could* go back?

If she went back ten years, maybe she could stop the accident from happening.

If she went back *twelve* years, to that summer, maybe she'd be able to see the way Finn looked at her, and maybe she could look at him the same way, and—

"Stop! Just stop. You cannot go back, there is only now. Finish the eulogy and send it."

She reread the words she'd written and found herself blinking back more tears as she sent it, thinking of Lily's loss, her grief.

She reached for her phone almost without conscious thought and heaved a tremulous sigh when Lily's face popped up.

"Zoe? What's wrong?" Lily asked.

"Do I look that bad?"

"You look perfect as always. Well, aside from the bluish smudges under your eyes. But you sounded like you were going to cry and you—"

"Never cry. But yes, I'm a little…tired, I guess."

"I know you love travel, Zo, but it's not a sign of weakness to take a break and stay in one place for more than a week."

"That's the plan after this trip. A home holiday. But right now, I just want to let you know the eulogy is in your inbox. Let me know what you think after you've had a chance to read it."

"Am *I* going to cry?"

"Maybe."

"Then I'll leave it until the morning," Lily said, voice quavering. "My sob quota has been filled for today. Oh. Hang on!" She pulled a tissue out of the box beside her and blew her nose.

"Where's V? She's there, right? You're not on your own?"

"She's been with me all day but she's staying at her parents' place. Do you need her? Should we dial her in?"

"No, don't. I was only calling to make sure you're OK. And because I was feeling nostalgic after writing the eulogy."

"I'm doing better, I guess. I have to do better, because there's so much to plan for the wedding and I can't, I just *can't*, let Victoria down. I'll probably be a mess at the funeral next week but that's got to be my closure point. I won't let myself fall apart after that."

"Closure point," Zoe said. "Yes, I understand that. I'm not sure I…"

There was a long pause, and then Lily said, "Are you thinking about the accident, Zo?"

"I was thinking about it tonight while I was writing the

eulogy. I still can't remember it, Lils. I know what I've been told about it, and there are fragments from that night that shift around in my head, but the detail…it's missing. And I have this feeling that I need to remember it. It's like I've left a piece of myself on that road in Hawke's Cove and I have to find it."

"You can always come home. We can find it together."

"I can't come back. If life was almost unbearable before the accident…"

"Yeah, *after* the accident it was becoming a full-blown fuss-over-poor-brave-Zoe-Tayler epidemic. I get it. So how do we find your missing part? How can I help you? Any of us? All of us?"

"I don't know. It's weird, but it…it scares me a little—the idea that I won't ever find that part. But equally, I think, that I *will*, which is probably why I've locked it away." She made an impatient sound. "That sounds stupid."

"You talk about Claudia's death, about Henry having to deal with that, but do you know this is the first time you've ever even hinted at how *you* deal with what happened? We almost lost you, Zoe. We almost *lost* you. And if you think the rest of us don't deal with that every single day, then…then maybe I'm going to fly over to French Polynesia, or Timbuktu, or Zanzibar, or wherever you're going next so I can help you through whatever's eating away at you. In other words, no it does not sound stupid, *it is not stupid* to be scared. You're allowed to come to terms with what happened whenever you want or never, and if you remember everything or half of it or nothing, no one's going to judge you. And now I'm crying again, thank you very much!"

"How about we gossip about Oliver and Todd?" Zoe said, forcing a dismal-sounding laugh. "We can rank them on our old Cove Hotness Scale from one to ten. Will that cheer you up?"

"The only guy who came close to a ten in those days was

Finn Doherty, Mr. Off-Limits-To-Good-Girls—and do not come back at me with Brad Ellersley because he was a solid eight (and incidentally he's now dropped to a seven). Oliver and Todd are so perfect I'd be jealous if I was remotely interested in having a love life. And for the record, I'm one hundred percent *not interested*. I'm too busy with the restaurant and the wedding and a million other things."

"You don't miss having someone?"

"Do *you* miss it?"

"I never had someone so how would I know? Not even Brad. Not really. But I'd like to know what it's like to be in love."

"Oh Zoe, you were always the one to zero in on a target and hit the bull's-eye dead center. Why don't you take aim at someone while you're in French Polynesia?"

"The only guy who's interested in me here is an American journalist, who's admittedly a nine on the scale—or at least he would be if he'd stop asking things like 'Can paraplegics still have sex?'"

"No!"

"To be fair he asked Cris, not me—he wasn't quite that tactless—but I heard it. You should have seen the withering look she gave him!" She laughed. "I'm having room service tonight just so I can avoid him."

"Room service? You? This is dire! OK, there's nothing for it. I was thinking it would just be me and Mrs. Whittaker who ended up loveless, sharing a quaint cottage with four cats and a parrot in a cage, but I'll look for a place with three bedrooms so you can join us."

"You know you're going to give me nightmares with that image, right?"

"I'm going to give *myself* nightmares!" Lily said, laughing. And then she sighed. "Promise me you'll get some rest after this trip, Zoe."

"I promise I'll go straight home to Sydney and I'll stay there until the wedding if you promise to stop stressing over every minute detail about the wedding, the funeral, the restaurant, the—"

"OK, OK, message received!" Lily laughed again, then her face softened and she blinked, blinked, blinked. "I love you, Zo."

"Love you too," Zoe said, "but we are not going to get into a cry-fest."

"Not possible, you don't cry."

"Yeah, well, let's not put it to the test."

"OK, I'm going back to my lists," Lily said, laughing as she disconnected.

Zoe blew out a long, slow breath.

Rest.

Home to Sydney.

A prospect she should be looking forward to, but that odd sense of dislocation that had been digging at her so often lately was back, full force. Tiredness, sameness, that fear she'd tried to explain to Lily—that something was missing, the absence of not-knowing-what's-next now Finn had left. There really was nothing to do *except* go home to Sydney.

And who knew, maybe she'd write that novel she'd always dreamed of writing. Reverse "Rapunzel."

Or maybe she'd write the mermaid story.

She gasped as the memory came at her, fast and painful. Finn smiling at her as he held up the pearl they'd found, swinging it back and forth on its platinum chain as though hypnotizing her, offering the perfect title for the story, *their* story he'd called it: "Mermaid's Kiss." He'd said it represented the waves tumbling onto the sand, two worlds meshing—the mermaid's ocean and the mortal's earth. A brief kiss before the waves receded, dragging the mermaid back to the ocean and leaving the mortal on the sand waiting for the next kiss, and the next, and the next, unable to anchor his love to his world, but waiting for her as long as it would take, even if that was eternity.

Their story. She'd thought he meant the fairy tale they were dreaming up together but what if he'd meant—

Zoe's phone pinged, and the memory of Finn smiling at her vanished as she saw the email from mum.dad@taylers.co.uk.

Time to tuck the fantasies away.

Finn had rebuffed her last night. Eternity aside, she was twelve years too late to wonder what he'd meant.

She opened the message to read that in the wake of her rare visit home last Christmas her parents had gone ahead with plans to remodel a wing for her because maybe one day she'd decide *not* to live on the other side of the world.

Automatically she started to write back, telling them she was very, very happy in Sydney.

And then she stopped, because that was a lie. She wasn't very, very happy in Sydney. She couldn't remember the last time she'd felt very, very happy.

"I'm not happy and not one person knows it," she whispered, as though the thought was a sacrilege that should not be uttered at all.

A sacrilege…but true.

She wasn't happy, she wasn't even content. What she was, was in a rut. Unfulfilled. Bored.

Lost.

A eulogy…travel stories…a blog…but no novel.

Finn's words from last night now seemed to her to be a reflection of everything that was wrong with her life. She'd wanted to be a novelist more than anything. Wildly, passionately wanted it. And yet she'd locked away those story ideas, only remembering them when Finn brought them up.

So much for zeroing in on a target and hitting the bull's-eye. She'd become a passive piece of flotsam, drifting from her blog to travel writing, filling her downtime writing web content for her wheelchair support group Chair Chicks, occasional speeches for her father when he had to attend conferences, and now a eulogy.

But no novel.

Could she write a novel?

She couldn't even remember what she'd written to her parents since she'd arrived on Sunday!

Resolutely she pulled up all those emails, casting a critical eye over the words, stunned at how dull and meaningless they were, how soulless. She was in paradise and that was the best she could do? No wonder her mum and dad were shooting her anxiety-riddled messages four times a day. When had she become this pathetic shell of the person she'd dreamed she'd be?

Well, that was going to change forthwith!

She started her reply to their latest email with a quick line about the renovation: fabulous, she'd be home in August for Victoria's wedding and again for Malie's wedding but no going overboard.

And then she drumrolled her fingers either side of the computer, and sifted through mental images of today's fishing trip, this morning's gym workout, yesterday's snorkeling cruise. Last night's dinner—not about Finn (she didn't want to give her parents a heart attack) but about the flavors she could miraculously taste right that second even though she hadn't been aware of tasting them last night. Her bold new friend Matilda. Cristina's budding romance with the dashing Captain Joe. The story of the legendary Kupe Kahale. The texture and scent of the air, the feel of the sun on her skin, the brooding silence of the rainforest and gentle swash of the lagoons, the crystal clarity of the water, the vibrancy of the blues, the magical colors of an underwater paradise.

Weren't those things all symbols of the life she'd wanted? The daring, romantic, go-out-and-grab-it life for which she'd moved away from home? Of course they were. And her parents, who loved her devotedly, deserved to share that piece of her.

She started tapping the keys, the words suddenly flowing:

Mum and Dad, are you sitting down? I have a story to tell and you'll never believe it.

It's a story about a guy hitting on a girl by making her catch a fish! Yes, today I caught my first ever fish, and I have to tell you, it was as disgusting as I'd always imagined it would be.

Fifteen minutes later, Zoe hit send, feeling a new energy surging through her, and decided it would be a waste to take that energy to bed.

"I think the orange dress with the floral embroidery around the hem," she announced to herself. "And a wreath for my hair made of the frangipanis in the bowl in the bathroom."

No one was going to keep her marooned in her bungalow—least of all a man who forced her to catch a fish and then tried to steal the damn thing!

fourteen

FINN HAD BEEN WEAVING THROUGH TĀMA'A SINCE six o'clock, never sitting to eat, instead snatching quick bites in the kitchen between excursions into the dining area (much to Gaspard's annoyance).

The other journalists arrived and he went to their table to welcome them, staying for a glass of wine in the hope one of them would let slip where Zoe was, but the gleam in Matilda's eyes soon had him retreating. Matilda couldn't possibly know what was eating at him but he had a sinking feeling that she did.

He checked the restaurant's dinner reservations. No joy.

Checked with transport to see if Zoe had booked a ride to a different restaurant. Nope.

Cristina arrived with Joe and he thought about going over and asking her outright where Zoe was, but before he could turn thought into action Daniel called out to Cristina and for his trouble got a look of such disdain Finn's courage deserted him.

But Cristina had seen him.

She frowned as she pulled out her phone (presumably to call Zoe and break the news that big bad Finn Doherty was still on the island) and then she froze for one second, two, three... before putting the phone away. Her frown cleared as she looked over at him again, replaced by a look of—dear God, amusement!

Disgruntled, he turned his back on Cristina and went to check the room service orders even though it was inconceivable that Zoe would have stayed in her room because she never—

Whoa!

Bingo!

There it was. A room service order to Zoe's bungalow.

Fishing; room service—both completely unexpected choices resulting in a wasted day. He was going to have to get his head together and do some serious planning if he didn't want to chase her around the island like a crazed stalker for the next five days. (And he most assuredly did *not* want to do that!)

He headed to Manuia, took a seat at the bar and ordered his usual vanilla rum from self-named "Tiki mixologist" Tepatua.

"How about I make you something more interesting, boss? A Yaka Hula Hickey Dula, say?"

"Er...no," Finn said, sparing a thought for how his regulars at the pub in Hawke's Cove would have reacted to that suggestion. He imagined looks of horror, wary backsteps, a chorus of hasty, *"Just the pint thanks, Finn lad!"*

"Then how about I make the rum a double? You look like you could use the extra shot."

"The single's fine," he said—not because he couldn't use the double—he could!—but because he was over the sympathetic looks and sly smiles and laughing eyes that seemed to be running rampant at Poerava.

When he got his drink he did nothing more than look at it, recalling his thoughts last night about sitting on the "right" side of the bar.

"Hey, Tepatua," he said on impulse, pushing his drink back across the bar. "Move over. I'm on the clock tonight."

"You, boss?"

"Me."

And it felt good to get behind the bar and say, "What'll it be?" to his first customer in ten years.

An hour later, Matilda came to the bar. "I see it but I don't believe it!" she said, and ordered a bottle of champagne.

"I'm a man of many talents," Finn said, putting a bottle of the best in an ice bucket on a tray. "How many glasses?"

"Three."

He started polishing the glasses.

"One for me," she said as he placed the first glass on the tray, "one for Corinne from *Island Rendezvous*," second glass, "and one in case Zoe turns up... Aaand there it is!" she said triumphantly as he dropped the last glass.

"Sorry," he said, ignoring that added-on comment of hers, then quickly polishing a fresh glass and positioning it. "The champagne's on the house. Can you manage it or do you want Tepatua to bring it to your table?"

"I'll take it, and respectfully ask that if Zoe does turn up you bring another bottle to the table because I may need reinforcements—either to distract Daniel from Zoe or monopolize her so he can't pester her like he apparently did on the fishing trip today."

Finn's hackles rose hard and fast. "What do you mean, pester her?"

"Nothing like that, no need to growl. Let's just say there's a reason Zoe ordered room service and it wasn't me she was avoiding." Pause. "And of course it wasn't you she was avoiding since we all thought you were flying out today?"

"There's an issue."

"Of course there is."

"Not what you're thinking," he said. Winced.

She tinkled out a laugh. "Fresh bottle of champagne. Don't forget."

She sauntered off and Finn kept serving, but when he mixed up two orders—a Tahitian Sunset and a plain old rum and Coke—and Tepatua was forced to rescue a beer before he gave it a six-inch head, he knew he was going to have to call it quits for the reputation of Manuia.

So it was fortunate that five minutes after the beer incident, Zoe arrived.

Or perhaps not fortunate, because the rush of blood to his head boded ill for managing a casual conversation.

Nevertheless, he got the champagne ready, got three clean glasses and a rum for himself, and headed over. Zoe was slightly separated at one end of the table, a seat conveniently vacant beside her—*thank you, Matilda.*

Zoe's eyes lit up as he put the tray on the table and his heart actually leaped like a…like a… Hell, it just leaped, that was all.

"As you can see I got delayed again," he said, taking the seat next to her. "Looks like I'll be here until Monday." Deep breath. "So, room service, huh? I thought you never did that."

"Wow! You Poerava people really do know everything that's going on in every part of the resort."

He poured her champagne, keeping his eyes occupied as he asked, "Does it bother you that I know?" He was surprised how much he needed to know the answer, as though that would be a "go" signal.

"N-no," she said, but the uncertain stammer had him reaching for his rum, downing a quick swallow. "Then again it's not like I'm doing anything especially *interesting.*" Freeze, as she looked at him.

Interesting.

What did that mean?

Ah hell, he didn't know, but it figured it was suggestive

enough to be classified as a "go." "Then we'd better fix that," he said.

Her eyes went wide. "Oh, I didn't mean... That is, it's not that I'm not having a wonderful time."

But no, he wasn't backing off. "Now you see, that's the polite Hawke's Cove Zoe talking to Mrs. Whittaker, not rocking any boats. I prefer Crab Shack Zoe who was always honest with me. So tell me..." jerking his head in Daniel's direction, "how did it go today? Asking for a friend."

"Asking for a—" She broke off, laughing. "You are *not* asking for a friend."

"I *am* asking for a friend, Zoe. I'm asking as *your* friend."

The laughter died. She gave him a searching look. "*Are* we friends, Finn?"

Friends. Ah geez, he didn't know. But at least the promise of a path to closure was floating between them. A touch, that was all he needed, one touch. "We can try for this week—no, five days—can't we? I mean, if I promise not to tell you how lucky you are that you always have a seat wherever you go."

And the laughter was back. "I don't know how you know that's what happens. Oh! Yes, I do! Jed. Your architect."

"Yeah, Jed's told me all the trials and tribulations." He hesitated, but with closure in mind decided he might as well get it all out on the table. "But I already knew a lot because of my mother."

"Your mother? I don't...?"

"She was in a wheelchair the last few months. It wasn't the same for her as it is for you, she wasn't a paraplegic, she could stand, she could walk. She just couldn't walk and breathe at the same time."

"I didn't know."

"That's what I figured."

"I mean I heard about..."

"Her death? It's all right, Zoe, you can say the word."

"I heard, but not when it happened. Not until later. When I was in Chicago."

"That would have been three months after she died."

"Oh you…you know when I was in Chicago?"

"Google, blog?"

"Yes. I see."

"Don't worry, I hadn't expected you'd fly in for the funeral."

"I would have…" But she gave up, her shoulders rising, falling, her hands going to her thighs, rubbing agitatedly.

"What? Sent a sympathy card?"

"Yes, I guess," she said, diffident. "Or…or something."

He took another sip of his rum, tasted nothing because he was too busy digesting that, wanting to let it go, knowing he couldn't. "Lily's mother was at the funeral. She made me a million casseroles. I figured Lily would've told you."

She shook her head. No words now, just a stricken look that infuriated him because it made him want to grovel for her, tell her it didn't matter, that he didn't care, when it *did* matter and he *did* care. His world had collapsed and he'd been stranded, alone, adrift, the entire purpose of his life gone in an instant. With Zoe's last words in that hospital room buzzing in his head as they'd been doing for months: *If you need a pity project, go back to your mother.*

His mother. His kind, smart, gentle, generous mother. A *pity project*? And now to discover Zoe hadn't had the decency to ask her friends about his mother's death?

She reached for his hand. Too late. He was already jerking it up to his heart as though he could rub the ache away. No touching. Not now. Not *now*.

"Finn!" His name sounded like it was wrenched out of her. "You don't understand. The first year, that year after I left, I didn't talk to *anyone*. Even the girls I talked to only once, on my birthday. My parents—"

"Took you on a holiday to get over the trauma, I know, we all knew."

"Not a holiday. That's just what we told people so that…" She shook her head. "Not a holiday. My parents were looking for a cure, and we didn't want anyone pestering us for updates because if it didn't work we… I…needed to be able to break down in private when the hope was gone."

He closed his eyes, absorbing the force of that dizzying blow. He'd been wrong. Completely wrong. *Face it, face her!* He opened his eyes. And knew he could rub his heart until the end of time and it wouldn't help, not when he could see in her face that she'd been carrying the pain of that lost hope for ten years and it was still so raw she couldn't touch it. So *raw*…and yet last night he'd asked her to dig it up, to remember it so *he* could heal. "I'm sorry, Zoe, I'm so, so sorry."

"Don't look at me like that. Like you want to save me. Like you *can* save me. Just don't, Finn, please don't. I can't bear it. From anyone else, yes, but not from you, never from you. I thought… I used to think…you understood that."

"No," he said. "If I understood I wouldn't have—" No use. The words choked inside him. That night. She didn't want to talk about that night.

"My injury, it's not complete," she went on, the floodgates brutally open. "I still…feel. Nothing much. Tingles. Pain—which is really annoying." Short laugh. "I can't describe what it's like. A ghostlike sensation…a dream of what *could* be, almost. Mum and Dad…they took those signs to mean I was going to walk again. I had to give them a chance to try and find a miracle."

"Give *them* a chance?"

"Yes, them," she insisted. "I knew there was no miracle but how could I not let them try and fix me? They'd always have wondered if there was something they could have done and blamed themselves for not giving it their all. It wasn't until we got to Sydney that I broke down and begged them, *begged* them to stop, to let me just live. Live my life." She dragged in a breath, attempted a smile that didn't quite get there. "If I hadn't fallen apart, we'd probably still be traveling, nine years later, on an endless, futile quest."

"Why didn't they take you home with them, Zoe?"

"Superstition," she said.

"I don't understand."

"Superstition. Mine, not theirs. Can you imagine what it's like living your whole life as though you're about to drop dead?"

"Actually, yes," he said. "I don't remember a time when my mother wasn't sick."

Her hand came up, hovering as though she'd touch him. He stiffened because no, no this was not going to be the time she touched him, out of pity. As though reading his mind, that hand floated back down to settle in her lap. "Yes, I see. And I remember, yes, I *do* remember, Ewan at the Crab Shack asking you every day how she was. People coming in, looking at you but being too scared to ask."

"My reputation preceded me." A ghost of a grin. "Thankfully, I scared them off. There's nothing worse than everyone asking… Well, you know."

She smiled sadly at him. "I guess that's why you understood me better than anyone else and never asked me how I was. The daily hazard of living in Hawke's Cove. Everyone waiting for an illness to carry me off." Pause. "And in the end I was my own self-fulfilling prophecy. Poor Zoe. Sick Zoe. Frail Zoe. When there was nothing poor, sick or frail about me…until at last there was, and I was bitter enough at the time to think, *great, now everyone will finally be happy and leave me alone.*"

"Is that why you never go back?"

"Yes, it's why I don't go back. It's why I had to leave. And so… I did leave. Though it wasn't exactly the way I planned my exit. And you left too. And the rest, as they say—" She held up her glass, a toast-like gesture.

"Is history," he said and clinked his glass against hers, and sipped.

"What are you drinking?" she asked.

"Vanilla-infused rum. Distilled in Tahiti. Want to try it? I can get you a glass."

She held out her hand. "I can just drink out of yours."

They'd done this before, shared milkshakes. And yet…this was new because when she took the glass she twisted it so the section of rim where his mouth had been was where she would put *her* mouth. She licked her lips, took a deep breath, raised the glass, sipped from the exact same spot.

Oh boy, that hit him in the solar plexus. Go. Go! Another signal, stronger.

And like a lightning bolt, a plan rocketed into his head. He had the boat, now he had the strategy—not to find a way back to what he and Zoe once were, but to move forward.

"But since we're here in the present for the next five days," he said, "and since you're not on a junket and would prefer to live like a local, and I know my way around a wheelchair, as well as being something of an expert on this part of the world despite being an Irish-English-kind-of-Australian, I'm perfectly placed to be your escort. I can take you to a bakery to buy a baguette so good you'll think you were in Paris. To the local *roulottes* for the most delicious crepes to be found outside Normandy. Snorkeling off a deserted *motu*, swimming at a pink sand beach, on visits to locally run vanilla and pearl farms. Pick one and let me make it happen for you. Or pick them all and we'll challenge ourselves, see how many we can squeeze into our five days."

"Let you make it happen for me," she repeated, and frowned. He mentally kicked himself because those were the words he'd said ten years ago in that hospital room when he was too young and arrogant and stupid to know he was promising the impossible. He hoped, he really did, she didn't remember them now.

She shook her head as though shaking off a thought—whew!—and laughed her sunshiny laugh. "Hmm, well, I've had someone make *fishing* happen for me today—he even wanted to bait my hook—so the competition is fierce for that particular honor."

"Bait your—"

"He wanted to land my fish for me, too."

"And you haven't beaten him to a pulp? You'd better give me the whole saga so I know what level of idiot we're dealing with."

"Are you asking as the boss of Poerava, because I don't want there to be any ramifications for—"

"Told you before, I'm asking for a friend."

"Oh, on *that* basis…" She leaned a little closer, twinkling and telling secrets like the old days. "He told me that the way I swam, he knew that with a little work I'd be out of the wheelchair in no time."

"What the f—"

"Cris was *not* amused. In fact, she told him to… Let's just say that what she told him to do would be anatomically uncomfortable!"

"And what did *you* do?"

"I explained my gym workout, which is what keeps my upper body strong."

"Very…*patient* of you. What other clangers did he make?"

"He told everyone on the boat what an inspiration I am."

"And you definitely didn't swing at him?" he said with the air of someone getting their facts straight. Then his sense of humor deserted him. "Of course you didn't. You took it all, didn't you?"

"What?" she said, all faux outrage. "Are you saying I'm *not* an inspiration?"

"I'm saying he's a tool. And I suppose he pushed your chair for you like he did on the boat."

"Hmm, he *tried* to."

"And lifted you out of it."

"Offered to."

"Definitely a tool. And I warn you, Zoe, I'm very tempted to do something *anatomically uncomfortable* to him."

She laughed, and it caught at his heart the way it always did, and then she opened her mouth, closed it, opened it.

He waved one hand in a *bring it* gesture. "Come on."

She blushed...hesitated...squared those stubborn shoulders. "I just... I want you to know that even though I can do everything for myself, sometimes I *do* let people push my wheelchair. Lift me out of it, too. People I know, people who understand me, people I..." She paused. He saw, could almost feel, the breath she drew in, watched her tongue dart out to moisten her bottom lip. "People I trust." Another pause. Her hands were going up and down her thighs but she kept her eyes on his and he knew she was about to say something vital. "Some people—the ones I trust—don't even have to ask, they can just...do what needs to be done."

Ooooh. This was bad. Good. Bad. Perfect. Oh God, how was he supposed to handle this? "I...I used to push my mother. Lift her. She taught me...so much. How to, when to, what not to do." He shrugged, feeling stupid.

She smiled. "I figured as much."

"She taught me not to overstep."

"Smart."

"Are you telling me you trust me, Zoe?"

A heartbeat. She drew in one more breath. Nodded once, twice.

The invitation was there. To touch her. It would be so easy. He wanted to feel her skin, breathe her in. But he *wasn't* going to overstep, not for anything in the world.

All he did was reach a hand toward her hair, and yet he felt the shiver that rippled through her. Her eyelids drifted closed. She was holding her breath, waiting for him. He traced the tip of one finger around a single frangipani bloom, and that shiver came again. He looked down and yes, her nipples had gone hard, and God knew he was hard as a damn rock just at the sight of them.

"I like the way you wear these," he said. His voice was revealingly hoarse but he didn't care. Let her hear what she did to him, let her know, it was time. "The flowers, the clips, the crystals and pins."

"My version of a tiara," she said breathily as she opened her eyes. "I've always wanted one."

"Princess Zoe in the tower." His fingertip lingered on the petal. "The frangipani tree is strong, but the flowers bruise easily."

She looked steadily at him. "Then I guess I'm like the tree, not the flower. I don't bruise easily, Finn. Not then, and definitely not now."

Oh, how he wanted to touch her, wanted to do more than touch, wanted to put his hands, his mouth, all over her, wanted to make her moan his name. He hovered on the brink of asking her to come to his bungalow, let him do all the things he wanted to do...

His hand started shaking, so hard he had to pull it away.

Wrong move.

He saw embarrassment in her eyes, felt her withdrawal as she crossed her arms over her chest. She thought he didn't want to touch her, when he wanted to touch her so much it was terrifying.

She nodded as though to say, *It's OK, I get it*, and laughed a laugh that somehow wasn't hers. She called up the table to Matilda, "Hey, Tilly—I thought you said there'd be Long Island Iced Tea?"

"Oh, there will be," Matilda called back. "Finn, catch us up on the champagne! Once it's gone I'm taking my extra special tea recipe to Tepatua."

Swallowing a *you blew it* sigh, Finn poured the champagne.

fifteen

ZOE WOKE TO TWO EMAILS.

The first: from Lily thanking her for the "perfect" eulogy, with a postscript reminder from Victoria to send her measurements. The second: from her parents, saying how much they'd enjoyed reading about her fishing expedition and—in the same spirit, they said—sharing the goings-on in the village as well as including a reminder, passed on via Lily (whom they'd seen the night before at Lily's restaurant, The Sea Rose) that Victoria was waiting for Zoe's measurements. That was Lils—covering everyone's bases twice no matter what was happening in her own chockablock life.

Zoe frowned when she came to the end of that second email because something was off about it.

It took her a minute to pinpoint the problem: it wasn't something off it was something missing; the reminder about her measurements was the *only* instruction in it.

She distinctly recalled mentioning in last night's email that she'd be spending the day at the beach and would be trying out the resort's all-terrain submersible wheelchair. So where were the warnings about sunblock and heatstroke? Where was the request for details on the chair's safety certification? Where was the reminder to put her phone in a waterproof bag, not forget her painkillers, et cetera, et cetera?

How…interesting.

Zoe was impressed that Matilda made it to the beach not only on time but looking remarkably fresh for someone who'd probably been in the bar half the night.

"Hangover?" Matilda said, sounding surprised when Zoe quizzed her. "I never get them! I don't drink that much."

Zoe raised a questioning eyebrow. "And here I was thinking you were planning to woo Mr. Doherty over that Long Island Iced Tea I never got to try."

"Oh, it was Daniel I was wooing last night," she said blithely. "I plied him with enough booze to fell an entire football team."

"Tilly! You didn't!"

"Someone had to console him after you ran away so early."

"It wasn't early and I didn't run away. I left because I got a call about a brief I wrote for that surf school documentary I told you about. And I wasn't talking about you consoling him—go ahead with my blessing—I was talking about getting the poor guy drunk."

"OK, confession time. I know you don't want anyone fighting your battles for you, tough girl, but Daniel said something about you being too pretty to be in a wheelchair and Finn looked ready to murder him so I figured I'd better step in as a lifesaving measure."

"Oh." Zoe wasn't sure how to respond. A bubble of delight was trying to effervesce inside her but she knew that was a bad, bad idea so she opted for outraged dignity given *she could look after herself* as she'd already told Finn and…and he didn't seem to want to do anything…anything *important* with her, anything she actually *wanted*. "Just because Finn Doherty has a savior complex—"

"If that's what he's got, I'm ready to be saved!"

She started laughing. "You're way past saving, Tilly."

"Savior complex or not, Mr. Doherty looks mighty fine behind a bar. He's the one who decided to mix the Long Island Iced Tea. Apparently, he used to work in a pub. But of course you know that."

A memory. Finn, serving drinks at the pub a week before the summer ball. Claudia was there. Zoe had felt confused, uneasy. Something else. Ashamed?

"Zo? Are you OK?" Cristina asked her.

Blink, blink, and the memory was gone.

"Fine," she said. "Just remembering…" She lost her train of thought because that memory fragment had shaken her. She'd felt it, actually *felt* it. *Stop. Shake it off. Not now, on a beach, in public.* "Remembering the Great Barrier Reef." *Smile, Zoe.* "Cris, how would you compare the snorkeling here?"

"Wait!" Matilda, wide-eyed. "You've snorkeled the *Great Barrier Reef*?"

"Snorkeled?" Zoe waved a dramatically nonchalant hand. "We've *dived* there."

"Dived?"

"Dived!" Zoe confirmed with relish.

"Of course you dived. You don't do 'easy,' do you!"

"If I did, it wouldn't be good for my character."

"Oh, if we only did things that were good for our—" Matilda stopped abruptly, then whipped off her sunglasses. "Well, well, well, our favorite bartender approacheth."

Gulp. Skittering pulse. Drying mouth. So hard to resist the urge to look behind her and an even more powerful urge to check that her hair was perfect.

"He thinks he's so stealthy with all that stopping to chat with the hotel guests," Matilda went on under her breath, "but anyone with eyes can tell what he's up to."

Zoe swallowed, hard. "So it *did* go well last night after I left? You and Finn?"

Matilda gave an oh-so-casual shrug. And OK, Zoe had to look. Just once. Fast.

There he was, and yes, he was talking to one of the hotel guests, and dear God he looked amazing. Board shorts. A loose, short-sleeved cotton shirt that did nothing to disguise his muscles. The jaw-dropping *strength* of him. Even his feet, in flip-flops, were sexy.

He darted a look in their direction and she whipped her head back around—in time to intercept a look between Matilda and Cristina. "What?"

Matilda rolled her eyes. "Don't get me wrong, Zo, but it's not for me he's full-steaming-ahead. More's the pity."

"Huh?"

"The only person who can't see that Finn Doherty is hunting you is that lovable rogue Daniel."

"Oh puh-lease!" she scoffed but she had to admit it sounded a little bit like the lady protesteth too much.

Matilda raised that highly articulate eyebrow of hers. "Remind me who Finn invited to a private dinner Monday night?"

"That was work!"

"And who popped in and out of Tāma'a all night, searing us all with his deliciously blue searchlight gaze? And who, when he didn't find the one person he was looking for, decided not to join the rest of us but instead eat in the kitchen?"

"You can't know he was looking for me, or that he ate in the kitchen."

"I've got spies everywhere."

"You're crazy!"

"Not as crazy as you if you have no idea how many times he looked at you on the cruise on Monday."

"He looked at all of us."

"He may well have done, but not like he wanted to strip us naked."

Zoe sucked in a spluttering breath. "You have seriously got to meet my friend Malie!"

"So I can talk to her about your boy trouble?"

"No, because she said the sa— Oh never mind."

Up went Matilda's other eyebrow. "I think I can guess the rest of that sentence."

"You're crazy!"

Matilda rolled her eyes. "Uh, repeating yourself!"

"She's not crazy, Zo," Cristina said, entering the fray. "But it's not a strip-you-naked look. At least, it is. I mean it *was*, that the first night at the cocktail party, so intense it was kind of scary. But now... Well now, the 'strip you' thing is still there, no doubt about it, but it's tempered by something more...romantic. Quite *desperately* romantic, if you ask me."

Zoe rubbed her hands up and down her thighs. "I'm *not* asking you. Because the...the way he looks at me is...is meaningless. If anything were going to happen between me and Finn, it would have happened twelve years ago, but it didn't happen because I was like...like a sister to him."

Matilda gave Zoe an incredulous look. "Guy looks at his sister the way he looks at you, I'm going to call the police!"

Zoe giggled despite her embarrassment. "Stop it!"

"OK, let's cut to the chase. If you're not interested, you won't mind if I have a crack at him, hmm?"

Zoe opened her mouth to say, *Go right ahead*...and out came, "Oh shut up!"

Matilda started laughing. And then Cristina started laughing. And of course, Zoe started laughing.

And then, suddenly, Finn was there, asking, "What's so funny?" and they were laughing even harder.

"Nothing," Matilda wheezed out. "Just...nothing."

"Um...so..." Finn darted a look from one to the other of them, "are any of you interested in vanilla? I've got the use of a pontoon boat and there's a plantation on an island not far from here." He looked only at Zoe then. "The 'live like a local' thing we talked about. Most of the tourists go to Taha'a but this place is off the tourist track and since I'm going there anyway..." He cleared his throat. "Well, I'm leaving at eleven. There's a beach on a *motu* just off the island if you want to swim afterward and I can arrange a picnic lunch. If you want to come."

"Oh, I—I do," Zoe said. "I mean, I want. To come. I'm interested. In vanilla. And *motus*. They're the tiny islets, right? Lunch. Yes. Yes, please." Oh God! Three pairs of eyes were on her and knew she sounded like a complete imbecile. The urge to bury her face in her hands was so strong it took a huge effort to fight it. "So eleven at the pier? See you there."

As the three of them watched Finn's departing back, Matilda waved her hand fanlike in front of Zoe's face. "Do you need a moment to cool down, Zo?"

"Shut up!"

"I just hope that 'vanilla' wasn't a euphemism," Matilda said and winked at her. "You know, *vanilla*."

"Vanilla?"

Matilda threw up her hands. "As in sex, of course! Geez." She let out a gusty sigh. "It would be too depressing if that bad boy didn't get a little dirty in the sack."

"As in— A little dir— A little—" But it was no use. Zoe had collapsed with laughter. Almost snorting with it, she said: "Village gossip is he's plenty dirty in the sack, nothing vanilla about it."

"In that case," Matilda said, "I'm wearing my red bikini for that swim and giving you a little competition."

"I see your red bikini," Zoe said, "and raise you a purple two-piece 1960s swimsuit with ruffled skirtlet—"

"Ruffled *skirtlet*?"

"Adorned with sequins! My fashion designer girlfriend Victoria found it in a vintage shop in London and tweaked it for me."

"Hey! Unfair! London, fashion designer girlfriend, vintage, skirtlet—whatever the hell that is—*and* sequins?"

"I'll have a handicap, though—and no it's not my wheelchair, it's my hot pink rash vest. The clash is eye-popping, and not in a good way."

"Um…so buy a new rash vest?"

"Hell no!" Zoe grinned. "This pink one is from Malie's godfather's surf school in Hawaii and it's a reminder to get me some 'boy trouble.'"

And all three of them started laughing again.

sixteen

"CLOSE YOUR EYES...IMAGINE THE TASTE OF VA-
nilla from your childhood...ice cream...cupcakes." Silence.
"Now imagine that innocent sweetness overlaid with an adult
complexity. Rich, intense, luxurious, aromatic." Silence.
"Spicy...sensual...juicy..."

Matilda and Cristina were rapt, but from where Finn was
standing, well back from the group, Zoe's reaction was a level
up. It was as though all of her senses were exquisitely, almost
painfully, attuned to the scent, to the words, and he decided it
had been worth every pain-in-the-butt moment it had taken
to arrange this visit with Orihei, who as a rule didn't allow
tourists.

"That is the smell of paradise," Orihei said, and let the silence
stretch for a dramatic moment before clapping her hands—a
hypnotist bringing her subjects out of a trance.

Matilda and Cristina instantly started talking animatedly

to each other, but it took Zoe a moment to shrug off the spell before joining in.

Zoe's hair was kookily—not seductively—styled in two enamel-pin-studded knot-like buns high on either side of her center parting. No hat today, but a crownless sun visor—to accommodate the hair-knots presumably. She wasn't wearing the visor at the moment; it was hanging over the handle of her wheelchair with that bedazzled-to-hell-backpack she carried everywhere. She was wearing a modest ankle-length skirt, white with pale pink flowers, and a long-sleeved T-shirt in white.

She should not have looked sexy, but God help him, she did.

Her nipples were clearly defined despite the two layers covering them—the white and a haze of purple beneath—and he was desperate to feel them, taste them, lick them, suck them, and he tried—he really did—not to watch only her, but his eyes had other ideas.

He strained to hear what the three women were talking about but caught only stray words: vanilla…dirty…skirtlet—what the hell was a skirtlet? And was that? Huh? Sequin? And holy sh— Had he really just heard the word "sex" being giggled over?

"Vanilla" again.

A repeat of some of the things Orihei had said. Intense, sensual, juicy, spicy.

And then Zoe's face was in her hands, and she was trying to smother that endearing guffaw thing she did, and his chest was aching so hard he wanted to punch himself in the heart to get it to stop. But he couldn't do that. Orihei was walking toward him and he had to don the professional mantle of the owner of Poerava.

"Gaspard's vanilla," Orihei said. "Will you take it with you?"

"Yes," he said, his eyes straying inevitably back to Zoe as he heard the word "sex" again.

Beat, beat, pulse, pulse. Vanilla. *Click*. Sex. *Click*. Intense. Spicy. Sensual. Juicy. *Click, click, click, click*. Dirty. *Click*.

"She has a nice laugh, your Zoe."

Zoe. His. What would it be like to taste vanilla overlaid on Zoe's lemon scent?

He looked at Orihei, saw she was giving him the glinting, knowing smile he was becoming way too familiar with. He thought about insisting she wasn't "his" Zoe but knew it would be a waste of time so he simply said, "Yes, she does, she always did." It was the truth. "We knew each other, a long time ago, in England."

And there it was again, the laugh, and he dared not look at Zoe this time because Orihei would pounce on it and that would be irritating as hell. But also because the sound of that laugh was making his chest ache again. The way it had always done. He'd hated that ache...but never enough to make him want her to stop laughing. He'd always wanted her to keep laughing, at herself, at him, with him, for him.

Nostalgia, he told himself, even though he didn't believe it, and bent to kiss Orihei on the cheek. "Thanks for today. We'll head over to Motu Marama and get out of your hair."

He strode over to Zoe, Matilda and Cristina, and announced: "Beach. If you're ready, let's get back on the boat."

The beauty of *Little Micky*, the pontoon boat Finn had borrowed from Kupe's friend, was that it could be beached, which made it easy to get the all-terrain wheelchair from the boat onto the sand.

Finn disembarked first, giving the women privacy on the boat to change. While he waited he set up a portable table on the strip of sand separating the water from the dense circle of vegetation at the center of the *motu*, in the shade of three rogue palm trees that stretched across the beach in an arc almost to the water's edge. Stools on three sides of the table, a space on the fourth for Zoe. Two cooler boxes—one for drinks, one for food. Four neatly folded towels on the sand, a mask and snorkel on three of them; a mask, snorkel and noodle on the fourth—Zoe's.

By the time the women disembarked—Cristina pushing Zoe in the all-terrain wheelchair, Matilda already stripped to her swimsuit—Finn had the champagne poured.

He handed them each a flute as they reached the table.

Matilda immediately raised her glass. "A toast, to Finn," she said.

Obviously, Finn couldn't drink a toast to himself—no loss; as the boat operator he was drinking water—so he waited while Zoe and Cristina smilingly echoed "To Finn" and sipped.

And then, "OK—" he began, only for Matilda to raise her glass again.

"And of course to..." looking from Finn to Zoe, her lips twitching, "vanilla."

Zoe lowered her eyes and choke-snorted before hastily taking another small swallow of champagne, Finn sipped his water, and Matilda managed a hefty glug before saying to Cristina: "What do you say we get into the water?"

Cristina shook her head. "I have to help Z—"

"I'm fine," Zoe cut her off. "I need to do the whole sunblock routine."

"But that chair, you can't—"

"Finn can push me." Zoe looked at him, her chin jutting a challenge. "OK?"

"Of course," he said.

Cristina was clearly still reluctant but Matilda waggled what could only be described as vaudeville eyebrows at her while shooting Finn a meaningful side-eye. Cristina's mouth formed an O. It was all over then. Cristina nodding, taking a last taste of champagne before whipping her dress over her head. Twin swoops to grab their snorkels, an extra swoop by Matilda to snag her waterproof camera, and with a warlike yell Cristina and Matilda were gone, leaving Finn alone with Zoe and no idea what to do except take the seat opposite her and try to make conversation.

"So, vanilla," he said. "You found it…amusing?"

Zoe jerked, sloshing her champagne over the rim of the flute glass. "I was…er…telling them about the…the vanilla milkshake Ewan concocted as the seasonal special at the Crab Shack that summer."

He left the moment there, suspended.

And then he said, "Well, there's vanilla…and then there's vanilla. Take imitation vanilla. Production line stuff. Easily produced. Cheap." He leaned across the table, forced her to keep her eyes on his. "And then there's the real thing. Labor intensive, focused, dedicated. Each flower of the vanilla orchid blooms for only six hours and has to be pollinated by hand before the flower closes. Timing, technique is everything. Worth its weight in gold." He held her gaze, refusing to let her look away—*two can play at this game*. "That wasn't just a vanilla milkshake at the Crab Shack, Zoe. It was a *vanilla fondant milkshake with clotted cream*. Vanilla isn't always vanilla. It can be much, much more."

She blinked, blushed, finally looked away. Her hands were going up and down her thighs, her eyes searching for Cristina and Matilda, as though she needed reinforcements.

"So what's next?" he asked.

She licked her lips. "I guess we'd better get undressed." She jolted, looked at him, blushed harder. "I didn't mean—I meant—not *undressed* undressed. Dressed for swimming. Snorkeling. I have my swimsuit on. Under my clothes." And as though to shut herself up she removed her visor and yanked her top up over her head.

Finn's mouth went dry, his heart went whomp, and although he really, truly wanted to avert his gaze, he was stuck looking at her because his eyes would not move. She was wearing a minuscule bikini top covered in sun-catching purple sequins. And he was remembering what she'd said last night in the bar, that she let people she knew, people who understood her, people she trusted, touch her, lift her out of her chair, without asking…

How he wanted to put that to the test. Wanted to drag her out of that chair and onto his lap. Wanted to devour her, wanted to beg her to feel the same, to want him the same way, or any way at all as long as it wasn't as the genderless friend-zoned coworker she'd slummed it with that summer she'd had a holiday job.

Holiday job. That stopped him.

Her *summer* job had been his *real* job.

She is not for you.

God, he had to stop thinking like that or she would *never* be for him.

Zoe pulled the pink rash vest she'd worn for Monday's snorkeling cruise out of her backpack, as oblivious of his torment as she'd ever been. She looked at the vest as though debating whether or not to wear it and he wished, wished, wished she'd put it on, cover up, wrap a towel around herself for good measure, because he didn't trust his willpower.

He got to his feet, moving a few safe steps away as she gave an infinitesimal shrug and dug out the Factor 60 and started performing the by-rote activity of covering every centimeter of her exposed skin with it. At least, the parts she could reach. She was having trouble with her back but making an effort nevertheless.

Finn glanced around to see if Cristina or Matilda was available to offer assistance but they were both still swimming.

Sunblock was an innocent thing, wasn't it? Harmless. People put it on each other's backs all the time. If Zoe would let him push her wheelchair surely she'd let him put sunblock on her back. And maybe, *maybe*, the mystery of her would then be solved, he'd find that touching her wasn't such a big deal after all, that skin was just skin, and closure would be achieved.

Technically, though, closure wouldn't be achieved, would it? That would only happen when *she* touched *him*.

But at this precise moment, with every nerve in his body stretching toward her and his hands trembling with need, did he really care about that technicality?

Right. He was going to do it. He was going to ask her if she wanted him to put the stuff on her back and if she said yes then he was going to just...just do it.

He unclenched his jaw ready to speak...just as Zoe tugged that pink rash vest over her head, and the sunblock offer was rendered null and void. He was relieved. No he wasn't. Yes he was. Not relieved. Yes. No. Oh for God's *sake*.

She made an adjustment to her hair, refixing a hairpin. Her hands went to her skirt next, unzipping, wiggling it under her backside, down her legs, off.

And good Lord, his eyes were going to melt the sequins right off her if he stared any harder at the playful little ruffled skirt attached to her shimmery bikini bottoms. The "skirt-let," obviously. She was twitching at it, unconsciously drawing his attention to what was hidden beneath, and he thought it was lucky she was concentrating and therefore not looking at his face because his tongue was ready to roll right out of his mouth at the thought of what it was hiding from him. But he knew what he wanted was more than sex. He wanted to be as close as he could get to her, to be part of her, to be one with her, his soulmate.

Oh God, he was in trouble. Because there she went, putting more Factor 60 on her legs, making another adjustment to her hair, and he could tell himself that he saw the physical signs that she wanted him but emotionally she had to be as oblivious as ever or she'd be freaking out at being alone on the beach with a man who was clearly desperate.

As though feeling his laser gaze on her, Zoe looked at him, her eyes flicking from his face to his chest, and she licked her lips, and he imagined her licking *him*, all the way from his collarbone to his—

"Are you wearing your shirt in the water?" she asked, sounding as breathless as he felt.

His fingers went to the buttons of his shirt, and then stopped. She'd never seen him shirtless. In the old days he'd been self-conscious because his ribs stuck out. He hadn't been aware of deliberately covering up here in the islands. If anything, he should be eager to show her that he wasn't skin and bones anymore. And yet his shirt was somehow…armor. Once it was off…once she saw him…if she liked what she saw… Argh, where was he going with this?

"What's wrong?" she asked, giving a breathy little laugh. "Do you have girls' names tattooed across your chest like notches on a bedpost? I'd like to read those. It'd be like a school reunion. A hundred names I know, and probably another hundred I don't."

"No tattoos," he said.

"Seriously?" Another breathy laugh. "And to think there I was all those years ago imagining you covered in tattoos like all the other guys in your—"

"Gang?"

"I was going to say group of friends."

"Gang will do, Zoe."

"Well, what kind of gang member are you to have not one measly little tattoo?"

"The kind with a mother who wouldn't have approved," he said, meaning it as a joke, but neither of them laughed.

"No, she wouldn't have, would she?" Zoe said with such… such *poignancy*, and it damn near crushed him.

He thought of Gina, wanting to talk about his mother and always being blocked. Waiting on a decision he couldn't make about a UK property because it would mean going back to Hawke's Cove. All those years he'd thought he'd sloughed off that life he'd left behind, and yet he knew he wasn't free of those years—they were still part of him, both driving and shackling him.

He wasn't free of those years, that life. And he wasn't free of Zoe, who could read him, *feel* him, wound him, own him body and soul.

He'd intended to let his frustrated yearning for Zoe go twelve years ago. Ten years ago he'd thought he had. But it seemed he'd only buried it—so deep it would have taken a psychological earthquake to uncover it, but there it was nevertheless. And now here she was. Tiny and glowing, smelling like sunlight, as indomitable as ever. Wanting to go only forward, not back. His earthquake, ripping out his soul, reminding him that she was part of everything he'd become and it still wasn't enough because even as he told himself he wanted her not to matter to him anymore, she mattered more than ever.

He returned to the table, sat. "It's still a part of us, isn't it, Hawke's Cove?" he asked, and although he hadn't intended to ask that—was disturbed that he had—he found that he really wanted to hear her answer.

She took a moment, stuffing her visor, skirt and sunblock into her bedazzled backpack, putting the backpack on the sand beside her, looking at it for a frowning moment. "I thought… But lately…" She brought her eyes up, her hands going unerringly to her thighs. "Lately I've felt…" She made a sound redolent of frustration. "Felt something I can't describe. Not quite homesickness but a need for…for closure that I can't grasp because of the memories not being whole. Maybe there *are* things I'd change if I could go back. But there's no time machine so we can't go back, can we." She said the words, didn't ask them, but he heard a plea in them.

"I don't know, Zoe," he said.

"Finn…" It was almost a cry, but she brought herself up, shook her head. "Nothing. I just—" She gave a helpless little shrug. "Nothing."

"You know you can say anything to me, Zoe. Even if I don't have the answers I can listen."

"I could...and you did...once upon a time."

"You can and I will now."

She took a deep breath, nodded. "I just wondered if... H-have you ever been back? Because I haven't. At least, I have... but I haven't. That is, I had to go because...not for me...but..." She slapped her hands over her face, said something that sounded like "Gagh" and then dropped her hands to reveal a ruefully laughing countenance. "That didn't make sense."

He smiled. "You've been back but only once, last Christmas, and in answer to your question, no I've never been back, not even once."

"How do you know it was at Christmas? No, don't tell me, I know. Google! Though why you'd want to look into how many times I've been back to Hawke's Cove and when—why those details would even pop up in an online search..." She gave a *words fail me* shake of her head.

"Google provides me with general information so I don't have to waste journalists' time with superfluous questions. For example, I don't have to ask you how many wheelchair users there are in the world because the answer—seventy-five million—is readily available. I also prefer to do my own research about the style of articles journalists write. If I read the stories they've filed in the past couple of years, I don't make the mistake of inviting them to a destination they've already covered, plus I get an idea of whether they're more into natural wonders, the spa experience, nightlife, cuisine, whatever, so their experience at our resorts can be tailored. Along the way, though, it's inevitable that I'll find out things I don't need to know, things I wasn't necessarily looking for." He paused. Hell, why not? "For example, if X is single, if Y has a husband, if Z lives alone."

Her hands were on her thighs, moving up and down. He

knew the moment she became aware that his eyes were on her hands, because she stopped the action.

"Yes, no, yes," she said, "if you want to know those things in relation to me."

Relief surged but he kept his expression neutral. "Those were general examples but if you want something specific, I know Victoria got engaged in Hawke's Cove at Christmas to some rich hotshot department store owner because I saw it on the local paper's website. I assumed you were there, and I guessed that was the only time you went back to the Cove because there's no mention of going home in your blog. If you can wax lyrical about your hair clips it makes sense that you'd chronicle your trips home."

"So you weren't—" She stopped, blushed. "I mean, you didn't..." Her hands came up to cover her face again, and she made that adorable *I'm-an-idiot* explosion of sound. A moment only, then the hands were falling, and there was laughter on her lips and in her eyes. "No, of course you didn't...you weren't... whatever I was trying to say."

Ah, what was he doing? This was like...like sand, trickling through that hourglass—one grain at a time but inexorable, telling him that time was running out. Four days left after today, and then he'd never see her again. And he needed her to know. "Actually..." Oh God, he couldn't do this to himself.

She blinked at him, the laughter draining out of her, expectation filling the gaps.

Do it. Say it. Let her know. "Actually, I did and I was."

She licked her lips. "Huh?"

"I did want to know if you were engaged or married or living with someone. And I absolutely searched for the answers on Google." Long, *dare you* look into her pale green eyes. "Just for the record."

She sucked in a breath, let it out slowly. "So you lied."

He conceded that with a tilt of his head, a half smile. "Yeah.

I do that sometimes, when the stakes are high. Then again, you lie sometimes too. You lied to me about fifteen minutes ago on the subject of vanilla milkshakes."

"Oh," she said, and spluttered out a laugh. "Well, OK, you got me. But vanilla milkshakes are not in the same league as… as cyberstalking someone."

"But how do I know that if you won't tell me the truth? Come on, play the game," he challenged. "Truth or dare."

"Dare," she said and out came her chin. "I *dare* you to take off your shirt."

He raised his hands. Surrender. "Fine," he said, and stood. "I'll even let you watch while *I* explain to *you* the joke about vanilla."

"How could you know?"

"We both know I've been around the block a time or two," he said, undoing one button. "And if you want to talk vanilla…" Another button. "I'm definitely the fondant vanilla milkshake with clotted cream." One more button, very slowly because her eyes were fixed on his hands.

She swallowed as the last two buttons were undone. The air was almost sizzling and it had nothing to do with the air temperature. He started to shrug off his shirt, stopped as she squared her narrow shoulders. "A shame," she said with an oh-so-innocent toss of her head. "I was kind of hoping for… I don't know, a Dirty Rocky Road Milkshake, maybe."

"You've got me there, Zoe, I don't know what that is. How about you tell me?"

She opened her eyes exaggeratedly wide. "You don't know? *You*, Finn Doherty? Well! A Dirty Rocky Road Milkshake's got Jack Daniel's, toasted marshmallows, rocky road ice cream, chocolate syrup, whipped cream and sprinkles."

"Sprinkles, huh?" he said and removed his shirt.

She looked him over, her eyes snagging on the front of his board shorts, and he knew exactly what she was seeing because he could feel it pushing against the cotton, pushing and full-on throbbing. The air wasn't just sizzling now, it was sparking like firecrackers, only those firecrackers were inside him, singeing every cell in his body.

Up came her eyes, direct and sure. "I'd *insist* on the sprinkles, Finlay, just so you know."

Finlay.

Finlay.

Just a name. *Don't get carried away.* It was nothing, it *meant* nothing that she could say it so easily, as though they had indeed gone back in their time machine to Hawke's Cove when one of them had been head over heels and the other had been safely, securely oblivious.

"But if you want to fight about flavors…" She faltered. Took a breath.

"I don't want to fight, Zoe. About anything."

"Fight your big battles to the death, but don't sweat the scrappy skirmishes if you want to win the long war," she said. "Do you remember saying that to me?"

"Yes. I remember it. I remember…that time I said it."

And it was there, stretching between them, the memory of that one time he'd dared to touch. It was so vivid, so real, he could almost believe she could see it the way he did, feel it the way he had. The silk of her hair, the tremble in his fingers, the want in him.

"Zoe…" he said. "I wish I'd—"

"Gotcha!" Matilda said, and they both startled, then turned their heads to see her waving her camera. "If I had to caption that photo it would be: *No longer kids who once upon a time didn't hang in the same circles.* Whaddya think?"

Finn looked at Zoe. "How about *Not all milkshakes are vanilla?*"

"Or *Not all bad boys have tattoos?*" Zoe counteroffered.

"Or perhaps *Matilda has no idea what the hell is going on?*"

Matilda said. And then "Riiight," as neither of them responded. "I'm going swimming. Something the two of you might want to consider some time this century. Zo, do you need me to help?"

Zoe's hands hovered over her thighs. Finn knew she was barely restraining herself from taking up her favorite nervous habit. "No," she said and shook her head with something that looked a lot like defiance. "I already told Cris, Finn's going to push me."

As Matilda headed back to the water, Zoe looked up at him. "Don't tip me over."

"Zoe Tayler, are you *scared*?"

"It's a question of dignity, not fear."

A heartbeat's pause. And then, seriously, he asked, "Does anything scare you, Zoe? Like, *anything*? 'Cause I've never seen you afraid."

"Yes," she said, and faced the lagoon again. Silence. Unbearable, and yet he would have waited all day. "If I've been in the water too long," she said at last, "and my arms are tired and I find myself too far from the beach or the boat or the pontoon, I sometimes think I'll keep drifting, and drifting...and end up like George Clooney in space in *Gravity*—only the marine version, floating out further and further until there's only me, and water, and no way back." A beat of silence, and then she looked at him, and gave a shrug and a laugh that sounded forced, and Finn guessed she was self-conscious about that confession. "Well, maybe me, a great white and a giant clam."

He smiled, but he didn't laugh. "I won't let you drift too far, Zoe."

She tilted her head, looked hard at him. "You won't always be with me."

"Hey, no time machine, right? There's just today."

seventeen

THE URGE TO WRITE WOKE ZOE AN HOUR EARLIER than usual the next morning.

She sat at her computer and without thinking started an email to her parents, describing the vanilla farm and Motu Marama, signing off with a jaunty "Princess Zoe" because that was how she pictured herself, under the palm trees, surveying her lagoon kingdom.

She stared at the word "Princess," thinking of that fractured fairy tale about Rapunzel and the idiot prince she and Finn had laughed over on Monday night. She understood why she'd woken with the need to write: sometime between laughing with Finn about the meaning of vanilla on Motu Marama and the end of the dinner Finn had hosted for the media in Tāma'a last night, that awful feeling of suffocation had lifted. It was as though she'd gone back to Hawke's Cove in that time machine after all and Finn Doherty was daring her into climbing into Sir

Gaden's stolen dinghy and she was feeling reckless because she was with him, restless for something to happen. Feeling...alive.

Alive, but not in the naive way she'd felt at sixteen. Not even in the way she'd felt on Monday night when she'd so calculatedly decided to ask him to have sex with her only to lose her nerve.

Ever since Finn had stripped off his shirt on the beach yesterday the unsettling swirl of feelings she used to have when she looked at him had been meshing and merging with something new, something hot and needy and hungry. There was nothing calculated now about the way she felt, nothing intellectual about it, it was just there—like the shivers that wracked her when he was near or even when she was only thinking about him. She thought of those shivers as a visible manifestation of a craving she'd always had but hadn't truly comprehended until she'd seen him that night with Jess Trewes. Yes, she wanted the fun and fairy tales of the past, but she wanted more, and the more she wanted was the Finn Doherty of *now*.

Last night at dinner he'd been every inch the owner of Poerava. Charming, commanding, in his element. Magnetic rather than handsome. Darkly, exhilaratingly so. Zoe had been at a different table and he hadn't come near her, but he'd looked at her often and that eye-locking thing had happened over and over again, making her breathless with longing for what would happen next.

The feeling that something wonderful, something exciting, was possible was there in the words she'd just written to her parents, in the words she'd written to them last night even though she hadn't understood the truth until this moment—that Finn was responsible for that feeling.

So...why hadn't she yet told them about Finn being on the island?

Of course she wasn't going to trumpet the news that she was in lust with the man. That would likely send them into apoplexy. But she could—she *should*—tell them he owned the resort. She *owed* it to Finn to tell them. *See, I tried to tell you he wasn't a no-hoper!*

OK, she was going to do it.

She rubbed her hands together, then wriggled her fingers over the keyboard, and taking a quick breath popped in a throwaway line at the end.

She reread the line. Shook her head.

It looked out of place.

Delete.

She tried again, higher up in the email. Decided it didn't work there either. Didn't work in the next place she selected, or the next.

It was too short. Too bald. And because it was too short and bald it looked too...too *weighty*. They'd read something into it she didn't want them to read.

OK, so she'd just describe how he looked. A show-not-tell thing. What he'd been wearing last night. Tailored charcoal trousers and a crisp white shirt—not the scruffy jeans and T-shirt her parents would remember. His hair, perfectly cut. His shoulders, so broad. The strength of his chest and arms and thighs. And his eyes, like the sky only brighter and bluer and...

Ugh!

No good.

She could not write about the way he looked.

She thought of other things she could say about him. What he'd told her that night in his bungalow, or at the bar, or on the beach...

No, they were too...well, *private*. He'd always seen her parents as the enemy; it would be tantamount to a betrayal to reveal to them anything he'd said to her.

Hmm. She'd have to find the words tomorrow and write about him in her next email. So...send.

Whew. Gone.

She turned as Cristina came out of her bedroom. "Ready to hit the gym?" she asked. "I want to challenge myself today so I'm going to up my weights."

And of course, because Zoe had pushed herself to her absolute limit and was a bedraggled, sticky-haired mess at the end of her allocated hour, Finn just had to turn up at the gym.

He was wearing the loose singlet and shorts she'd visualized him in, muscles rippling, looking vital and virile and squeaky clean, and he was striding over to her like a man on a mission.

"Glad I caught you both!" he said. "I understand you're booked into the spa with Matilda today."

"That's the plan," Zoe said, surreptitiously sniffing herself.

He smiled his chipped-tooth smile and Zoe's heart started flopping around in her chest even though that smile was directed at Cristina. "If Zoe can spare you I thought you might like to dodge the spa and take a cooking class. It's a short boat ride away but Captain Joe's free to take you."

Zoe tried to listen as he talked about the acclaimed French chef who'd be teaching his signature dish, but she caught only snippets because she was shivering again and wondering if she could wheel just a little bit closer. Duck breast...blah blah... Tahitian honey...blah blah... *If I get closer I might be able to smell that aphrodisiacal soap...* Puff pastry...blah blah... *No, stay where you are, Zoe, you stink...* Sweetbreads...blah blah... *Hang on— is that one dish or an entire menu?* Risotto, blah blah... *OK, Zoe, snap out of it.*

Finn ended with, "So what do you say?"

The light of the true food zealot was glowing in Cristina's eyes, making Zoe smile because she'd seen Lily look exactly like that.

"Lily would kill to take that class," Zoe said.

But Cristina, after a scrunched-eye moment, shook her head. "No, if it's on a different island I can't go."

"Sure you can," Zoe said.

"No, Zoe."

Geez. Not this again. "I'll be with Matilda," Zoe remonstrated. "I'll be fine."

Another shake of Cristina's head. "I can't leave you for that long when I won't be able to get to you quickly if you need me."

"Then how about I do the class with you?" an exasperated Zoe offered, not wanting Cristina to go into full-on self-sacrifice mode. "That way I can share the recipe with Lily and she can maybe give it a local Devon twist and put it on The Sea Rose menu."

Cristina ping-ponged a deer-in-the-headlights look between Zoe and Finn. "What about the spa?"

Zoe brushed that aside with a flick of her wrist. "I can go to a spa anytime. And I haven't done a cooking class since Thailand. Remember when we made *Yam Pla Dook Foo*? It'll be fun."

There was an arrested moment where nobody moved, nobody spoke; then Finn picked up Zoe's baton and ran with it.

"Good idea," he said, and got a sharp look from Cristina. "I wonder, though, if The Sea Rose might be more interested in seafood dishes. I mean, you know, the *sea*."

Zoe didn't know how the conversation segued to the Doherty & Berne food philosophy, which was all about fresh produce sourced locally, but segue it did. And as Zoe reefed out her notebook and started jotting down a few notes for her article (and for Lily, who would absolutely agree with everything Finn said), the discussion became focused on French Polynesian specialities. And somehow, by the time Zoe's pencil stopped scratching on the page, the cooking class was now being conducted in Poerava's kitchen by Finn's head chef, no boat ride required. Furthermore, they'd be preparing *poisson cru* because it would be a "crime" to leave French Polynesia without learning how to prepare *the* dish of the islands. In fact, it was about time Finn learned how to make it himself, so he'd join them if that was all right.

Next minute, Zoe and Cristina were on their way back to their bungalow and Zoe had no idea how that transition to Poerava and *poisson cru* had actually occurred.

Nor why Finn would bother joining them when he could invade the Poerava kitchen anytime.

It was the first thing Zoe asked Finn when they joined him at the entrance to the kitchen after the breakfast service had finished.

"Every time I've tried I've been called away," he said. He ushered them into the kitchen and over to an unenthusiastic-looking man.

"Gaspard," Finn said after the introductions, "Cristina is quite a chef as well as a fishing aficionado. Why don't you run through the essentials with her?"

"You like fishing?" Gaspard said, eyes sparking.

As Gaspard started talking to Cristina, Finn raised his eyebrows at Zoe, simultaneously rolling his eyes toward the conversing couple and jerking his head toward the other side of an enormous table that was being cleared of kitchen paraphernalia by one of the staff. Quite the performance.

Zoe heard something about the catch of the day being yellowfin tuna and deciding that was as detailed as she needed to get, she followed Finn.

"He doesn't want to teach us, does he?" Zoe hissed, because it was *so* obvious.

He didn't bother contradicting her. "She'll win him over."

"But why?"

"Because he's temperamental but she's one of his kind."

"No, I mean why are we here and not on that other course?"

He huffed out an exaggerated sigh. "Zoe, surely you saw the look of entreaty Cristina gave me when you offered to make that duck-whatever-it-is with her. Pretty sure it has something to do with your *Yam Pla Dook Foo*. I read about it in one of your blogs."

Zoe gasped. And up went her hands, over her face, and she was choking on laughter.

"Hey," he said, "could have been worse."

She dropped her hands, still laughing. "I assure you it couldn't!" She grimaced. "So I ruined her lesson."

"How so?"

"She'll be disappointed she missed out on the advanced class."

"I'll make it up to her. Just remember next time I suggest a cooking class you're not allowed to offer to go with her. She'll never say no to you, you know that. No one ever could, Zoe."

"That's not true."

"Yes it is. So work with me, OK?"

"Fine!"

"And yeah, she might be disappointed when she sees that *poisson cru* is nothing more than raw fish marinated in lime juice and soaked in coconut milk—"

"You already know how to make it? Seriously, *why* are you here?"

"I want to see what you think of our kitchen and our chef. For the article."

"I can see your tongue in your cheek," she said.

"OK, OK. I've made *poisson cru* a few times, *but* I haven't made *poisson cru ananas* and that's what Gaspard's showing us. It's much more complicated."

"How complicated?"

He grinned at her. "You add pineapple slices."

"Oh! You!"

"And I don't think Gaspard will cope with a *Yam Pla Dook Foo*-style disaster so I'm here to take the heat when it all goes down."

She gasped out a helpless laugh, which was interrupted by an impatient Gaspard telling them he was ready to start.

Gaspard waited until everyone was settled, then waited an extra few beats—for dramatic effect, Zoe thought, and had to squelch a giggle at his seriousness. And then he said: "Most dishes here in French Polynesia will have a French and a Polynesian name. *Poisson cru* is French and translates into raw fish. Simple, no?"

Zoe and Cristina dutifully nodded.

"But here at Poerava," he continued, "we prefer the Polynesian name: *e'ia ota*."

"And what does that mean?" Zoe asked.

Gaspard gave a Gallic shrug. "Raw fish," he said.

Finn burst out laughing, which made a giggle erupt from Zoe. Both of them were threatened with being evicted from the kitchen.

"But when I say it is simple," Gaspard intoned once order had been restored, "it is *not*!"

Over the next twenty minutes, Zoe scribbled furiously as Gaspard waxed lyrical about the best types of fish to use—sashimi grade yellowfin tuna, which they would be using today, jackfish, striped marlin, even mackerel (ergh, mackerel!) as long as it was fresh, fresh, fresh… The zest of the marinade resulting from the exquisite balance of lime juice—so fresh—and salt… The delight of massaging the marinade into the flesh of the fish… The joy of choosing vibrantly colorful vegetables to make the dish a feast for the eyes as well as the palate—fresh, fresh, the freshest!… The choice of pineapple—the crunch, the juiciness.

"And of course, the coconut milk," Gaspard said, and waited a beat. "What do we say this must be?"

"Fresh," Cristina said, as serious as Gaspard, who beamed at her, his star pupil, while Finn caught Zoe's eye and pulled a cross-eyed face that had her biting her trembling lip.

"Above all," Gaspard said, finishing his course introduction with a grand flourish of both hands, "time is of the essence. We must be fast. Any longer than *eleven minutes* in our marinade will overcook our fish, and the flavors will invade the flesh. We do not want an invasion, we want a relationship!"

"No invasion," Zoe murmured, her shoulders shaking as she bent over her notebook. No way was she going to let Finn catch her eye this time or she'd be in hysterics.

Not that the food itself was funny. Far from it. From what Zoe could tell, *poisson cru* in any of the permutations Gaspard rattled off was about as close to sustainable eating—the virtues of which Lily was always extolling—as it was possible to get. Always made with the freshest of ingredients, all readily available and abundant throughout French Polynesia.

It was while they were chopping their fresh-fresh-freshest vegetables that Finn moved his chair closer to Zoe and whispered, "Remember that time you asked Ewan if you should freeze the cod for the next day's fish cakes?"

"Yes! He chased me out of the kitchen."

"Dare you to ask Gaspard what he does with the fish that's left over from the catch of the day."

"No!" Zoe said, feeling a giggle bubbling up.

"Double dare you."

"Finn, I'm holding a knife!"

"That you barely know how to use. I'm safe to triple dare you!"

"Shh," Zoe hissed back, struggling not to laugh.

"OK, you asked for it, quadruple dare you."

At which point they were interrupted by Gaspard demanding irritably: "What's going on over there?"

Finn cast Zoe a speaking look and mouthed: "Quintuple dare."

She bared her teeth at him but then blinked limpidly at Gaspard. "I was just wondering what you did with the leftover yellowfin tuna, Gaspard. Do you freeze it?"

Gaspard stared at her for one awful moment. "Do not talk to me of frozen fish," he said grandly.

"Sorry, Gaspard," she said, pretending to be chastened as Gaspard returned his attention to his star pupil, Cristina.

Finn was practically wheezing as Zoe tried—and failed—to glare at him.

"Just for that, Finlay Doherty," she said out of the corner of her mouth, "I'm going to make you *eat* my *poisson cru ananas*."

There was a short burst of laughter, which Finn swallowed as Gaspard swiveled to face him with a threatening look in his eye.

"Sorry!" he said meekly, but he did the cross-eyed thing at Zoe the moment Gaspard released him from his ire, and she had to clench everything in her entire body to stop from giggling.

Zoe gave it her best shot but for all of Gaspard's instructions, Cristina's assistance, and Finn's cheekily offered hints (or perhaps *because* of those), her *poisson cru* ended up looking like minced slime.

Finn, to his credit, despite sending her a *please don't make me look* that had her giggling again, swapped plates with her, and while she ate his marginally more appetizing offering he manfully swallowed hers, complete with over-the-top grimaces that somehow made her heart feel as light and sweet as sponge cake.

And then the lesson was over.

Finn went to consult with Gaspard about the farewell cocktail party that was planned for Sunday night and she and Cristina chatted as they cleaned up their respective stations at the table.

It had been the most uncomplicated fun Zoe had had in… hmm…she couldn't actually remember. Even at Christmas when she'd been with the girls on the beach drinking champagne the mood had been shadowed by what was going on with

Victoria and Oliver, and the time in Hawaii with Malie had been complicated by Malie's conflicted feelings about Todd.

That was what love did. Made even the fun things messy.

She thought back to her conversation with Lily about wanting to know what it was like to be in love and there—twisting inside her—was that strange sensation, the tide that kept pulling her, like a…a grief, almost. For her friends, for the past, for Devon, for what might have been. But also there was what Finn had promised on the *motu* yesterday, to not let her drift too far, and that was like an anchor to who she was now. It felt as though her past and her present were colliding, and she wasn't ready for the impact.

She pushed the thoughts aside. The past had waited ten years; it could wait three more days. As for the present, the whole afternoon stretched ahead of them and Finn—heading purposefully toward them—would have a suggestion for how to fill it from his "live like a local" list.

"Cristina," he said when he reached them, "if you ever want a job in the resort kitchen, let me know. It's not easy to impress Gaspard but you've done it."

He touched Cristina, just a small touch on her elbow, and Zoe held her breath hoping he was going to touch her too. Elbow, hand, arm, hair, somewhere, anywhere. *Please!*

Notepad. He'd almost brushed fingers with her on Monday night when he'd held it out to her, so maybe if *she* held it out to *him*?

"Finn," she said, and bravely offered it, page open at the *poisson cru* recipe. "Could you maybe check that I got the thing about the vegetables right? I need it to be perfect before I send it to Lily. She…she's fussy about this stuff."

He looked a fraction too long at her mouth before his eyes dropped to the notepad, and then he looked a fraction too long at that. His lips parted, his fingers seemed to spasm, his jaw

clenched. Zoe waited, expectant, hopeful, her silent wish—
touch me!—hanging unvoiced in the air.

The moment stretched, stretched...

And then Finn said: "Gaspard's the one to ask about that."
He smiled, but his eyes didn't crinkle at the corners. "But right
now I'm needed elsewhere. I'd better rush. Let Aiata know if
you need anything."

"Oh," Zoe said, and swallowed. "Of course. Thanks. For
the lesson."

"My pleasure," he said, but it was at best a perfunctory response, and he strode out of the kitchen without a backward
glance.

"I'll check it for you, Zoe," Cristina offered, taking the
notepad, scrutinizing the words. "Looks fine. But maybe *type*
it out for Lily instead of scanning it. So what do you want to
do this afternoon?"

"Hmm?" She'd been so certain Finn would come up with
a suggestion.

"Tilly's sent a text saying the Taurumi massage is swoon-
worthy."

"Taurumi massage?" *Of course* Finn had work to do. At least
she hoped he did, hoped she hadn't said or done anything to
make him run away. Maybe she should go over it all, moment
by moment...

"Er... Zo? Anything in particular you want to do?"

"Sorry." Zoe gave herself a mental shake, looked at Cristina,
caught a soul-destroying flash of sympathy in her eyes, made
somehow worse by the fact it was so quickly concealed. What
did she want to do? Go to bed and cry her eyes out. But she
wouldn't do that. Never, ever.

OK, snap back. She could go to the spa. She could laze on
the beach. Visit the newly opened Giant Clam Sanctuary—Gaz
could arrange it with thirty minutes' notice. Call Kupe Kahale
and make arrangements to go to Heia Island, ask a few supple-

mentary questions for her article on him, have an early dinner at his famous restaurant and snap his photo, which would mean she could bow out of the Saturday dinner gracefully.

But, "I think I'll go back to the bungalow," she said. "I owe Mum and Dad an email. Why don't you go and get that massage?"

"If this is like the fishing trip and the cooking class, and you're shooing me off for a massage because you think it's what I want—"

"I promise this is all about me," Zoe assured her. "I want to tell them about the cooking class and I need to do it before the details fade."

And to her surprise, Zoe realized that wasn't an excuse, it was the truth. She knew it would make her parents smile to hear about the class, the way she'd felt their smile in their last two emails to her. They'd got back to her so quickly after she'd sent that email this morning, telling her how much they'd loved her description of the beach, and that Matilda sounded like Malie, and Daniel like Brad (who, she'd be interested to know, had become somewhat "unfit" since becoming a father). Again, no cautionary paragraphs, no safety reminders, no suggestions for ensuring her safety. It was weird but it was also wow, and she was determined to keep sharing her life with them, and making them smile and showing them she was not…not lost.

eighteen

NANIHI'S OFFICE DOOR WAS AJAR, WHICH MEANT
staff were welcome to enter. Finn, as the owner, would be
doubly welcome, and yet he paused outside trying to figure out
what he could ask her given there was nothing about Poerava
he didn't already know.

He was only there to vacate the lobby so Zoe could leave
without talking to him. Talking now would be...not good.

"Finn, is that you out there?" Nanihi called from inside the
office. Finn entered, deliberately leaving the door open because...just because. Air, he needed air, because of that.

"Just interested in the forward bookings for June," he said.

Nanihi started tapping on her keyboard and suggested he
come to her side of the desk. He stood there, not listening as
she explained the data in the file she'd opened, flicking his gaze
between the computer screen and the open doorway.

And there she was. Zoe, with Cristina, crossing the lobby.

Something scarily like a whimper came out of his mouth.

"Finn?" Nanihi's voice recalled him to sanity.

She said nothing else, but looked through the doorway just in time to see a back view of Zoe as she wheeled herself out of the building. Going...going...gone.

"Right, where were we?" he asked Nanihi, and saw that her eyebrows were up.

"What?" he said, feeling the hideous heat of a blush flushing up from his neck.

"You seem...troubled," she said calmly. "Are you unhappy with the occupancy rates?"

He scanned the report on the screen. Occupancy rates were nudging ninety percent. Everything was perfect. He started to tell Nanihi so and found she was biting her lip.

Dammit! How many more people were going to slap that trying-not-to smile routine on him? "I'm not troubled," he said, with as much sangfroid as he could muster. "You're all doing an amazing job."

"I'm glad you think so. I was only wondering because..." her lip was definitely wobbling, "there seemed to be no reason for you staying on for the week."

He had no answer to that. All he could do was breathe. In. Out. In. Out.

Nanihi made a tiny sound and covered her mouth with one hand.

Right, he was going to call Gina, fly out tomorrow. He didn't think he could take any more people sly-smiling at him and laughing behind their hands. Joe and Orihei and Aiata and Tepatua and Cristina and Matilda and Nanihi and even Gaspard with his "not invasion, relationship" stuff, and—

Gaspard!

Why hadn't Gaspard stormed after him demanding either satisfaction or a raise? Finn had, after all, with no notice, forced him to give a lesson he hadn't wanted to give; he'd insisted not only that a table be moved into the kitchen but that it also be piled with assorted utensils so they could have the lesson seated without Zoe guessing the table was newly there specifically to accommodate her wheelchair; he'd encouraged Zoe to giggle her way through the class and hadn't taken one moment of it seriously himself even though he knew disrespect annoyed Gaspard…and Gaspard had *let him get away with it all.*

"Gaspard!" he said in accents of loathing.

"He'll be hard to replace if you fire him," Nanihi said, oh so deadpan but with an unmistakable twinkle in her eye.

"You know!" Finn accused.

She raised her hands, palm out, placating. "I know nothing except that only for a romantic emergency would Gaspard allow his kitchen to be used in such a fashion. I told him he was imagining things."

"Then at least someone here isn't an idiot."

"I told him he was imagining things," she went on, implacably serene, "but now I know he wasn't."

Breathe in, in, in. Out, dammit! "I ought to sack the lot of you."

"Kupe Kahale has been doing his best to poach staff from Poerava so please make up your mind fast. By Monday, perhaps?" She was full-throttle smirking now. "That's when she flies home, isn't it?"

At which point Finn stormed out of the office, intent on bearding the lion in his den.

The sound of Nanihi's laughter, which she was making no effort to stifle, floated after him.

He tore into the kitchen only to pull up short at the sight of Gaspard leaning a hip against the counter, arms crossed over his chest as though he'd been expecting Finn to arrive at just that moment.

"So!" Gaspard said. "You return to the scene of the crime."

"Crime?" Finn said, ready to come over all boss-like.

Gaston shuddered. "Her *poisson cru? Exécrable.* A crime, committed in *my* kitchen! *Impardonnable!*"

Finn grinned, despite himself. "At least you didn't have to eat it!"

Another shudder from Gaspard.

"Listen, Gaspard, I'm sor—"

"She is delightful, my dear Finn," Gaspard interrupted. "But it is my duty to warn you that if you go there you will have to do all the cooking yourself. Or perhaps hire someone for the home."

"What do you mean, go there?"

"You know what I mean."

"But I'm not. Going there. I'm not."

"Of course you're not," Gaspard said, and he didn't need to roll his eyes because his voice was one major eye roll in itself.

"I'm not!" Finn insisted.

"Is that not what I just said?"

"No, that's not what you just said. At least it is but that's not what's happening."

Gaspard looked at him with a weary kind of patience and that annoying, knowing smirk everyone was giving him. "If that's not what's happening, why are you in my kitchen arguing with me?"

Unanswerable.

Finn turned without another word and swung out of the kitchen.

It didn't do his temper any good to hear Gaspard laughing his head off. Worse than Nanihi. It would serve Gaspard right if he made him teach Zoe how to make his fussy passionfruit soufflé.

The thought of which had Finn, unbelievably, grinning like an idiot as he made his way back to his bungalow, because she'd probably make Finn eat it the way she'd made him eat her *poisson cru.*

But as he let himself into his bungalow the grin faded.

Zoe hadn't been here since Monday night and yet he could still smell her. Lemon and sunshine and white flowers.

He closed his eyes as the memories crowded. Not old memories, new memories. *Now* memories. The cocktail party, her voice saying, *I'm not lost.* Swimming off the platform on *Pearl Finder* with a purple noodle but not one moment's hesitation. The jut of her chin, the rise of her eyebrows, the tilt of her head, the waves of her hair glinting in the sunlight. The dreamy delight on her face as she sniffed the vanilla air. Hair clips and sequins and sparkly shoes, the ridiculous pink rash vest that was her sole fashion incongruity. That gaze out at the water yesterday when she'd talked about overcoming her one fear, the way she'd tried to laugh it off. Her tolerant self-possession at dinner last night when Daniel leaned his elbow on the rim of one of her wheels as though her chair was a tabletop, the warning look she'd shot Finn as he half rose from his seat at his own table to intervene because she could look after her damn self, thank you. Choking on laughter in the kitchen, writing in her notepad, *We do not want an invasion, we want a relationship* and underlining it *five times* as she waited for her shoulders to stop their giveaway shaking.

Holding out that notepad to him.

That notepad.

He'd intended to suggest that Zoe give Cristina the afternoon off and come back with him to his bungalow. To interview him—she could ask questions about Poerava for her travel feature or he could…dammit, yes he *could* he could give his pathetic poor-boy-makes-good story. To swim with him in his pool. To watch TV or a movie or the rainforest. To talk about anything, everything, nothing. To have another crack at making *poisson cru* or bake a cake or crack a coconut in half or just open a packet of peanuts from the minibar. To do whatever she wanted.

But the minute she'd held out her notepad and he'd seen her

handwriting up close, the despicable truth of *why* had burst in his head: why he'd gone barging into her hospital room after staying away from her for two solid years.

The first time he'd seen her handwriting was when she'd shyly offered him her journal to read and told him that no one, not even the girls, got to see it. The entry was about sneaking out to go surfing with Malie and it was so funny and charming it was easy to see her as a novelist-in-waiting, but her penmanship had gobsmacked him. How could someone so delicate, so meticulously put together, have handwriting that looked like a drunk spider had dipped its legs in ink and staggered across the page?

He'd thought of it as her one flaw, that handwriting.

Until he'd discovered her second: the way she ate, shoving food in and dripping sauce down her chin—mainly because she was thinking of something she considered more important, like getting more food into *him*, or she was too busy talking, or listening, or laughing.

He'd liked those flaws, had thought them quirkily adorable.

But there was a truth darker than liking them for their own sake, and that was that those flaws made her less perfect, and if she was less perfect she was more attainable for someone like him.

Less perfect. More attainable.

Not attainable enough for him to take his courage in two hands and ask her out, but enough for her to be with him in… well, whatever way it was that they were when they were together all that summer.

But then summer was over, and the fact that she'd moved on to her "real" life while the Crab Shack and the gym and the pub remained his full-time-forever reality was rammed home to him when she'd dragged her boyfriend over to meet him. Finn had wondered, cynically, if Brad Ellersley—who'd had the protect Zoe shtick down pat, shooting a *keep your distance* warning at Finn over Zoe's head—had been preallocated to her from her birth.

The difference between him and Brad had been so marked Finn had accepted the truth at last: she definitely was *not* for the likes of him; she never would be. But it had hurt. It had hurt to even *see* her with the guy. Hurt to see her at all, knowing she was always and forever out of his league.

Call it self-preservation, call it whatever you like, but from that moment Finn had methodically rebuffed her every time she came up to him, whether she was with Brad, or those shiny-pretty girlfriends of hers, or on her own. Even after the accident, when it had half killed him not to see her, he'd stayed away… until the night one of the patrons at the pub had confided that Zoe Tayler's parents were taking her on a long overseas holiday—how brave of them to take that on!

The moment his shift had ended he'd rushed out of the pub, not stopping to brush his hair or change his shirt. Disheveled and smelling of the beer someone had slopped onto his sleeve, he'd hovered outside Zoe's room for five minutes, asking himself why she'd want to see him when he hadn't had the guts to visit her even once in the three months since the accident.

He'd been about to flee the scene…but then he'd overheard the breakup, and Brad Ellersley had come out and leaned against the wall, crying. Finn had hissed in a breath wanting to punch the guy, and that had drawn Brad's attention. Brad had had the nerve to give him another *stay away* warning look. Finn had no idea what expression had been on his face, but all it took was one step in Brad's direction to send Brad running away like he'd come face-to-face with the grim reaper.

And of course Finn had had to go into the room because everyone knew people needed support after a breakup, and multiply that need by a thousand in Zoe's circumstances. Yes, she had three best friends and a million other friends, any one of whom was better than him, but there was no one else waiting out there, not even her parents, so the job fell to him.

And so he'd entered the room, and she was lying there. Not crying. Just…broken.

Broken.

So broken the perfect guy didn't want her anymore because *she* wasn't perfect anymore.

She was really, truly attainable. At last.

It had all come pouring out then. How *he* felt, what *he* wanted, what *he* could do for her.

He felt again the chagrin, the humiliation as she'd yelled for her parents, begged them to get him out of there. And as they'd hurried in, his hopeless longing for Zoe had turned to something else, something savage and cold, something that was almost hate, and he'd wanted to hurt her as she had hurt him.

You're lost, Zoe, and you don't even know it, do you? Poor lost Zoe.

He'd seen the anguish in her eyes when he'd said that and he hadn't cared.

But she hadn't been lost.

Seeing her now, in his mind, in that bed, he knew what she'd been was young and scared and so, so badly hurt, her life in tatters, deserted by the guy who was supposed to be hers for life. She hadn't been lost, and she hadn't been broken. Not her spirit.

She'd kicked him out, hadn't she? Good for her, he'd deserved it.

And then, valiant as ever, she'd forged that life she'd always wanted. She'd conquered the world and she was now showing him that if anyone was lost it was him.

So lost he had to pay a florist to put flowers on his mother's grave twice a year—on her birthday and deathday—because he was too much of a coward to go back and do it himself, to go back to Hawke's Cove and *be* himself.

So lost he couldn't bring himself to open a document and look at a property proposal because of a dot on a map.

It might have taken Zoe ten years but she'd managed to do what he could not; she'd gone back—to the place that had made her a paraplegic. Talk about guts. And he'd had the gall to ask her about time machines?

Zoe was in the right of it there. Why look back when you could move forward?

He closed his eyes, tried to imagine being with her. Being *with* her. *Being* with her. But the picture remained elusive. How could it be that she seemed to be within his grasp at last and yet even more impossible to claim?

It made no sense.

And yet it made perfect sense.

Because the problem wasn't her, it was him.

Talk about fighting your big battles to the death; he felt like he'd been fighting a battle for twelve years, ever since the day Zoe had smiled at him over a table full of salt shakers and he'd known that even though she was too good for a scruffy nobody like him he belonged to her.

But it was way past time to leave the battlefield. To say that goodbye to a fantasy that was never his to own. No, not *say* but *feel* it.

He dragged out his phone.

"Buy the place in Scotland," he said, when Gina answered, as usual, on the first ring. "I'll fly out tomorrow."

Alone in her bungalow, the word "lost" kept echoing in Zoe's head.

Lost. Alone. Adrift. Floating out to sea. No anchor.

She was not ready to write that email. But maybe she was ready to talk?

The girls. They'd enjoy hearing about the cooking class, about Gaspard, about Matilda, about Cristina's burgeoning romance. And of course they'd be interested in Finn.

Hmm, maybe she could leave Finn out of the conversation.

That chorus of *Zoe and Finn sitting in a tree, K.I.S.S.I.N.G.* the girls used to sing *sotto voce* whenever they'd come into the Crab Shack was the last thing she needed when she was trying to work him out herself. And Lily... After that last phone call, Lily would smell the most gigantic rat if she mentioned Finn. She'd *definitely* leave Finn out.

She did a quick calculation of time zones. She'd get Malie. V might still be up. Lily would be awake because dinner service would have ended an hour or so ago and she'd only just be getting home...but she'd already off-loaded on Lily once this trip and Lily had enough on her plate; Zoe wasn't dragging her to the phone at midnight for anything less than a Lost Hours situation. And however "lost" Zoe felt, this wasn't Lost Hours business.

No phone call then.

She sighed. In the old days a fit of melancholia would have had her reaching for her journal.

But she didn't keep a journal anymore.

She hadn't kept one since the accident.

The last entry had been the day of the summer ball.

And the memory was suddenly there. Like a flash, a shock, a blow she couldn't ward off.

That night, at the pub.

She grabbed her phone, hands shaking as she called Victoria. Victoria, who'd been drinking soda water, not champagne like the rest of them, because she was driving, so she'd have had the clearest head of any of them.

Oh God, how could she talk to V about this when V was planning her wedding? Happy times, moving forward. No, she had to—

"Zoe? What's up?"

Too late to hang up. "Ah...just wondering how the wedding plans are progressing."

Beat, beat, beat. "Fine and a lot finer if you'd send me your measurements." Pause. "But that's not why you're calling."

"I didn't realize how late it was. I'll talk you tomorr—"

"Now. You'll talk to me now."

Deep breath. "OK. The truth is I remembered something and I…I need you to tell me if the memory is true or my imagination. That night…the accident… I was wearing a blue silk dress, silver shoes. I think there was a photo. *Was* there a photo?"

"Yes, there was a photo, there *is* a photo. And yes, you were wearing a blue dress, *ridiculously* high-heeled silver shoes, and a circlet of fake aquamarines on your head. You looked…" Victoria's breath hitched. "You looked like a princess who'd wandered off the page of a fairy tale. I've got that photo at my studio. I can scan it, take a photo of it, get a copy of it, send it to you any way you like."

"No, no I don't… No, not yet. But I think… I think I can see it in part of a memory. The four of us. You, me, Devil, Lils, our arms around each other. We were laughing. So happy and free and young and…" She stopped there, too emotional to continue.

"Innocent, hopeful," Victoria said softly. "We thought the world was ours for the taking."

"I'm not sure that I really did think that, V."

Pause. And then, "What's the problem, Zo?"

"Memories. Half memories. The absence of memories. Memories I can't find but want to reclaim. I called you because I suddenly remembered that night at the pub and you were the only one who hadn't been drinking so I thought maybe your own memory would be sharper and you could give me some clarity. I remember Finn—" Stop. Breath. "Finn Doherty working behind the bar. He wasn't going to the ball."

"No, he wasn't going to the ball. Not his scene even though he could have had his pick of partners."

"Definitely not his scene," Zoe said, and it was suddenly so easy to remember the way he'd looked at them all that night, like they were...well, what they were. Eighteen-year-olds at their first grown-up party. It had made her feel as though that holiday in Ibiza had been for kids toting fake IDs. "I doubt he'd have gone even to his own Leavers Ball."

"Definitely not, because he dropped out of school the moment he turned sixteen. I remember that one of the teachers tried to talk him into staying but he flat out refused. He...he didn't have much but he certainly had pride by the bucketful."

"Yes, he did have pride," Zoe said, and wondered how Finn must have felt that night, seeing everyone in their new clothes, laughing and drinking and full of excitement about the life ahead, when his life was going nowhere. "Claudia was there, at the pub."

"Yes, Claudia. But not Henry." Pause. "Claudia was flirting with Finn, doing it on purpose, thumbing her nose at all of us."

"Yes, they were flaunting it. Claudia...it was like she wanted to make Henry jealous even though he wasn't there. The sad thing is that I'd seen her do it before and everyone could see that Henry couldn't have cared less. As for Finn..." She trailed off as those feelings from that night came back to her. Confusion. Uneasiness. Shame. Finn flirting with Claudia...looking at Zoe while he did it...and Zoe was so jealous, and that was wrong, it was bad, because she had Brad. And yet whenever Finn's eyes met hers Brad ceased to exist.

"Finn the bad boy, Claudia the bad girl," Victoria said. "Lily said they were a better match than Claudia and Henry. But Malie said no, Finn was yours."

"A teensy problem with that. I already had a boyfriend and Finn had...well, he had just about every girl in the village."

"Don't get me started on your boyfriend."

"At least Brad didn't abandon me."

"I beg your pardon?"

"I mean as a friend. He came to see me in the hospital so many times, not only before we broke up but after, always bringing flowers or chocolates or books."

"Yeah, I think that's called a guilty conscience."

"I don't think so. He had nothing to feel guilty about, not really. I…didn't *want* him, V. I really didn't. And he stood by me, as a friend. In fact he still texts me on my birthday every year. The last few years he's attached a 'happy family' photo of him with his wife and son. In fact, I'm expecting a text this weekend, probably at nine o'clock on Saturday night because the reminder will pop up on his mobile phone at eight o'clock Sunday morning and he won't think about international time zones, seeing how he's Hawke's Cove to the bone marrow. And it…it won't hurt. It truly doesn't hurt, V."

"And there you have it. Brad being Hawke's Cove to the bone marrow and you being nothing of the kind. Funny, I would have said Finn Doherty was Hawke's Cove to the bone marrow as well but he proved us wrong by leaving. Maybe Malie was right. Maybe he had all the girls in the village except the one he really wanted."

"You know he never came near me after that summer we worked at the Crab Shack."

"I know you kept dragging us over to him despite that. And the way I remember it his eyes were always on you. Who knows what might have happened if you'd given him the look he was always giving you."

"Oh, the look!" she dismissed.

"The look, yes!"

"I struggle with the whole concept of 'the look.' What exactly is it? How do you know someone's giving it to you? How do you give it back to that person? How did it work with you and Oliver?"

"I don't think it's something you can control. I looked at

Oliver and it was… I don't know, it was just there. The feeling, the knowledge that he was the one for me. Why are you asking, Zo? Is there someone you *do*…"

"Want?" She tried to laugh, but it sounded forlorn, even to her. "Is there someone I want? Yes, there is," she admitted, and oh the joy of saying it out loud. "But I don't know how… how to recognize if he's returning my look, if he's even *seeing* the way I look at him."

"Is it the American journalist Lily told me about?"

"Daniel? No! It's someone more…well, more interesting."

"Interesting… Hmm. Interesting's good. But it's not necessarily…"

"Not necessarily what?" Zoe prompted.

"Not necessarily safe. Then again, one thing I've learned since meeting Oliver is that playing it safe isn't an option when it comes to love. You need to jump, no parachute."

A zip of panic raced all the way up one of Zoe's arms and all the way down the other. "It's not love, it's lust. That's all. L.U.S.T. Lust."

"Oh well, if it's just L.U.S.T.," Victoria said, "by all means *do* play it safe."

"Yes, yes, got that! Birds and bees, no getting carried away and forgetting the basics."

Victoria's expression warped from serious to comical grimace. "Aaand now I feel like your mother!"

Zoe rolled her eyes. "Do *not* go there! Please! She'd be express couriering me a jumbo pack of—"

"Stop! Stop, I'm begging you! I don't need the image of your mother at the Hawke's Cove post office in my head."

"Mrs. Whittaker peering over her shoulder as the jumbo pack was furtively shoved into a Jiffy bag."

"Asking, 'So is Zoe *seeing* someone?'"

"Offering Bubble Wrap."

"And pontificating as to whether the climate control of air freight was conducive to the transport of such a delicate product!"

They both dissolved into giggles, which petered out slowly.

And then Victoria sighed. "Zoe, you are so lovely. So funny and smart and…and perfect."

Zoe held up a hand. "Don't. Don't say that. Perfect. It's not a word I…I like, really. I think… I really do think I prefer *im*-perfect."

"Ah, so can I assume the man you want isn't perfect? Maybe not up to Selena and Noel Tayler's standards?"

"No! Yes. No. Oh, I don't know. Not up to Mum and Dad's standards but…but…"

"But perfect for you perhaps?"

"I think…yes. I think he always was."

"Zoe! Who are we talking about?"

"Not who, what! Lust, I'm talking about lust. And now I have to go. I have to email those disapproving parents of mine about a charismatically tyrannical half French, half Polynesian chef called Gaspard."

"So it's a chef you're in lust with? Lily is going to be so happy!"

"She will be when she gets the recipe I'm going to send her," Zoe said, and then she laughed, blew Victoria a kiss, and disconnected.

For a long moment she sat perfectly still, doing what she'd initially planned to do—casting her mind back over that cooking class, every word, every look. She still didn't understand why Finn had run away at the end…but she knew that she was through playing it safe.

And she was now ready to write that email to her parents, but she was *not* going to tell them about Finn.

Finn was going to be her unsafe, lusty, dirty secret. She went to her computer and started typing:

Today, I learned that not everything sounds better in French. Take raw fish e'ia ota—doesn't that sound wonderful? Or in my case maybe *don't* take it, because as it turns out, I'm terrible in the kitchen even when something doesn't actually have to go into an oven...

nineteen

NO FINN AT THE GYM THE NEXT MORNING OFFER-
ing a tour suggestion.

Nor did he show up for the visit to the pink sand beach Aiata organized under instructions from Finn for any of the media that were interested—but with a cautious smile at Zoe that suggested to her that while it was a group outing it had been arranged specifically for her. Something to tick off her "live like a local" list, she presumed.

Well, a group outing was just fine by Zoe.

She was too busy taking a hundred photos trying to do justice to the shade of pink she was seeing—which managed to be simultaneously pastel and bright—to wonder at the reason for Finn's absence or to think about lust or about leaping without a parachute or time machines or fairy tales. Too busy making jokes about how her pink rash vest was finally *en pointe*. Too busy scribbling down notes for her article. Too busy raving over the picnic lunch provided by Gaspard, which featured nothing that wasn't pink, even the champagne!

In fact, it was a relief not to be trying to work out in what way Finn *looked* at her or searching for hidden meanings in what he said.

She was a journalist writing about his resort. Full stop. The end.

And strictly speaking, this trip fit under the umbrella of Finn "making it happen" for her. The same way getting Aiata to arrange a visit to Tiare Island's mini-version of Pape'ete's famous *roulottes* tonight for the *whole media group* could technically be considered "making it happen" for her.

It *did not matter* who did the arranging or for how large a group as long as she got to see and do everything. And if she could have sworn Finn's "make it happen" promise was supposed to be something more intimate than getting his PR manager to include her on a tour, then that was on her. Just as it was on her if being part of the larger group made her feel...feel...

Well, how *did* she feel?

A jumble of things. Bereft that she'd lost the ebullient mood in which she'd woken yesterday morning. Needing a Lost Hours call even though there was nothing actually wrong. Confused by the clutter of darting images in her head. V, Lils, Devil, breaking her out of "Palace de Prison." Cooking that detestable mackerel on the beach in Hawke's Cove. Staring at the coastal views from her parents' house and wanting to fly over the water to freedom. Early morning surfing with Malie. Sharing smiles with Finn at the Crab Shack. Finding that pearl on the beach, making up stories with Finn about it. Flashes of all the trips she'd done. All those returns to her apartment in Sydney. The trip to Hawaii, Malie talking to her about Finn the bad boy. Finn sitting on the beach at midnight...while she drifted in her *Gravity* way, out to sea, away from him.

She kept going over in her head that conversation with Lily

about being in love, telling herself Lily's ex Alistair was a salutary reminder that for every lucky woman out there with an Oliver (Victoria) or a Todd (Malie) there was a woman who'd had her savings stolen (Lily) or who'd wasted an entire summer mooning over a guy who hadn't had the courage to ask her out on one lousy date (Zoe).

Hey!

Hey!

Stop. Thinking. About. *Finn!*

He. Was. Not. *Interested!*

So they'd done some reminiscing about old times, and he'd told her about his mother, and he'd flirted about vanilla and wanted to know if she was single or living with someone or married, and they'd had fun in Gaspard's kitchen. There was nothing in any of it. It was just collateral information the same as the number of wheelchair users in the world. He was the professionally charming host of a media group. Nothing more to it. Didn't mean he was interested in her. Didn't mean he wanted to have sex with her.

And if he didn't want to have sex with her then she definitely didn't want to have sex with him! She *certainly* wasn't going to even *think* about including a reference to him in the email she'd send to her parents about today's activities. No point since it seemed unlikely she'd ever lay eyes on him again.

All fired up, she went straight to her computer once she was back in her bungalow and furiously started tapping out that no-Finn email, describing the day in detail. She threw in an update on Cristina and Joe's romance, another about Victoria's wedding to Oliver, plus one about Todd going with Malie to her next surfing competition, and added the news that one of her Chair Chicks friends had got engaged. It seemed fitting then to mention that Daniel, about whom she'd already told them and who was *a great guy*, had asked her to sit with him tonight when the media group visited the *roulottes* on one of Tiare Island's seven petals.

No, not "petals." Petal was too romantic a word for her current state of mind. "Peninsula" was the right word. *Peninsula.*

She made the correction, hit send with unnecessary force, and found that she was breathing as though she'd run a marathon. Harsh, ugly breaths, struggling around a lump in her throat.

No, not her throat. The lump was in her chest. That old sense of suffocation was back, her heart a hot, heavy stone. She suddenly knew the word for how she'd been feeling all day. The word was "lonely." *She* was lonely.

It made no sense—she'd been with people all day. And yet it was the truth.

She would feel lonely even if she called V, Devil and Lils. She would feel lonely if she checked in online with the Chair Chicks gals. She would feel lonely tonight.

Tonight.

She sighed at the thought of sitting with Daniel tonight.

Unfair. He *was* a nice guy, really. It was just that he wasn't…

No. Not finishing that thought.

Whoever Daniel wasn't, at least he was interested. And since she'd designated L.U.S.T. as her key driver, why not see if she could engineer a fling with Daniel?

Daniel was big, buff, handsome. Not the type to be afraid of a little passion judging by the overly enthusiastic way he manhandled her wheelchair.

Finn, on the other hand, looked tough but hadn't even come close to reading her "touch me" signals this week—on the contrary, he'd deliberately avoided touching her, even accidentally. He probably thought he'd bruise or break her. He'd only ever touched her (not counting the easily bruised frangipani because that *was not her*) once, twelve years ago—and even that had been just two tentative fingers on her hair. He hadn't even grazed her ear! *And* he'd pulled his hand back so fast he'd probably got whiplash of the wrist. He'd probably *never* looked at her like he wanted to strip her naked and have his way with her, so that whole *Zoe and Finn sitting in a tree, K.I.S.S.I.N.G.* thing the girls used to chant at her had always been ridiculous. She wished, how she wished, the girls could be here so they could see someone did indeed look at her like he wanted to strip her naked and that it wasn't Finn Doherty, and she was so *stupid* for starting to think anything different, and she would stop, stop, *stop* immediately, and conquer the ridiculous shivering that came over her whenever she thought about him while she was at it.

So. Freaking. *There!*

In a militant frame of mind she donned a shimmery gold dress and metallic-gold sandals, leaving her hair loose and weaving gold beads through the strands. Her version of Lust Goddess. And if she wondered whether maybe someone would report back to Poerava's owner that the journalist in the wheelchair was not only independent and gregarious and charming and fearless but also *gorgeous*, so what? Such reports would be out of her control. She'd rather die than ask anyone to pass on an observation about her to Finn.

Finn Doherty was her past.

She was focusing on a Finn-free future as of now.

You need a fling, Zoe reminded herself, as Daniel wolf-whistled when he spotted her and hurried to her side.

"What do you feel like eating?" he asked as they approached the cluster of brightly colored caravans parked across the sand. "Each van has a speciality. Grilled mahi-mahi, chow mein Tahiti-style, Japanese-style soba noodles, rotisserie chicken. But I hear the *poisson cru* here is—"

"Not poisson cru," Zoe snapped.

"Er… OK?" Daniel said. "Then how about—"

"Crepes," she said. Because yes, she was going to eat those crepes Finn Doherty had told her about. And she was going to make sure Finn Doherty *knew* she'd eaten crepes and that she'd eaten them with Daniel even if she didn't know precisely how she was going to achieve that given *she'd rather die than ask anyone to pass on an observation about her to Finn*. And she was going to enjoy every bite, even if she had a humongous lump in her throat and her heart still felt like a chunk of battered stone.

"How about I get the crepes and you and Cristina grab a table?" Daniel suggested.

"How about *I* get the crepes and *you* and Cris grab a table?" Zoe said, the snap in her voice still there because dammit! Just...dammit!

"Zo, how about *I* get the crepes?" Cristina, playing referee, no doubt wondering at Zoe's uncharacteristically combative mood. Well, Cristina could suck it. *Everyone* could suck it. The *entire world* could suck it. Because Zoe Tayler was *allowed* to be in a bad mood occasionally.

"No," Zoe said shortly. She wheeled herself toward the crepe truck, cursing under her breath when one of her wheels went fractionally off the ramp, then cursing some more when she heard Cristina's indrawn breath. Cristina had better not rush to help her or she'd...she'd *explode*. Yes, she would explode.

She got herself back on course, shifted slightly to give Cristina a peremptorily crisp version of their royal wave *I'm OK, as you were* signal, and saw that Cristina was looking not at her but past her, at the crepe truck.

And Zoe knew, because that shiver was running through her even before she saw him.

Finn.

Actually *in* the food truck. He was making the crepes.

Not looking at her. As in *deliberately* not looking.

She maneuvered herself into a turn and came back to Daniel and Cristina. "Actually," she said to Daniel, "the ramp's not firm enough for my wheelchair so yes, please get the crepes. And Cris, why don't you go and sit with Tilly? I'm sure Daniel will be able to help me if I need anything."

And *that* was definitely an order!

twenty

FINN SERVED DANIEL TWO PLATES OF CREPES.
With a smile.

He had to. He was the owner of Poerava. And the media visit to the food trucks had been his brilliant idea. And it wasn't Daniel's fault Finn hadn't got on that plane this morning after all, or that he'd decided to come tonight even though he'd spent all day telling himself he wouldn't.

At least cooking the crepes meant he could see Zoe (because he really needed to see her) but also keep his distance from her. And because she and Daniel had chosen the most secluded of the tables, half tucked behind the trunk of a palm tree, he was getting exactly what he wanted. He could see her...but only because she glowed like a golden shaft of sunlight even under the moon.

"Hey, Finn!" Matilda said, smiling at him in that hideous way he was unfortunately getting used to. "Cris has gone to play footsies with Captain Joe. Are you on shift all night or do you feel like joining me for an adult beverage and—dare I say it—some crepes?"

An automatic "no" rose to Finn's lips, but then an overloud trill of Zoe's laughter seared the air and he caught the quickest flash of a look from her that told him she was doing it on purpose and he knew his concentration was shot for the night.

"I'd be delighted," he said to Matilda. "Go back to your table and I'll bring the crepes over."

"Um, not that one you're currently incinerating, I hope?"

"What...? Oh! Go, you're distracting me."

"*I* am, am I?" she tossed over her shoulder.

Finn traded places with one of the local cooks and a few minutes later was plonking two plates of crepes on Matilda's table. "I hope you like lemon and sugar."

"I do, but this little catch-up isn't about crepes, it's about information," Matilda said.

"What do you want to know?"

Matilda jerked her head in Zoe's direction. "Why you're letting him have her."

Finn took a savage bite of his crepe, chewed, swallowed. "She's not my property. It's not up to me to let anyone have her. She has the choice. He's a nice guy. They make a great pair."

"And there I was thinking you were a fighter."

Finn made some kind of noncommittal grunt.

"*She's* certainly a fighter," Matilda said.

Another grunt. Yes, Zoe was a fighter, even if in that shimmery gold dress with those beads in her hair she looked like a fairy child. All she needed was a pair of gilded wings. Another savage swallow of crepe.

Matilda threw back her head and laughed—clearly the sight of him choking on food was amusing—and that drew Zoe's eyes to them. It felt so much like those times in the village when Zoe had seen him with another girl and had come over to him anyway, he could almost believe she'd bring Daniel over any moment.

But all she did was go back to her conversation.

Slowly, he put down his fork. He was tired of keeping everything inside. He wanted to ask for advice, wanted to know how to say goodbye, because he was flying out in the morning (again!) and he didn't know how to do it without tearing out his heart. And God, *he should not have come tonight.*

Matilda cut delicately into her lemon-and-sugar-soaked crepe, placed the bite carefully in her mouth, swallowed without allowing any juice to dribble onto her chin, and Finn wondered why he couldn't be attracted to her even as his eyes flickered in Zoe's direction.

"Whoa!" she said as Finn surged up out of his seat, clamping a hand on his wrist. She looked over at Zoe and Daniel. "So he's wiping her chin, big deal."

"She doesn't need him to wipe her damn chin. She's not a baby."

"No, she's not a baby, so what makes you think she needs you racing over to save her?"

For a split second what Finn would do hung in the balance, but just as he took a step in Zoe's direction Daniel backed off, making placating hand gestures. Finn settled back into his seat.

"Nice guy, huh?" Matilda said, amused. "They make a great pair? Tell you what. How about I take Daniel off everyone's hands because we both know they *don't* make a great pair."

"You don't have to sacrifice yourself."

"I'm not the self-sacrificing type so believe me when I say this is going to be pure pleasure. I'll get Daniel on the first run back to Poerava. You stay around for the second transfer. If you can't work out what to do—"

"I know what to do, Matilda."

"Could have fooled me," she said, and got gracefully to her feet. "Well, *au revoir!*"

Finn watched as Matilda sashayed her way over to Zoe and Daniel. Watched as Cristina and Captain Joe joined them. There was a conversation that looked like some sort of negotiation. Next thing he knew, Matilda, Daniel, Cristina and Joe were all heading for *Little Micky*, leaving Zoe alone.

No.

Wait.

Cristina was turning back. Her eyes locked with his. She nodded, then recommenced boarding.

So they weren't leaving Zoe alone, they were leaving her *specifically* with him.

Did Zoe know what they were up to?

He looked at Zoe, found her eyes unwaveringly on him, and his heart skipped a beat.

She knew.

Only four journalists, plus Aiata, himself and Zoe, were left to return to Poerava on the second transfer. Aiata and the others were clustered around the last caravan in the row of *roulottes*, which was operating as the bar.

Heart thundering, Finn made his way to Zoe. He had no idea what to say, but he had only twenty minutes in which to say it. That was when the boat would be back.

He took the seat beside Zoe's wheelchair. Saw that her hands were running up and down her thighs, which for once he was glad to see because it meant he wasn't the only one who was nervous. She said nothing, which he guessed meant the ball was in his court.

"Zoe," he said, and had to stop to clear his throat. "I…" Nope. He didn't know what to say.

Zoe looked at her phone, which was face up on the table. "Nineteen minutes until the boat comes back for us," she announced.

Sand sifting through that hourglass. Time, as always, running out. And she was actively watching the clock.

Now or never. He was going to have to blaze his guns a little.

"I don't usually play it safe," was what he came up with, and he immediately thought that was too tepid an approach to be classified as a blazed gun, but hell, everything was riding on these nineteen minutes and he wasn't going to stuff it up the way he'd done ten years ago.

"I know that," she said. "It's why I thought—" Stop. Chin jut. "Go on."

"I don't usually play it safe but I did…with you…that summer."

"And?"

"And I want to know…*need* to know…if you want me to play it safe now."

She pursed her lips. "You're going to have to be a little less inscrutable."

He shoved an impatient hand through his hair. "How can you not know what I mean, Zoe?"

"I don't *trust* myself to know. I don't think I ever trusted myself to know because…because I was me and you were you." Her hands were still moving up and down on her thighs. A glance at her phone. "Seventeen minutes. How about you to tell me exactly what you mean when you say you always played it safe and what it means to stop playing it safe. You say you need to know if I want you to keep playing it safe but *I* need to know if we're on the same page or if we're reading completely different books."

"We were always reading the same book, Zoe, but…it was a fairy tale, back then. Because, as you say, you were you and I was me and no one was going to let us…let us…be. Just *be*." He tore both hands through his hair. "Ah dammit, Zoe, you want to know what playing it safe meant? It meant not touching you. Not then, and not in the two years that followed."

Her hands stopped on her thighs. "I…I see."

"Do you, Zoe? *Do you?* You didn't back then, but if you see now then I guess at last we're reading the same book."

"I don't want the book to be a fairy tale," she said. "I want it to be real. I want to know it's real."

He laughed, a short, harsh laugh. "Last time I let myself be real for you, you called security."

"Finn—"

"Sorry, sorry, stop. Let's forget that night because this is now and things are different and time's running out and I'm wondering what it would feel like if you… I mean, if I asked you… I think what I'm trying to say is…" Stop. "I'm messing this up and I don't want to."

"Just say it," she said, staring intently at him.

"I want to know…" Swallow. "I want to know what you'd do if I asked you to touch me." There, said, done. But his head was like a newsreel, running on a loop. All those times he'd seen her touch other people, easily, effortlessly. Hugging, patting, kissing her friends. The timid stuff with Brad he'd hungered for even as he sneered at it. Strange, now, to know he would hate her to touch him the way she touched anyone else. He wanted a touch that was just for him. That she gave to nobody else. He wanted her to touch him because she couldn't help it. Passionate and needful and burning and in the moment only his.

"Well…" she said, deliciously breathless, "let's find out." A drift of laughter from the booze van. The scent of her. A throb in the air. "But I don't think it's going to work unless you come a little closer, Finlay."

Dear God. She was going to do it. It was happening, it really was. Here. Now. Zoe. His.

He edged toward her, hopeful, afraid.

"Closer," she breathed, and when he leaned in and she took his face between her delicate palms, the hope surged and the fear receded and he knew that if a bolt of lightning arced down from the sky and hit him he'd die happy.

They stared into each other's eyes for one heartbeat, two, three. No words, no smiles; this trembling moment of awareness was too precious, too serious, for that. And then she closed her eyes and the breath-distance between them, and laid her lips gently on his. He felt the shiver that wracked her, and twelve years of longing shuddered through him so that he started to full-on shake and he *did not care* that his vulnerability was palpable. Let her feel it, let her know what she did to him, what she'd always done to him. He would have stayed like that, tireless, unmoving, for eternity, just to have her mouth resting against his.

But then she said, right there against his lips, "How about a little reciprocity? You're not the only one who's been waiting, you know."

He thought about all the times he'd wanted to kiss her, wanted to run his hands all over her, and now, at last, he would know. He moved his lips against hers, coaxing her mouth open. More, he needed more, so his tongue came out, licking at her lips, into her mouth, drinking her in. When she opened wider, hunger writhed inside him and he deepened the kiss, helpless, wanting to devour her. Did she know he was hers? No time machine and yet he had been hers from the moment she'd smiled at him, he'd been hers ever since, he was hers now.

Emotion swelled in him so that he could barely breathe. He needed to tell her in case she still didn't get it. He pulled back from the kiss and as she moaned a protest, her hands slipping down from his face to grab fistfuls of his shirt to drag him back, he decided words could wait, he would tell her with his mouth. Kisses, a hot, hungry, sucking chain of them, each one a story. *I've been waiting forever for you. I want you. I love you, love you, love you, love you, Zoe. Zoe, feel it, feel what I feel.*

And then his hands were cradling her face, angling her so that her mouth fit seamlessly with his, wholly, entirely, completely, frantically. He wanted to drag her onto his lap. He could do it, she'd told him he could, that night in the bar. *I do let people push my wheelchair. Lift me out of it, too. People I know, people who understand me. Some people, the ones I trust, don't even have to ask, they can just do what needs to be done.*

And she trusted him. She'd told him so. And oh how he wanted to know what it was like to have her in his arms, wanted his hands in her glorious hair and his mouth all over her body, wanted to touch all the places she could feel and also the ones she couldn't because they were still her and he loved every inch of her, wanted to learn everything that made her tingle, know every patch of her skin, wanted all of her to be his to cherish.

A shout. A clang.

Time had run out.

He eased back from her, and when she murmured a protest, keeping a death grip on his shirt, kissed her again and groaned against her mouth, *"Little Micky."*

She slumped against him, her head on his chest. He ran a shaking hand down her hair, absorbing the shiver that ran through her. A long, long moment, and then her hands loosened and with a sigh she raised her head, sat back. "So I guess we should..." She gave a deliciously breathy laugh, a helpless little shrug. "Actually, I don't know what we should do."

Her trembling hands went to her cheeks as though they'd press the red heat out of them, then to her lips as though feeling his kiss through her fingertips.

Hunger for her roared through him. Words trembled on his tongue. *I know what we should do. Come to bed with me. Let me have you. Let me show you how I feel. Stay with me.*

His heart ached with the need to say the words but he forced them back. Yes, he knew what they should do, but ten years ago he'd had his heart mangled when he'd dared to say the words. What he needed before he offered his heart to her again was for *her* to say what they should do.

And so he bit back those words.

And he waited.

twenty-one

AT. LAST.

For all of her imaginings back in Hawke's Cove of Finn with those other, bolder, hotter girls, Zoe had not anticipated what his kiss would do to her.

The absolute scorch of it. The claim of it: you're mine. The tingling of her skin, the thrumming in her veins, the deliriously excruciating tightening of her nipples, as though she'd woken from a hundred Sleeping Beauty years, suddenly, vibrantly, brilliantly alive. And if she'd thought he'd given her the shivers before? Well…just *well*! She was a mess. A wonderful, glorious, lick-me-all-over-immediately mess.

He'd do it, too. Lick her all over. His eyes, so slumberously hot and hooded, told her he wanted to—and that he'd know how to make her beg for more.

How about a little reciprocity? You're not the only one who's been waiting, you know. She wanted to laugh at the primness of those words. What she'd really wanted to say was, *Touch every inch of me, with your hands and your mouth and your tongue, come inside me because you were always meant to be there, a part of me, and I want you with everything I have, everything I am, everything I ever want to be.*

"Actually, Finlay, I do know what we should do," she said, at the exact moment her phone pinged with an incoming email.

The screen, face up and glowing on the table, told her—told them both because Finn was looking at it too—that an email had arrived from mum.dad@taylers.co.uk and she wanted to bang her head on it. Not! Now!

Finn blew out a long breath as he blinked and blinked, as though he were waking from the same hundred-year sleep that had held her in its thrall. And then he smiled at her. The slow, diffident, crooked smile of old that had made the chip in his tooth endearing even though everyone knew he'd got it in a fight in which he'd knocked two of the other guy's teeth right out.

She wanted to touch his mouth, feel that chip in his tooth with her fingers the way she just had with her tongue, the way that had delighted her because it meant this was no fairy tale, it was real, *he* was real, this was happening.

"Better get that, huh," he said with a dip of his head that was almost shy. "I'll check in with Aiata about whether the boat can...maybe...come back for us?" He shrugged, delectably uncertain. "I mean, if you want to stay here a while."

"Yes, I'd like to stay for a while," she said, sounding way too eager but so what. If there was a time to be eager, it was now, here, tonight.

"Zoe, just to be absolutely clear..." Another of those uncertain shrugs. "I'm twelve years past being in the friend zone."

Twelve years past. So Malie had been right after all? The enigmatic, dangerous, hot-and-cold, sweet-and-angry, push-pull Finn Doherty could have been hers, *hers*, and she'd missed the signs. She wanted to weep. Wanted to shout with joy. Wanted to melt and laugh and...and exult, wallow, rejoice, sing. Wanted everything.

"You understand what I'm saying?" he said, so serious.

"Yes," she whispered, and then repeated, "Yes," stronger and louder to make sure he heard, he knew.

A searing moment. A glowing look, a wordless promise of more.

And then he smiled, and nodded, and strode off.

Zoe sighed giddily as she snatched up her phone and read the message from her parents. Then reread it. Read it again.

A tingle at the back of her neck, a hint of soap in the air, told her Finn had returned, but she nevertheless started when he said, "Trouble?" because she felt guilty reading an email from her parents with him standing there.

"Just an email from…" she hesitated, but Finn had already seen who it was from so, "my parents."

"Let me guess. Use sunblock during the day, wrap up warmly at night, be careful crossing the street, eat your greens, don't hang around with that Finn Doherty because everyone knows he's only interested in one thing."

She laughed. "*Are* you only interested in one thing?"

There was the smile, the glow, the heat, that promise. "Depends how you classify one thing."

One thing. The one thing was her. She laughed again, at the absolute wonder of it. "There's nothing in there about sunblock, crossing the street, wrapping up at night, or eating my greens."

"Uh-oh! Armageddon must be on approach!"

"Maybe, if they dare to read them!" she said, and realized that of course he had no idea what she was talking about. "My journals. They found some of them under the loose floorboard in my bedroom."

"Under the *floorboard*? Were they looking for buried treasure?"

"Got it in one. My journals are the treasure. I hid them because…well, because they were… Actually, there were two years' worth under the floorboards from that summer until… until the accident." Oh. The memory. There. Floating. Waiting. Taunting. Writing that last entry. About the summer ball, her plan to live a new life, the grand deflowering scheme that hadn't happened.

"Zoe?" Finn, crouching beside her chair, holding out his hand. She wanted to take that hand, wanted to press it to her heart, but another memory crowded into her head. Finn, holding out his hand, no, *both* hands, in her hospital room, pleading with her, *pleading*. And she was shouting, shouting for the parents who didn't want him anywhere near her, and they were racing in to save her, save her from Finn.

No! Not *now*, when things were so perfect! *Go away.*

"They're remodeling the house," she said, trying desperately to bring herself back to the present, make the email inconsequential because that was what it was. "Making a wing for me. Wheelchair-friendly, my own entrance, the works." Inconsequential…and yet his smile faded, his outstretched hand dropped.

"How about you tell me what your parents said about me in that email, Zoe," he said quietly.

And of course he'd think they'd said something, something bad, something to pull her away from him. How to fix it? *How?* "Nothing. Nothing, *really*, they were too busy extolling the virtues of their floor plan to mention anything else." The truth. The absolute truth. And because it was the truth, they were losing this moment. It was dying before her eyes, because he believed her.

"Nothing," he repeated, and his face blanked, closing her out.

He gestured to *Little Micky*. "Time for you to board."

"But aren't we…? I mean, don't you want to…? That is, isn't the boat going to…?" She covered her face with her hands, groaned into them, came up trying to laugh because of course that was what she did when she got muddled up, but she didn't quite make it.

"No, yes, no," he said, interpreting as expertly as always,

but coolly, without apparent interest. "The skipper has to clock off after this trip and Aiata needs me to stay until all the food trucks are locked up."

No, yes, no. Zoe tried to assign them in her head so they would mean what she wanted them to mean. No, they weren't staying. *Yes, he wanted to stay with her.* No, the boat wasn't coming back. Oh God, what should she do?

"But how will you get back to Poerava if the boat isn't returning?"

"I make my own way, Zoe." Did she imagine that slight emphasis on the I? An emphasis that had those words *You're lost, Zoe, and you don't even know it* ringing in her ears. "I'd offer to push you—these ramps aren't as steady as the ones at Poerava—but I see Cristina is disembarking." His lips twisted in that cynical excuse for a smile, the one she'd hadn't seen since her first night on Tiare Island, at the cocktail party. "She came back for you, which I guess was always the plan. The cavalry arriving. Playing it safe after all."

And as Zoe wheeled herself forlornly toward the boat, she thought about truth and lies, and why she hadn't told anyone from back home about him, and why she hadn't googled him the way he'd googled her, and she remembered what Finn had said on Motu Marama.

I did want to know if you were engaged or married or living with someone. And I absolutely searched for the answers on Google.

So you lied.

Yeah. I do that sometimes.

"As it happens, Finn, so do I," she said softly, echoing what she'd told him then. And then, still more softly, "I lie to myself, every single day."

Her own wing. In her parents' mansion. In Hawke's Cove.

Finn let those facts settle in his head and came up with the only possible conclusion: she was going home.

Maybe it wouldn't have mattered if the touch she'd decided on had been something simple like a brush of her hand against his arm. She could have chosen to live in Hawke's Cove, or Sydney, the Congo, Finland, wherever, and he liked to think he would have got over it, over her.

But she'd kissed him, she'd *chosen* to *kiss him*...and in that miraculous moment everything had changed.

At least he'd thought it had. He'd seen not the past but the future, he'd forgotten about achieving closure in favor of seizing an opening he hadn't dared to believe was possible. And so he'd gone to Aiata to talk about boat transfers. Aiata's knowing smile hadn't bothered him. He hadn't cared that he was so transparent. He was going to stay with Zoe under the stars and talk and laugh and dream and make love for as long as she wanted.

And then the crash, falling from the stars to earth.

One email from her parents, that was all it took, and she hadn't even been able to take his hand. He swore Noel and Selena Tayler were his nemeses.

He paced restlessly across the sand, telling himself to let it go, because it *was not fate*, that it had *never been fate* that she'd moved to Sydney, that she'd turned up here. It wasn't fate, otherwise how could he have decided to buy a property in bloody *Scotland* when he could have bought a property a stone's throw from Hawke's Cove, where Zoe was about to live.

Not. Fate.

Let. Go.

And yet...the lovely, subtle scent of her was in the air, and he craved it.

He closed his eyes, relived the kiss, felt her hands on his face, saw the glow in her eyes. For him. Felt the shiver tremble through her. For him.

He opened his eyes. He hadn't imagined those things. They were real. Not a fairy tale. And he'd be damned if he let her parents drag him away this time.

He threw back his head and gazed at the sky, at the stars. Remembered that night on the beach, when they'd found the white pearl. Spinning tales about mermaids. Lovesick Mathey throwing himself off a cliff.

Dammit, why *not* throw himself off a cliff?

And just like that he was back in the long war. He was going into battle for Zoe. And if anyone knew about fighting battles it was him. Every day of his whole life had felt like a battle to the death. Literally, in his mother's case. Well, he'd lost that battle, but he wasn't going to lose this one. He'd take on anything, anyone, anywhere, to have Zoe. If he had to win over her parents, he'd do it. If he had to become best friends with those girlfriends of hers, he'd do it. If he had to move back to Hawke's Cove, well, he'd do that too.

Time to go home.

He pulled out his phone, called Gina, waited impatiently for her to pick up.

She sounded sleepy as she said his name, "Finn?"

"Yes, listen, Gina—"

"Wait a minute, let me get up."

"Get up? But it's nine o'clock!"

"Yes, oh," she said wryly.

She covered the mouthpiece, said something. He heard a deep rumble in response, tested the concept of Gina being with someone else, found he was glad that she was moving on.

Moving on. Not looking back. What he had to do. No more talk of time traveling to the past.

A rustle, the click of a door closing, then she was back. "OK, what's the problem? Aside from the obvious fact that—again— you're not on your way to the UK."

"I'm sorry, Gina, if I'd known you were with someone—"

"Just tell me what the problem is so I can get back to him."

"Not a problem, just a decision."

"A decision?"

"Buy the property in Devon."

"But you said Scotland!"

"And I'm changing my mind."

"You're a pain in the—"

"Yeah, I know I am. But come on, you know it's the one you want to buy."

"Fine. Fine! But don't make plans for tomorrow, I'm sending you a bunch of legal documents. And don't bother telling me you're flying out in the morning. Talk about the boy who cried wolf!"

twenty-two

THE NEXT MORNING FINN APPROACHED THE TABLE where Zoe was sitting with Cristina and Matilda, having just finished breakfast.

He dragged over a chair from the next table and sat. "Cristina, that cooking class I mentioned the other day is on again. Are you interested?"

"As long as it's OK with Zoe," Cristina responded, and then looked at Zoe as though she was trying not to laugh. "Do you want to come too, Zo?"

"No!" Zoe said, laying a warning hand on Cristina's knee under the table: *do not mess this up.* "I mean yes, I mean no, I don't want to come, I mean yes, go, go, go. Please." She was babbling but she didn't care. She would not—*not*—let anyone stand in the way if Finn was offering an olive branch after whatever had happened last night, even if she didn't know exactly what *had* happened! That wonderful restless recklessness was flooding through her just because he was here and nothing was going to stop her being alone with him. If only she could work out how to issue an invitation he couldn't refuse!

"Joe will take you in an hour," Finn said to Cristina. "He'll be using his own boat so you can go fishing afterward if you like."

And then he transferred his attention to Zoe...*and* Matilda. Dammit.

"How about you two come with me to a Tahitian pearl farm?" he said. "It's a forty-minute boat ride. Small scale, exquisite pearls, unusual jewelry designs. We stock some of their jewelry in our gift store here at Poerava but the more exclusive designs are only available in a handful of big-name stores in London, New York and Paris."

"Not Tilly," Zoe said, gripping Matilda's knee with her free hand under the table. "She's busy."

"Yes, Tilly's busy," Matilda said without missing a beat, giving Zoe's hand a conspiratorial squeeze under the table. "Despite the almost irresistible lure of jewelry, she has a date with Daniel."

He smiled at Zoe, making her heart somersault. "Well?"

Zoe cleared her throat. "Is there a group of us going?"

Finn recoiled. "What, like a *junket*?" he asked, in such overwrought horror, Matilda laughed outright and Cristina covered her mouth with her hand so that she didn't follow suit. "No, Ms. Intrepid. This would be you and me." He stood. "I'd quintuple dare you but if you're not interested—"

"Wait!" she said. "I...I am interested."

Finn shrugged as though it didn't matter, although the heated look in his eyes told her it mattered very much indeed, and she realized then that that one-shouldered shrug of his had never been indifferent; it was the Finn Doherty equivalent of her rubbing her hands up and down her thighs.

"Then let's meet at *Little Micky* in, say, ninety minutes?" he said. "I have some paperwork to look over before we go."

Finn watched Zoe as she boarded *Little Micky* but didn't offer to help her.

Which was good, Zoe told herself, he wasn't going to mollycoddle her after all of her protestations of independence. (Although in her most secret heart she'd have preferred him to swing her up in his manly arms and carry her onto the boat.)

He cemented his understanding of her need for independence by taking phone call after phone call as he manned the controls, leaving Zoe to "enjoy the scenery" all on her own.

And when they reached their destination, again he watched as she disembarked—very closely but without touching her. At. All.

Hmm.

She wondered if she could find an opportunity to throw out a reminder that some people *were* allowed to help her, no need to ask permission.

It was at least heartening to note that he'd obviously been thinking about her, though: Poerava's teak ramps had made their way over to this island in advance of their arrival, which meant she could wheel herself without recourse to the must-be-pushed, less maneuverable all-terrain wheelchair. Not that she was averse to him pushing her. Gah! She was becoming pathetic.

She quickly realized tourists weren't catered for here, which meant her visit was a personal favor granted to Finn. Was it a sign that he'd gone to such trouble, calling in favors for her? Could it be deemed romantic?

Not so romantic that he stayed with her for the tour. He was on his phone almost the moment they entered the grafting house, out of sight and earshot.

Which was probably just as well because Zoe knew Tahitian pearls would make a fantastic story and she needed to concentrate.

She quickly learned the characteristics that sorted pearls into their quality categories according to size, shape, color and luster, but it wasn't until she was ushered into the showroom that the words became meaningful.

Zoe had seen exquisite Australian South Sea pearls in Broome a few years ago, but the iridescent range of colors of these pearls—from black all the way through to light gray—made her gasp. Calling the pearls such basic colors didn't do them justice. There were hints of green, purple, red, pink and gold that made Zoe think of rainbows on a midnight sky. They were almost poetic in their magnificence.

The myths that went with them were equally amazing. From the ancient Chinese belief that they were formed in the heads of dragons, to the Polynesian legends that told of the moon bathing the ocean in its light to entice oysters to the surface for impregnation by heaven.

She was in awe as she photographed the designs, and wasn't aware she'd actually stopped, phone lowered to heart level, as she gazed at a dazzling tiara—a stunning confection of Tahitian and white South Sea pearls, some round, some baroque teardrops, set in platinum amongst diamonds, sapphires and emeralds—until Finn reemerged from wherever he'd been.

"You said you always wanted a tiara so I knew you'd want to see that," he said.

"That's not a tiara, that's a *crown*," Zoe said reverently. "Something the Mermaid of Zennor would wear. Way too beautiful for a mortal!"

"So write that mermaid story you were always talking about and give it to her," Finn said, and checked his watch. "Right now, though, we'd better make a move if I'm to get you back in time to get ready for dinner."

"Dinner?" she said, and waited breathlessly for an invitation to his bungalow.

"The dinner at Mama Papa'e on Heia Island. No pressure, of course, if you really don't want to go, but just about everyone from Poerava is going."

"Will you be there?" she asked, as they reached *Little Micky*. "At the dinner, I mean."

One of those long, considering looks. "Yes."

"Then I'll go."

He started to say something…and then his phone rang. He looked at the screen and squared his shoulders. "Let's go," he said, and accepted the call.

He was on and off his phone for the entire journey back to Poerava.

Zoe tried not to listen in, tried to focus on the notes she'd taken at the pearl farm, but she couldn't help overhearing snatches of conversation. The name Jed—she knew who he was: the architect. She heard Finn mention Gina, then *call* Gina; apologizing but in a playfully coaxing way Zoe didn't believe anyone could resist. There was someone with whom Finn seemed to be talking financials. A mention of Finn's Sydney apartment. Gina again. A reference to Scotland—something seemed to have gone wrong there. Back to Jed. Then Gina again, talking about… Devon? Had she really heard Finn say Devon?

She looked at him questioningly, thinking she'd misheard, and he…he beamed at her, and her thoughts skittered all the way out of her head. She didn't care what he was saying or who he was talking to as long as he kept smiling at her like that. But then he started, as though he'd been caught out, and said into the phone, "I missed that last bit," angling to face away from Zoe.

It seemed she was a distraction.

How completely, utterly wonderful!

Zoe gave up on her notes after that and simply sat there looking out at the water.

It was beautiful. Peaceful.

Until she heard Finn say "Hawke's Cove" and her vision blurred, grief surging inside her so suddenly her breath caught, clogged.

Hawke's Cove.

He had definitely referred to Hawke's Cove.

And there was that relentless tide, pulling at her heart, dragging her soul out of hiding, telling her she didn't belong here, she belonged…there. The grief, the yearning, the longing she'd been feeling, was for home.

The first thing Zoe noticed about Mama Papa'e was that it was a restaurant literally on the sand. The dining area was semicircular. Massive stone Tiki sculptures ranged along the circumference edge and a long wooden stage was set up across the diameter, beyond which the lagoon made a glorious backdrop. The tables and chairs were a blend of Polynesian and Asian design made from local wood, and flaming torches were thrust into the sand at regular intervals.

Guests were each greeted by pāreu-clad staff draping garlands of flowers around their necks and offering cocktails and mocktails. They were invited to kick off their shoes and dig in their toes. Although Zoe wasn't going to be digging her toes into any sand she got into the spirit of the evening by removing her jeweled sandals.

The tables were long and narrow, meant for groups. There were ramps over the sand to two of them, which had been set aside for parties that included people with mobility issues.

There was one wheelchair user and two people with other mobility aids already at one of those tables, but it was the other table that was reserved for Poerava. Zoe felt a twinge of remorse at forcing the Poerava contingent to walk across ramps instead of sand to take their seats, and she seriously contemplated joining the other table until Matilda gave a loud whoop of joy.

"Close to the stage," Matilda said. "Perfect! *Plus* I'm all for a bit of sand but none of us can say we haven't had our fair share of it this week—seriously, I have sand in every orifice known to man and a few as-yet-undiscovered ones. Anyway, there's dancing later in that huge sandpit right in front of the stage and I, for one, will be out there doing my world-famous twerk, so let's not sand it up before then!"

Zoe accepted that message for what it was: solidarity. It made her think of Victoria, Malie and Lily, always so caring but discreet with it, no *look how virtuous I am giving up my fun for poor Zoe*, and those blasted tears were stinging behind her nose.

Food started coming out almost the moment the group was seated. No lining up at the buffet for Poerava's guests: everything was served on platters brought to their table.

Zoe's head was spinning at the array of food and the table was buzzing. And yet that sense of nostalgic melancholy wouldn't leave her, no matter how many lighthearted conversations she entered into or how many oohs and aahs she produced in response to the incredible menu which, face it, was wasted on her.

She wondered where Finn was, guessed those phone calls were still keeping him busy, and wished she hadn't come—especially when Kupe Kahale took to the stage to introduce the entertainment: traditional music and dances on the main stage, including what was purported to be a mesmerizing fire dance, and demonstrations on smaller daises positioned between the Tiki sculptures of the making of heis (flower crowns—and OK, that sounded interesting, she had to admit), Tahitian tattooing, carving and pāreu painting.

It was as the audience participation part of proceedings was announced that Zoe finally saw Finn.

He was standing to the side of the stage, talking earnestly to one of the staff who was gesturing in the direction of the Poerava table. Finn gave a vehement shake of his head, made a cutting gesture with one of his hands, and then looked over at her, smiled and started toward her…but then he stopped, and out came his phone, and with an apologetic combination of eye roll and shoulder shrug he moved behind one of the Tiki sculptures.

Kupe came on stage again, announcing the audience participation part of the entertainment, and he looked right at Zoe as she sat there petrified. How was she going to refuse to get on stage if she was publicly urged to do so, to twirl a flaming baton or have people dance around her or something else equally heinous? She would faint. No, no, she would do more than faint, she would die. D.I.E.

But to her immense relief it was Matilda and Daniel who were laughingly encouraged (admittedly without much resistance) onto the stage when the dreaded moment arrived.

Zoe was sure Finn would join the table for dessert and waited in a state of excitement as dish after dish arrived. So many dishes Zoe lost count, and then the plates were cleared, coffee was served… Still no Finn.

The dancing commenced, and almost as one group the Poerava gang headed for the sand. Only Cristina stayed, sitting beside Zoe, obstinately refusing to move despite Joe asking her to dance and Zoe encouraging her by insisting she had notes to write about the dinner. Zoe then had to start writing in her notepad to make good on her lie, even though she wasn't going to submit the story.

In the end, it was Kupe Kahale who solved her dilemma, looming suddenly beside her. "Ah, the little *meherio*. *Ia Orana*—hello! And *maeva*—welcome—to Mama Papa'e."

"*Meherio?*" she asked.

He leaned down and kissed her French-style, on each cheek. "Mermaid," he translated. "Finn described you that way. He says you swim like one. He also tells me dinner shows are not your 'thing' and threatened dismemberment should we ask you onto the stage."

She laughed. "He did?"

"Most definitely."

"Oh dear, I'm sor—"

He held up a hand. Stop. "I understand. There is no story in our show for you but Finn knew he would be busy tonight and wanted you to not be alone, waiting, and so you are here against your inclination, and we are not allowed to 'push' our luck. So now, since you already have your story on me, *ay*, let us move a little away from the noise and I will show you my favorite place on Heia Island. It's also a perfect place to take my photo…" flicking his hands inward, presenting his chest to her, "for which I wore my special shirt, and I will give you another story to thank you for coming."

He pointed to the left, past Mama Papa'e where, in the middle distance, Zoe could see a gazebo-style structure. "See? Close but not too close," he said. "You can wheel yourself most of the way, but I will need to help you to enter. Is that satisfactory, or would you prefer your friend's assistance?"

Zoe turned to Cristina. "Cris, why don't you go and find Joe and grab that dance?" She reached out her hand. Cristina took it, pressed it, released it with a murmured acceptance. "Give me, say, thirty minutes?" She looked to Kupe for confirmation and got a regal inclination of the head. "Yes, thirty minutes. Come for me then."

It was unusual for someone Zoe didn't know to lift her from her wheelchair. But it also felt natural for Kupe Kahale—who was built like an ox—to swing her up into his arms, in the same way it had felt natural for Malie's godfather to get her on and off the adapted surfboard at the surf school in Hawaii. It was impersonal, inoffensive, prosaic in a way it wouldn't have been if, say, Daniel was doing it.

Or Finn, of course. A whole other kettle of fish in his case. *Not* mackerel. Something much more delicious. Salmon. Lobster. Caviar.

Kupe settled her in a well-cushioned cane seat, sat in a larger one opposite her, then spent a moment looking her over as she pulled out her phone ready to take his photo. The part of her that seemed to interest him the most was her hair, which was loose and studded tonight with *tiare mā'ohi* blossoms, Tahitian gardenia, which she'd worn for Finn.

"You like flowers." A statement.

A shiver shook her as she remembered Finn touching the frangipani in her hair that night at the bar. All she could do was nod.

"Then you will enjoy this tale. At its heart is the rarest flower in the world. A flower called the *tiare apetahi*."

"Tiare apetahi," Zoe repeated, liking the sound of it. She was already intrigued—the combination of the name of the flower and the hypnotic voice of Kupe Kahale.

"What makes it so rare?" he went on, as though she'd asked the question. "The fact that it grows only in one place in the world, on Ra'iātea, our most sacred island. And even on Ra'iātea it grows only on Mount Temehani—a volcano," quick grin, "that is mercifully extinct. Many attempts have been made to transplant the *tiare apetahi* to other parts of the world, to other parts of French Polynesia, even to other parts of Ra'iātea. All have failed. Not even the best botanists in the world can understand why."

"That's...extraordinary."

"It is a beautiful flower, unique, as delicate as you, little *meherio*, and it smells..." closing his eyes and breathing in, "ahhhhh...like heaven." He opened his eyes, took her hand, turned it palm up, splayed her fingers. "Imagine each finger as a petal..." closing her fingers around his thumb, "closing as the night descends..." opening her fingers again, "and opening at dawn with the sound...of a crack."

He released her hand. "Ra'iātea is the spiritual heart of my people—all of my people—Polynesian, Māori, Rapa Nui,

Hawaiian. Ra'iātea means faraway heaven. And we believe that when our spirit leaves us, our souls swim beneath the waves to Ra'iātea. At dawn, with the opening of the *tiare apetahi*, our spirits are released to the heavens, and as we soar upward, we take one flower with us to keep our heart forever beautiful."

"That's so…so wonderful. Romantic. Oh, I can't describe it."

"There's more, little *meherio*. A legend. A myth. I will tell you my version, a story of a beautiful young woman, a king and the sea.

"Tiaitau was the daughter of a fisherman and the beloved of King Tamatoa. One day, the king rowed away from Ra'iātea, heading for battle. He told Tiaitau not to worry for his safety—he was guarded by his best warriors. But Tiaitau had a feeling, a foreboding, that she would never see him again, and her heart compelled her to climb Mount Temehani to watch the sea for his return.

"What she saw was his oar floating on the sunlit waves, his empty canoe bobbing in the water. In despair, she plunged her arm into the ground, where it broke off, and she threw herself into the chasm of Apo'o hihi ura, unable to bear the thought that he would not return to her.

"Her arm grew from the ground into the *tiare apetahi*. According to the legend, should the king return one day he will smell her scent on the wind and grasp the white flower that is her hand. As long as he does not, the cracking sound made by the flower as it opens to hope every morning is the sound of her breaking heart.

"*This* is the reason the *tiare apetahi* can grow nowhere else. Because Tiaitau remains there, waiting for her love."

"That's so sad, *too* sad."

"Not all love stories have a happy ending, little *meherio*." He smiled at her, a definite twinkle in his eye. "But many do, even when the wait has been long."

"I like stories that have a happy ending," she said, twinkling back at him.

"Then we hope, no we believe, that your story will be such."

"Kupe, that legend..." she said, as an idea took hold, "is it possible for people to go to Ra'iātea?"

"But of course!"

"And see the flowers?"

"But of cou—" Abrupt stop. His eyes flickered to her wheelchair, a short distance from the gazebo. "Yes," he went on, but the twinkle in his eyes had disappeared, "it is *possible* for people to travel to Ra'iātea, and it is *possible* to go to one of the two plateaus on Mount Temehani where the *tiare apetahi* grow. But it is an arduous hike up a steep slope."

"Oh! Oh, of course," Zoe said, understanding immediately.

"If there was a way—"

"Please! Please, it's all right."

"I am sorry, little *meherio*, I didn't tell you the story to distress you."

"I'm not distressed," she responded, her voice sounding thankfully normal despite the cursed tears building behind her nose. "Anyway, let's move on. I need to take your photo, remember." She raised her phone, snapped, snapped, snapped. Peered at her phone, flicking through the shots until she had herself under control. Then she lifted her eyes to his. "You're very photogenic. Perhaps one more, standing, at the entrance."

Kupe dutifully positioned himself, and Zoe took another series of photographs. "That should do it. But now... Can you give me a few minutes? I need to make a call about the story, send the photos."

"I'm not sure it's a good idea for you to be alone."

She held up her phone. "Believe me, I'm a phone call away from the...the cavalry. Cris will come riding to the rescue in a flash if I need anything."

He hesitated, looking from her to her chair.

"She'll be here in ten minutes," she reassured him. "Or you can come back for me yourself, or ask Cris to come in five minutes. That's all I need. I'll be safe in the meantime. I always am, you know. Safe."

Another moment before a reluctant Kupe bowed and left... but the look on his face when he passed her wheelchair and glanced back at her had Zoe silently cursing. She'd seen that look on faces everywhere her whole life. She knew he was going to go straight to Cristina to tell her Zoe was alone. Cristina would be running for her without waiting even a minute.

Drastic action needed.

In a flash she had her phone out and started tapping out a text:

About to jump on a call with

Hmm. Who? Who would Cristina believe she was calling? Well, they'd done nothing but eat all night, so...

Lily. Sent her pics of the food so she wants to talk. See you in 10, not before.

She put her phone away, willing a sense of peace to descend so she could get her stoic-inspirational-Zoe facade in place before Cristina came for her.

But there was no peace. There was only frustration that her high hopes for tonight had been reduced to enduring a dinner she'd known she wouldn't enjoy, about which she wouldn't write, and instead of finishing the evening with the man she'd done it for, she'd ended it hearing that the most beautiful story she could imagine writing—a story that seemed to encapsulate the mood of this trip; the beauty, the magic, the melancholy— was impossible for her to experience to the full. Matilda, Daniel, any of the other travel writers here tonight could go to Ra'iātea and climb Mount Temehani and see the wondrous *tiare apetahi*, but she could not.

The fact that she'd managed to recruit a new member of the Keep Zoe Tayler Safe At All Costs brigade was the icing on a very unpalatable cake.

Safe. She'd told Kupe she'd be safe.

And now all she could think about was what Finn had said to her last night.

*I don't usually play it safe. But I did, with you, that summer. And I want to know…*need *to know…if you want me to play it safe now.*

She closed her eyes, seeing the longing in his eyes as he'd asked what she'd do if he asked her to touch him. She finally understood what Malie had meant in Hawaii when she'd said it had been impossible to get served in the Crab Shack when Zoe and Finn were on shift together because they'd been too busy getting lost in each other's eyes. She had been lost in Finn's eyes last night. She wanted to get lost in Finn's eyes again. Wanted to get lost in *him*, all of him. She needed to know what to do to make him look at her like that again. There was only one more day left, and she was panicking.

If only she could be as confident as Malie, laying out for Todd what she wanted, taking what she wanted.

Malie!

Of course.

She'd call Malie.

Out came her phone, an unthinking dash against the screen.

A moment later Malie's bleary, squinting-eyed face appeared. "Hmnhu?" she said, and then, "Oh! Zoe?"

Zoe was instantly stricken with remorse. "I'm sorry! I forgot the time."

She heard an indistinct mumble in the background and grimaced.

"Hang on!" Malie said to her, and then, over her shoulder, "Ask her yourself."

Next second Todd's equally bleary, squinting-eyed face appeared. "Hey, Zo!" he said. "Everything OK?"

"Yes, fine. I just... I forgot you guys were in the same time zone."

Todd's eyebrows went up. "You forgot? World-traveling globe-trotter, expert in all things tourism, forgot the time zone? This must be serious!"

Zoe giggled. "Shut up, Todd!"

He chuckled, and with a quick swoosh of vague darkness, Malie had the phone back and was walking with it out of the bedroom. "Right," she said, "spill because he's right, it *must* be serious if you can forget it's—hang on, what time *is* it?"

"Half past eleven," Zoe said, but couldn't immediately get another word out because the hideous scorch of tears was not only behind her nose now but in her throat.

"Oh well, that's not late. I've got all the time in the world."

"But what about Todd?"

Malie rolled her eyes. "I keep telling people we're not joined at the hip. Why won't anyone believe me?"

Zoe had to laugh at that. "Because I think he wants to be joined at the hip?"

"Yeah, it's not the hip he's thinking of!"

Another laugh, and the world righted itself. "Anyway, it's really not important. I just...just missed you. And I thought how much you'd like this place, where I am tonight. Hang on, I'll do a quick 360-degree swirl with the phone. I'm sitting in the most gorgeous wooden pagoda—"

"Wow!"

"Yes, isn't it wow? That's the lagoon...at least I think it is, I'm holding it over my head so I can't quite see."

"Yes, it's a lagoon and frankly I prefer a killer wave to still water."

"And that's a patch of rainforest. And there, not too far in the distance, can you see those massive statues? That's the outdoor restaurant where we had dinner tonight. The tables and chairs are right on the sand."

"I want one of those statues! And that sand is so... I don't know...white, I guess! Or is it the moon making it glow like that?"

"Partly the moon but the restaurant's called Mama Papa'e, which actually means pure white, so maybe it always glows a bit. This isn't Tiare Island, by the way, this is Heia Island, and the guy who owns the restaurant—a real personality—told me the most beautiful story tonight about where he's from..." Again, her throat closed over and she had to stop to take a few quick breaths.

"Zoeeeee. What. Is. It?"

"I told you, I miss you guys."

"Not buying it."

"It's true, I do miss you...but OK, I've just been wondering...lately...if I'm missing something...something else, too. I mean, what am I really doing?"

"In French Polynesia?"

"No, more...more existentially than that."

"Well, interpreting the 'existential' thing since I'm not a hundred percent sure I know what it means, I'd say you're living the life you always wanted. Traveling, writing?"

"Well, yes, I'm traveling and I'm writing..."

"But? I know there's a 'but' so get to it, babe."

"It's just... I started that blog of mine as an outlet to keep my sanity while Mum and Dad were dragging me all over the world, and the blog led to the travel-writer-for-hire thing, and I... I've never stopped to think about it, you know?"

"And you're thinking about it now because?"

"Because of myths, and legends, and fairy tales and...and take that story Kupe Kahale shared with me tonight."

"Kupe Kahale, huh? I hope you're about to tell me he's doing more for you than spinning a tall tale."

"What? No!" Zoe laughed. "He's married to one of the most gorgeous women I've ever seen. That story's just an example.

But there are others. Stories from Devon and Cornwall and… and…" Nope. She'd choked up again.

"Are you… I don't know…homesick maybe, Zoe? Because that's OK. Even when you hate a place you're allowed to miss it."

"I guess. A little. Not the place so much, but homesick for you and V and Lils. No, it's more than that. I'm homesick for… for what we lost. And…and the truth is, I'm asking myself at the moment if anyone would *care* if I stopped writing travel stories. I mean, if I gave it up tomorrow, there are so many other journalists who could pick up the baton as though it had never been dropped. They're already there, in fact some of them are *here*, in French Polynesia. I've met them."

"Hang on. There are other travel writers there who are wheelchair users?"

"That's not what I mean. I'm the only one on this trip but… but there are so many other terrific travel writers who are wheelchair users. Like Rolf, the guy I replaced on this trip. But I'm talking about more than my wheelchair. *I'm* more than my wheelchair, even though that's a part of me as a writer. I'm talking about just…just excellent writers, who are working for newspapers and magazines, and producing content for blogs and tourism organizations and online travel sites, who would slot seamlessly into my place the way I slotted into Rolf's this time. I can't even claim my photography is anything special. Rolf's images are a thousand times more evocative than mine and Tilly, one of the friends I've made here? *Her* photos are extraordinary."

"So what are you saying, Zo? You're going to give up?"

And there it was. Not just the question but the answer, so simple. It had been somewhere in her head since Finn had said today: *So write that mermaid story you were always talking about.* It was in the vision she kept having of Finn sitting on the beach in Hawke's Cove at midnight, spellbound by a tale they'd once woven from nothing more than a pearl on a chain. The reverse take on "Rapunzel." And so many other story ideas, about smugglers and treasure and true love, that she'd pushed to the back of her mind.

"I'm going to write novels," she announced.

Malie let out a whoop! "Serious?"

"Serious."

"Write one with sex in it! I've got stories that are worthy of a *New York Times* bestseller!"

"Of course you have!" Zoe said, and started laughing helplessly.

"Meanwhile, do another 360, will you? I want to imagine me and Todd on that white sand."

Still laughing, Zoe complied. "Just to whet your appetite…" she said as she slowly directed her phone, "there's also a pink sand beach where you could get hot and heavy with a surf school rash vest and—"

"Wait! Stop! Stop right there! Who the…? Who is *that*?"

"That?" Craning to see. "Probably Kupe Kaha— Oh. Oh! Gotta go!"

"Zoe Tayler, don't you dare hang up on me!"

"Seriously gotta go."

"Zoe!"

"Birthday call tomorrow. Speak then. Bye. Bye, bye, bye."

Zoe disconnected, and turned off the phone, and waited with a hair-trigger heart for Finn Doherty to arrive.

twenty-three

THE FIRST THING FINN NOTICED AS HE ENTERED the gazebo was Zoe's hands rubbing her thighs. Up, down, up, down.

"You don't have to do that, Zoe," he said.

"W-what?"

"Your hands."

Her hands stopped. "It's a…a nervous habit, that's all."

"And I make you nervous."

"No. I mean…no. Oh I don't know what I mean. Yes. Yes? Yes, you do, because I don't know what you're thinking when you look at me like that."

"Like what?"

"Like…that. Malie says you used to look at me like that but I was sure she was wrong. And I still… I mean how could you possibly? Except that sometimes…like last night…at the food trucks… And now here I am, and my chair's over there, and I don't want you to think—because I don't think. At least I do but I don't. I mean, I thought… But I know you're busy. Two resorts to manage and you were supposed to be in the UK, and you're so late… I really don't know why you're here. Tonight—but not…not *just* tonight. I mean here and not in the UK. But you have guests tonight so I'm not expecting—I mean, they're dancing and maybe you want to as well. And that's OK because I—grghahgah!" And her hands were up off her thighs, covering her face.

Finn waited for her to come up laughing so he could tell her answers to all those questions, but the sound he heard emerging from between her fingers wasn't a laugh, it was a sob.

"Hey!" he said.

She shook her head. What did that mean? Stay away? How could he stay away when she never cried and yet she was crying? His wonderful, indomitable Zoe, crying alone.

For a second he hesitated, but he couldn't bear to see her distressed. She'd said—hadn't she said?—that people she trusted didn't need permission. And she trusted him. Against all odds, she trusted him.

One more heartbeat, that was all it took to decide, and he was gently, carefully scooping her up, bringing her with him over to the larger chair, cradling her on his lap.

He waited for a fraught moment, ready for her to tell him to let her go; instead she burrowed closer, her hands still over her face.

"Are you trying to break my heart?" He kissed her hair. "I can't bear to see you cry."

She shook her head but didn't remove her hands.

"OK, so how about I answer your questions?"

A nod.

"Last night at the food trucks, I wanted to see you, I wanted to touch you. I'm here tonight, I'm here this week, only for you. I wanted you to come tonight because I had business to attend to and I didn't want you to be alone, waiting for me at Poerava. I'm late because of that business but nothing was going to keep me away. I know your chair is out there, and when you're ready to leave, I'm going to carry you to it if you'll let me, but if you prefer I'll call Cristina. My resorts can wait, just like the trip to the UK is waiting. I have guests, but as you said, they're dancing. And here's a deep dark secret for you—I dance like a flailing trout, so me dancing ain't happening anywhere except in the privacy of my own living room. Or I can dance for you, now, if you could use a laugh."

Obligingly, she gave a watery chuckle.

He nestled his cheek against the top of her head, crushing one of the *tiare mā'ohi* flowers she'd pinned into her hair and breathing in the intoxicating scent that was so heartbreakingly Zoe. "Now, how about you share a deep, dark secret of your own to make me feel better about the whole trout thing? One that isn't your abominable handwriting or the fact that you always manage to dribble your food down your chin or that you can't cook?"

And at that, the watery chuckle turned to a snort of laughter, and she emerged from behind her hands.

She smiled at him and his heart turned over. "I don't have any deep, dark secrets to match the flailing trout."

"I'd say you definitely have one secret at least, even if it isn't trout-worthy," he ventured. "Why the tears?"

To his utter amazement, she snuggled into his arms, resting the side of her face against his chest. "Because tonight I feel… lost. Like you said I was, all those years ago."

He went perfectly still. "You're not lost, Zoe. You're right here, with me."

Long, long moment. And then, tentative: "Have you been to see the *tiare apetahi*, Finn?"

"Yes."

"Kupe told me the story, and I asked… I asked if I could go to Ra'iātea and see them and he said…he said…" Another sob wracked her tiny frame, and Finn had to exercise superhuman restraint not to crush her in his arms, so closely did he want to hold her because he *knew*: it was something she'd never be able to do.

"Zoe, the *tiare apetahi* is a beautiful flower with an incredible story, but truthfully? I'm sorry I ever went up Mount Temehani to see them. If I had the chance to hike up there again I wouldn't do it. There are only about twenty plants left, and that's because they've been loved almost to extinction."

"Are you trying to make me feel better?" she asked into his shirt.

"Yes, but it's also the truth. That flower is sacred to Polynesian people. Do the rest of us really need to traipse up to see it? We can hear the stories, we can see the photos, there are other exquisite flowers we can smell. Isn't that enough?"

"Yes, yes, I guess that's enough," she said, and sighed as she burrowed closer.

He wondered if she knew that she was fiddling with the buttons of his shirt. If that was a replacement for rubbing her hands over her thighs he was all for it. He waited for what she would say. He knew in that moment he'd waited forever for her. That he'd keep waiting for as long as it took.

"When I have to attend a party," she said haltingly, "I try to get there early so I don't have to barge through people with my chair. But on a tour, I aim to be the last person to do things so everyone else doesn't have to maneuver around me. I'm the last into the water because I'm not as strong as other people so I don't have as long to swim. And I have to be the last one out so I don't get in anyone's way. The *Gravity* thing...well, you already know about that, and that's not really a secret because the girls know about it too. But they don't know...nobody knows...that sometimes I fall out of my chair, and when that happens, it can be so, so hard to get back into it. The last time it happened I sat on the floor and cried for an hour." She drew in a breath, huffed it out. "I guess those are deep dark secrets.

The crying thing especially. Because I don't want anyone to know that I do cry, sometimes."

Again, that urge to crush her in his arms, absorb her hurt, take it into his own body, his own soul. This was hard to hear, hard to bear.

"I've had sex, you know," she said, into his shirt again. "Yes, I have. And it was not good. Not. Good." A hitch in her breath, a caught-back sob. *Ah, Zoe.* "Just because I can't feel my legs doesn't mean I can't feel everywhere else, and just because I'm small and…and skinny doesn't mean I don't want… I don't know…passion instead of all the…the gentle and…vague and… and scared…blah, and…argh, I just… I can't talk about it!"

"You don't have to," he said, his hand stroking into her hair, soothing, yearning, aching, wanting.

"I tried online dating once." Nodding furiously against his chest. "And you know what I found?"

He wanted say, *That it sucks?* but decided to keep quiet instead.

"I found," she said, with a laugh that managed to sound like utter despair, "that there are wheelchair devotees out there. Wheelchair devotees, like…like *fetishists.*"

Yep, he was glad he'd kept quiet on that one.

"Not that there's anything wrong with that," she went on, really tugging on his buttons now. "If both sides are getting something out of it, go team! But I've had enough of people fussing over me, *through my entire childhood*, without bothering to find out who I really am on the *inside*. I don't need someone worshipping my wheelchair now. Do you know how many people tell me I'm an inspiration? How they admire my bravery? That they're proud of me? Or conversely that they pity me? And I don't want any of that. I just… I want to be me. But instead, I have to pretend to not mind that people see me as some kind of…of mirror to make themselves feel good, or a mission, or a little pet in need of stroking. Sometimes I want to punch them! Or just…just *scream!*"

One of his buttons came off, ripped from his shirt. "So go ahead," he said.

She was looking at the button in her hand as though she had no idea how it got there. "What?"

"Punch me. I'm strong as an ox. Lay into me."

Up came her head, her eyes blinking. "I'm not going to punch you, Finn."

"OK, then scream."

"No!"

"Why not? The show's over in Mama Papa'e. The guests are all dancing and the music's loud enough to drown out a scream or two. Kupe and Chen have gone home, and home's on the other side of the island."

"I'm not going to scream, Finn!"

She sounded so shocked! God, she was adorable. "OK, we'll save the scream for tomorrow but the option to punch me still stands."

"Wait. What. Tomorrow?"

"And Zoe," taking her chin in a gentle hand, "for the record, you are an inspiration, and I do admire your bravery, but it's got nothing to do with your wheelchair."

More blinking.

"Do you remember that entry in your journal you showed me? The one about surfing with Malie at dawn? You hid Malie's board in your parents' boatshed because her parents wouldn't let her surf anymore and yours would have had a fit if they'd found out what you were doing?"

"They *did* have a fit when I told them I was going surfing with Malie in Hawaii in February."

"And yet you went, and that was the trip you did without Cristina."

"Thanks to Malie cornering Mum and Dad last Christmas and promising them she'd go 'the full Rottweiler' to keep me safe."

Finn laughed. "And did she go 'the full Rottweiler'?"

"Oh, she did," Zoe said, laughing with him.

"I'd like to have seen that!" He smiled at her, then cupped her face with one reverent hand. "But the thing is, I knew from that journal entry that surfing scared you and yet you still went to Hawaii because it wasn't about the surfing, it was about…about you. About courage. A symbol of your friendship with Malie. And then today, I read your article on the surf school and—"

"What? How did you…? Oh." She giggled. "Google!"

"And I knew all those things were still there, the defiance, the courage. The loyalty that's making you wear that godawful pink vest!" Another giggle, and it made his heart swoon for her. "And I saw in that article that you conquered surfing the way you've conquered—the way you *conquer*—everything. It was in every line you wrote. I would have thought you'd feel more vulnerable than ever lying on your belly on an adapted surfboard but nothing I read suggested fear."

"Because I wasn't scared. I don't know how but I lost the fear and just loved it. It's like I'd grown into the freedom of it. Don't get me wrong, I'm never going to be like Malie, fiercely and fearlessly catching giant waves, but hey, *no one*'s as good as Malie on a wave! But I can still love it."

He trailed a thumb across her cheek. "Snorkeling in still water must seem tame by comparison."

"Tame? When there's every chance I could be consumed by a giant clam?"

He hooted out a laugh. "I'll man up and save you, I promise."

She snuggled back into his arms, and when he felt her shiver, he drew her closer against his chest. "So on the subject of Malie…"

"Hmm?"

"What was it she said?"

She looked up at him. "I don't—what?"

"You said, *Malie said you used to look at me like dot-dot-dot.* And then you said she was wrong. So fill in the dots."

She was back to fiddling with his shirt, but this time, she was sliding her finger inside the gap where the button was missing, tracing a small circle with it over and over. Unconsciously, he was sure. It felt…aaah…like heaven. If only she'd rip off a few more buttons, put her whole hand inside. Oh God, maybe not, he'd never be able to concentrate.

"Okaaay," she said. "Malie said…" her finger stopping, "that you looked at me…" licking at her lips, "like you wanted to…" closing her eyes tight, "strip me naked and have your wicked way with me." She opened her eyes and blinked up at him, clearly astounded that she'd said it.

He wanted to kiss her so, so badly. But this had to be finished, understood. "Well, Zoe, I have news for you." He threaded his fingers into her hair. "Malie was *not* wrong. She was one hundred percent right. That's how I used to look at you. And that's how I was looking at you when I came into this gazebo. It's how I'm looking at you now. And I can assure you I'm not scared of passion and I'm unlikely to be gentle—unless that's what you want me to be in which case that's what I'll be, because I'll be whatever the hell you want. I am not a wheelchair devotee or fetishist or whatever you want to call it. I just want you. Inside and out, from your hair clips to your jeweled feet and everywhere in between. So how about you let me do it? Strip you naked? I mean, come on, we both know I moved into that bungalow for a reason."

One breathless beat of a moment.

And then she twined her arms around his neck. "Am I allowed to strip you naked too?" she whispered.

"Ah, Zoe," he said unsteadily. "You are allowed to do whatever you want to me. Nothing is out of bounds. Absolutely nothing. Remember when we talked about vanilla? Well, choose whatever flavor you want and I will home deliver it and you can help me choose the sprinkles."

twenty-four

SO THAT'S WHAT ALL THE FUSS IS ABOUT.

Zoe woke with those words in her head, then grabbed Finn's pillow, brought it to her face and inhaled.

True to his word, he had *not* been gentle last night. Well, actually he had. When he'd whispered that he had to be—that he needed to be, *for her*—as he'd eased inside her, telling her it was wonderful, that she was everything, all he could ever want.

Other than that, though? Whew!

In the lead-up he'd found every single part of her body that could feel and made every single nerve explode. He'd done it effortlessly, easily, exuberantly, with hot words spilling out telling her what he was going to do next. *Lick you, suck you, kiss you here, put my tongue there.* And even better: *Do it back to me, I am so hot for you I'll let you take anything you want, do anything you want.*

Zoe didn't know what she'd expected, but it hadn't been anything quite so vocal!

And yet it had been perfect.

The fact that she was sporting a series of love bites all over her breasts was amazingly good. The fact he was sporting them all over his chest too? Even better. He was hers. She wanted him marked as such.

She wished she could do it all again immediately.

Except he wasn't there.

She remembered a soft kiss pressed to her mouth, a murmur that he'd be back, a stroke of her hair.

She eased up onto her elbows, and saw that Finn had brought her wheelchair in from the living room and positioned it absolutely perfectly beside the bed.

It wasn't until she was in the chair that she noticed a small box on the bedside table, sitting on top of a handwritten note, which read:

Happy birthday, my heart,

Had some work to do so the room is all yours until 9:30, when I'll be back with breakfast. I'm bringing extra napkins for when you slurp mango juice and get it all over your face.

Cristina knows where you are and isn't expecting to see you until it's time to get ready for tonight's farewell cocktail party—and no, I didn't call her, she called me when she couldn't get you on the phone so don't punch me when I get back, or do punch me, I can take it. (Memo to Zoe: turn your phone back on.)

Today we're practicing screaming. Don't worry, we're going off-the-grid, there'll be nobody else around.
Finlay

XX (The kisses seem kind of girly, but since I used to run with a gang I figure I can get away with them.)

PS: A travel writer once told me a girl can never have too many hair clips. Actually, she didn't tell me, she wrote it in a blog, and I found it online.

Zoe stared at the note for a full five minutes, not understanding why she was crying but crying anyway.

With one trembling hand she picked up the box and stared at it for so long anyone would have thought it was a bomb and she was working out how to neutralize it, but then she lifted the lid, and inside were two perfect hair combs, studded with black pearls and diamonds.

And it was at that precise moment that Zoe fell in love.

"Ready to scream?" Finn asked, once they were in their swimsuits.

Zoe looked so freaked out Finn almost laughed.

"Snorkeling it is, then," he said. "This is where we sort out the *Gravity* thing once and for all. And no need to rub your thighs like that, just trust me." He crouched down beside her, took her face in his hands and kissed her. "I'm going to strip you naked and have my wicked way with you tonight and nothing's going to stop me. You can therefore take it as a given that I'm not going to let you drown."

She laughed, as he expected, and he stood. "This *motu* we're on is uninhabited, and so is that one…" pointing to an islet to the right. "Between these two *motus* is a channel where the current peaks. It's not strong like a rip, but you also don't need to expend any energy to get from one *motu* to the next. All you have to do is float and let the current carry you—it's called 'drift snorkeling.' This is one of my favorite places in the world so I know what I'm doing." Crouching down again. "And Zoe, I will not, *will not*, let you drift more than a foot away from me. Understand?"

"Yes," she said.

He kissed her again, short and hard, and then grabbed the purple noodle and handed it to her. "OK for me to pick you up now?"

"You didn't have to ask."

"I'm asking anyway. We both know I'd be perfectly happy having you in my arms twenty-four hours a day so best not to let me take anything for granted."

"Oh well, if this is going to be a regular thing—"

"Count on that!"

"Then we're going to have to work out a signal—like the signal I have with Cris, the royal wave we call it, that lets her know to back off."

"Yeah, I've seen that wave. How about if I do this..." he laid his forehead against hers, "and if you're OK with it, you put your hands...ah hell, put them anywhere and—"

"How about for yes, I put them here..." she said, giggling as she wrapped her arms around his neck, "and here..." she shifted, so her hands were pushing against his chest, "for no."

"I can work with that. As long as you tell me, as we go along, how you want me to do it, what works, what doesn't, if I hurt you, whatever. No Hawke's Cove/Mrs. Whittaker/snowdrop Zoe, mind; I want Crab Shack oak tree Zoe giving it to me straight. Deal?"

"Deal," Zoe said, and rewound her arms around his neck before burying her face against his shoulder. "But just so you know, I kind of liked it when you hauled me out of the chair last night when we got to your bungalow."

"Note to self," he murmured as he carefully lifted her, "in moments of extreme passion, haul Zoe out of chair." He kissed her again, just because he could. He *could*! He was breathless when he raised his head and looked into her face. "I hope you realize that on that basis I'll be manhandling you just about every time I see you so you'd better practice our signal." One more kiss, all the more wonderful because they were both laughing. And then, "Let's go defy gravity," he said.

True to his word, Finn didn't stray more than one foot away from her for the next hour.

And when he carried her back onto the beach and she ripped off her mask and snorkel, and he'd settled her on a towel on the sand to dry off, she said, "Finn?"

"What do you need?"

"I need…" she said, giggling like a naughty schoolgirl.

"You need?" he said, laughing because it made him happy just to look at her.

"To SCREAM!" she screamed, and then she threw back her head, and did it again.

"My work here is done," Finn said.

And then he thought, *why not?* and he screamed too.

Zoe chose her favorite dress for dinner—a Victoria Scott design, because she always wore V's clothes for important events.

Her makeup was flawless, her hair twisted into an elaborate updo. All that was left to do was position the hair combs Finn had given her but she didn't want to do that until the last possible moment because she liked looking at them and wasn't about to spend the next half hour sitting in front of the mirror just so she could see them.

She took the combs with her to lay beside her computer while she wrote another long email to her parents, describing last night's dinner and today's snorkeling adventure.

They'd left her a "Happy Birthday" voice message while she'd been snorkeling, reminding her to open the gift they'd sent to her in Sydney to be opened on her birthday and not a moment before, which she'd dutifully packed (five diamond butterfly hair clips), but surprisingly there had been no anxious email making sure she was all right when she hadn't responded to their phone call. Not that Zoe was complaining.

She hovered over a mention of Finn (it really was time to tell them) but when a call came in from Victoria, Malie and Lily—her birthday call, right on schedule—she hit send because there was already too much to do and no time to choose the right words for such a delicate topic and any mention of him might elicit one of those *please be careful Zoe* emails and she did not want one of those, not on this perfect today.

She was, however, going to blurt it out to the girls, just as soon as the "Happy Birthdays" were done.

But before she got a chance to say a word, Victoria said: "Zoe! You look divine!"

Zoe beamed at her. "Thanks to my fashion designer girlfriend."

Victoria blew on her nails and gave them an over-the-top polish against her shoulder. "I know you love blue but I adore you in every shade of green—that dark color looks amazing."

"It's perfect for tonight's farewell cocktail party," Zoe said. "It reminds me of the iridescent green you see in Tahitian pearls—black pearls—which of course aren't really black, at least not black like onyx, more like deep peacock. I got some gorgeous new Tahitian pearl hair combs today as a birthday gift and they'll go wonderfully with this dress. Poerava, the name of this resort, actually means black pearl."

"Speaking of gifts and resorts and...and whatever," Malie cut in none too smoothly, "that certain someone I saw last night striding across the sand, why have you been holding out on us?"

Zoe laughed. "Well..."

"I *knew* it was him!" Malie pounced. "Zoe and Finn sitting in a tree, K.I.S.S.I.N.G.!"

"*Seriously*, Zo?" Lily said. "You knew Finn Doherty owned Poerava all along and didn't tell even one of us, not on any of our calls?"

"I didn't know until—hang on, how did *you* find out Finn owns...? Oh." Eye roll. "Don't tell me. Google!"

"I've got something better than Google," Lily said, looking smug. "Mrs. Whittaker! She stopped by for a cup of tea today with my mother and told her Finn Doherty had bought that manor house just outside Hawke's Cove. You know the place?

The one with the fortifications? Very run-down. I've hoped for so long someone would buy it and turn it into a boutique hotel. The view is spectacular. And if they do it right there's an opportunity for a wonderful restaurant. You know what I say about—"

"Restaurants," Malie, interrupting. "Yes, yes, the more good restaurants in one location, the easier it is to become known as a cuisine location, blah blah, Devon, potential food capital of sustainable eating! But get to the good part."

"The good part," Lily echoed. "That would be the part about it being Finn's *sixth property*! How did nobody know? Why didn't you tell us, Zoe?"

But Zoe, sitting like she'd been poleaxed, could only gape.

"Nope," Malie said, and hooted out a laugh. "Look at her—she didn't know the whole of it!"

"According to Mrs. Whittaker nobody knew, at least nobody in Hawke's Cove," Lily said. "I mean, really, even *she* didn't know? Of course, he hasn't been back since he left forever ago so it's not exactly surprising that no one knew but—"

"That's not the good part!" Malie, interrupting, and blowing an errant curl out of her eyes.

"Sounds pretty good to me," Victoria said. "I mean, *Finn*?"

"I'm getting to the good part if you'd let me draw breath, Malie!" Lily said. "Sheesh, that's what I get for telling you first! Right! So strictly speaking it's Doherty & Berne, a company, that bought the property, not Finn personally. He hasn't even seen it. He left the negotiations up to his *wife*."

Zoe's entire body went numb. "Wife?" It was her voice, but she didn't recognize it. No. Not true. *Please* not true!

"Not *wife*," Malie said. "*Ex-wife*."

"Ex-wife?" Zoe, still not recognizing her own voice.

"So!" Malie again. "What do you think of that?"

Zoe shook her head, trying to clear it. "I…I don't think of it."

"Oh Lord, that's Todd yelling at me!" Malie said, and turned around to call out, "Hang on a sec! Need to pick Zo up off the floor, metaphorically speaking, and see her new hair clips!" Back to the phone. "That's the phrase, isn't it, Madam Writer? Metaphorically speaking?"

She had to get off this call. Had to vomit. Had to faint. Had to die. "Actually," Zoe said, and forced out a laugh, "my new hair clips are awaiting placement so I'd better go and…and place them. You go, Devil. And V, I'm sure you have a million things to do. And Lils, the funeral, I can't imagine what you're dealing with. And I…I…that cocktail party tonight… hair clips…things to do…"

"Zo, you're babbling," Victoria said, frowning. "What's wrong?"

"Nothing."

"Liar!" Malie said, bringing her face all the way up to the phone.

Zoe's heart was aching so badly she couldn't think. But there was one thing she knew. "I miss you all so much."

"Nah. Not buying it. I mean, I am buying it because I miss you guys, too, but nah, that's not it."

Zoe's breath hitched. "It's that thing I talked to you about, Malie, about being homesick."

"So come home," Victoria said gently.

"It's not that simple, not now, not anymore," Zoe said, and dragged in a shuddering breath. "Listen, I really have to go. I'll call you and tell you all about everything when…when I can. And don't forget we've got your birthday call coming up soon, V! Meanwhile I'll email my measurements. And I have a recipe to send you, Lily. And Malie, my surf school story is up so I'll send you a link. But right now—"

"Zoe, wait!"

"Zo!"

"Zoe!"

"That's Cris calling me, and I still haven't finished doing my hair. Gotta go!"

Zoe disconnected, wheeled herself back into her bedroom and grabbed a tissue from the shell-encrusted box on the dressing table. A dab at the corner of one eye where a tear had started to escape but otherwise she was ready.

Except that she was not ready. Not ready to see Finn.

How was she supposed to live in Sydney with him there?

But how could she go home to Hawke's Cove knowing that Finn and his ex-wife—an ex-wife he hadn't mentioned even in passing—had bought a property there together and she could run into them at any time?

Where did she belong?

"Nowhere," she said. "I don't belong anywhere and I don't belong to anyone, and I never will."

"Zo?" Cristina called from the living room. "Ten minutes?"

"Ten minutes," Zoe confirmed.

She thought about the Tahitian pearl combs beside her computer and shook her head.

Malie had a butterfly tattoo at the base of her spine. A symbol of freedom, of rebirth, of moving on.

Perfect, she thought, and picked up the butterfly clips her parents had given her.

twenty-five

FINN HAD JUST FINISHED A WALK-THROUGH OF the Poerava Ballroom, enclosed tonight because rain was expected at some point, and was going through the order of events with Aiata when Zoe entered.

He broke off midsentence to gaze at her. Even Aiata's undisguised chuckle didn't have the power to bring him to his senses because Zoe looked…he didn't know how to describe it, but he figured heart-stopping came close.

She was wearing a shimmery green-black dress that fitted her like a second skin, draped lovingly across the small swell of her breasts, hiding those passionate marks he'd left on her last night. Two impossibly narrow shoulder straps held the dress in place and spangled silver spiderweb gauze attached to each of those narrow straps stretched tightly down her arms to her delicate wrists.

She was sitting straighter than ever in her chair, shoulders back further, head held higher, chin…jutting. Oh. And then he saw that her smile was stretched unnaturally wide and her eyes were glittering rather than glowing.

Something wasn't right.

He glanced behind her, to each side, ready to annihilate anyone who'd irritated, insulted or touched her, but except for Cristina there was nobody in the vicinity. Zoe had arrived early—because of course she had.

"Excuse me," he said to Aiata, and walked hastily toward Zoe, but Zoe wasn't waiting for him to reach her; instead she was making her way to the glass doors furthest away from him.

And then he saw the butterfly clips and stopped.

Zoe accepted a glass of champagne and said something to Cristina, carefully not looking in his direction, and it hit him that the person who'd irritated, insulted or touched her was him.

It didn't make sense; when he'd accompanied her back to her bungalow to get ready for tonight she'd given him an incendiary kiss at the door, running her hands across the hidden love bites she'd left on his chest, then up to the one very visible bite on his neck, and reminded him that raspberry was her favorite flavor if that gave him any ideas for tonight. He'd said it gave him ideas for right that second, with a *gigaton* of sprinkles, if she wanted to give Cristina a shock the minute they got inside the bungalow. She'd laughed and shooed him away and seriously, she'd thought he was joking but he absolutely was not.

OK, remembering all that, maybe he was overthinking this situation. Maybe she wasn't avoiding catching his eye. Maybe she wasn't wearing the combs because they didn't suit her outfit.

He reexamined her dress, looked at the toes of her shoes peeping from beneath the hem—platinum-colored sandals studded with black crystals—at the sparkling black evening purse on her lap. The combs he'd bought her were a glorious match.

So why was her hair studded with off-theme butterflies?

Well, he'd better ask her. Deep breath.

But two strides in he came to another stop.

Gina was entering the room, and although that didn't make sense either he was glad. It meant all the plans were in place, ready to be shared with Zoe.

Zoe knew who the woman was the moment she entered.

She was exquisite. Glowing with vitality. Gilded skin. Caramel hair in a sleekly simple chignon. Wearing a gown Victoria would have called Modern Grecian Goddess—a miracle of intricate folds in a rich cream color. No jewelry, no glitter: she didn't need anything more than what she was.

And just like that, Zoe Tayler, global citizen, intrepid travel reporter, drift-snorkeling screamer, was back in Hawke's Cove looking over at Finn with one of those bold, beautiful, confident girls, knowing he could never be interested in her.

She watched as the woman made a beeline for Finn, saw the surprise on his face give way to an unguarded smile, watched as he opened his arms and the goddess walked into them without a moment's hesitation, saw him fold her in close, whisper something to her as she touched that stupid, *stupid* love bite on his neck. And then he was laughing and turning that stunning woman in Zoe's direction; it seemed he was about to lead her over.

Zoe had never had a panic attack in her life but she wondered if she were about to.

"Who's that with Finn?" Cristina asked.

"His ex-wife."

"I didn't know he was married."

Click, click, click in Zoe's head. The phone calls yesterday on *Little Micky*. The reference to Hawke's Cove. There had been affection there. Love. "Her name's Gina. Gina Berne. I... I've heard him talking to her on the phone."

Gina had her hand on Finn's arm now, stopping him from bringing her over.

Good.

No! Not good! Bad! She was coming over all by herself. And Finn was *letting* her!

Calm down, Zoe. You are a successful journalist living your best life and—oohhh, her eyes are gold, and she is sooo beautiful, and she used to sleep every—single—night with Finn.

Gina came to a stop in front of her. She was smiling, but somehow not smiling.

"Can I get you a refill?" she asked, nodding at Zoe's glass.

Zoe looked at her glass. Empty. How had that happened?

Gina didn't wait for an answer, simply snagged a champagne flute from a waiter who'd been hovering near her—because who wouldn't want to hover near her?—and swapped it for Zoe's empty one before taking a glass for herself.

Gina tilted her head toward the glass doors. "How about we go outside?"

"The rain…" Zoe said.

"An hour away at least," Gina said, and turned to Cristina. "Do you mind if I borrow her?"

"That's my choice," Zoe said, emerging feistily from her near stupor.

Gina looked somewhat startled at the outburst, but nodded. "Of course. Shall we go outside, Zoe?" Oh-so-formal.

"Yes, let's," Zoe said, oh-so-sweet.

Gina moved around her to open the door and walked out onto the deck leaving Zoe to follow.

"We prefer it when we can open all the doors and lay down the extended teak floor but the grass also has charm for people looking for something a little more civilized," Gina said. "Have you had an enjoyable week?"

"Yes," Zoe said mechanically.

Gina took a sip of champagne, giving Zoe the impression she was fortifying herself. "So you know," she said, "our PR people send me links to all the media coverage associated with our properties. I saw a photo of you and Finn on Motu Marama."

"One of Matilda's stories," Zoe surmised.

Silence as Gina examined her, unsmiling.

Well, no way was Zoe going to break the silence. If this was some kind of showdown—and it certainly felt like one—it wasn't of her making.

And then it came, a bolt from the blue: "I don't want Finn to get hurt, Zoe."

Zoe blinked at her. *Finn* get hurt? "What makes you think I have that power?"

Gina smiled then, and it was rueful. "I researched you, Zoe Tayler. I know you're from Hawke's Cove, I know about your accident. I know all sorts of things." She flicked a hand at Zoe's wheelchair. "Finn has a savior complex. He couldn't save his mother, but maybe he thinks he can save—"

"I know about his mother."

"OK, so hear me out. When a man who hasn't even been able to go back to England to visit his mother's grave—about which he feels intensely guilty—who hasn't wanted to invest in property in the UK, who's had to be dragged kicking and screaming every step of the way, who reluctantly gives in but chooses Scotland because it's the safest emotional option, who somewhere in the middle of negotiations meets up with an old friend and looks at her like…like Finn looked at you in that photo, resulting in him switching out the Scotland option for the England option, and not just any place in England but a place so close to his old village it might actually be *in* his old village?" She gave a soft laugh. "Something's not right about that picture, so I have to assume he's done it for you, because nothing else has had the power to get him home."

"He hasn't done it for me," Zoe said. "If you've researched me, you know I live in Sydney, not Hawke's Cove."

Another of those soft laughs. "Don't you see, Zoe Tayler?

That makes it worse. Finn just mentioned the word 'fate' to me, about Poerava, about Sydney, about Hawke's Cove, and that is not the Finn I know. He's homesick, always has been, and you're part of that homesickness. He thinks you're going to take him home no matter where you live. An emotional home if not a geographic one. But you're not, are you? I've read your blogs, I know you've moved on, that you don't want to go back to Hawke's Cove. So let me say once more: do not hurt that man. Whatever power you have over him, let him go, please, and maybe instead of having someone else to save, he can go home and save himself."

twenty-six

ZOE HAD DISAPPEARED AND FINN HAD NO IDEA why.

He'd asked Gina, but Gina had been ridiculously cryptic. Instead of answering his questions she'd veered off-topic, talking about how Zoe had clearly outgrown Hawke's Cove, and how strong and independent and inspirational she was for choosing to live in Sydney on her own.

He'd laughed outright at the "inspirational" and said he hoped she hadn't said that to Zoe. Gina had said she and Zoe understood each other perfectly and Zoe hadn't taken offense at anything she'd said.

The cocktail party wound down and Finn made his way to the bar where Cristina, Matilda, Daniel and Joe were having a farewell drink.

He brushed aside their invitation to join them and said bluntly: "Where is she?"

"Packing," Cristina said.

"She's been gone over an hour."

"It takes her a while."

Finn dashed a hand through his hair. "Why aren't you helping her?"

"Er…" Cristina said. "Do you even *know* her? She likes to do it—"

"On her own, OK, OK, got it. I'll just go and see if she needs…anything."

"You do that," Matilda said, her lips so twisted with the effort not to laugh, Finn had to laugh himself.

"Shut up," he said.

"You two!" Matilda said. "Two peas in a pod."

But she said it to Finn's back; he was already striding out of the bar.

Finn paused at Zoe's door, feeling stupid about his mad dash. So she didn't wear the hair combs, she'd left the party early, she hadn't come up to him. She was packing, and when she finished packing she'd call him, or text him or—

Idiot. He hadn't checked his phone.

He pulled it out, holding his breath as he checked for messages, whooshing it out when he saw nothing, knowing she wasn't going to call or text him.

What she was going to do was leave him.

He put his phone away, rubbed a hand over his chest, over his heart, because it hurt, right *there*. Memories assailed him. The beach in Hawke's Cove… *Mermaid's Kiss*, two worlds colliding, inevitable as the tide. The look on her face every time she'd come up to him in the village and he'd rejected her—*keep away, you're not for the likes of me, everyone says so*. The hospital room, him begging, her rejecting *him*. Here on Tiare, insisting she wasn't lost, that she was independent, yet telling him it was OK for him to touch her, to lift her, unasked, because she trusted him. Her irrepressible laughter, that first kiss, the tears she never shed in front of anyone else as she poured out her deep dark secrets to him, the same way she'd shared her journal secrets only with him.

The fear was there, that he would lay out his heart and soul and she'd trample them.

But so was the fear that he would *not* lay out his heart and soul and he'd never know what might have been.

Sand through that damn hourglass. Last chance. Maybe it wouldn't work, maybe she'd leave him no matter what he said or did, but he wasn't a twenty-year-old idiot promising what he couldn't deliver, he was ten years wiser and he knew, *knew*, she wanted him, and he wasn't letting her go without a fight.

"All. Guns. Blazing!" he said through gritted teeth, and knocked hard on the door.

She'd know it was him. He wondered if she'd hide inside and refuse to see him.

But almost immediately he heard her, coming to the door. Of course she wasn't going to hide. Not Zoe.

She opened the door and led him wordlessly onto the deck. He took a seat, not because he wanted to, but because it put him at eye level with her. There was a bottle of vanilla rum on the table and a glass. She knew it was his drink of choice, and so he knew she'd been expecting him. He poured himself a measure, took a sip, waited.

At last she sucked in a breath, then jutted out her chin. Here it came.

"I didn't know you were married," she said.

He put his glass down, very precisely, on the table. "I'm not."

"I met your wife."

"Ex-wife. Gina. I know. I wanted you to meet her."

"I didn't know you'd *got* married."

"It wasn't a secret."

"Doherty & Berne. The surnames, they're different."

"Gina wanted to keep her name."

"She still loves you."

"And I still love her."

"You...you do?"

"I do. But not like..." He shrugged, sighed. "Let's not do this, Zoe. Not after last night, when you know how I—" Stop. If she didn't know what was the point? "What is this really about?"

"I heard about the property you bought in Hawke's Cove. I heard you now own *six* properties."

"And?"

"You never told me how many."

"You didn't ask."

"Well, I'm glad you're going home to Hawke's Cove."

"So are you," he said, although panic was etching an icy trail down his spine. "You're going home to Hawke's Cove too."

"No, Finn, I'm not."

A few seconds to process that. "Your parents...the renovation."

"That's pie-in-the-sky stuff. They got their hopes up at Christmas when I turned up, but I've told them I'm happy in Sydney so not to overdo the renovation."

He thought about that, decided it didn't matter. Who cared where they lived? "OK, what else? My ex-wife, my properties. How about we talk about why you didn't wear the hair combs?"

"I...I didn't want you to get the wrong impression. After last night."

"And what impression might I have got last night?"

"That there was...something...special...between us. I mean, w-we're friends, that's all."

"Friends, that's *all*?"

"Friends with a one-time benefit, and I...I thank you for that."

"Oh, you *thank* me, do you? Well, Zoe, leaving aside the fact

I told you very distinctly I have no intention of being in the friend zone this time around, how about you tell me—since that's where you're so determined to put me—why you haven't told your parents I'm here at Poerava. I'm sure you've told them about your new 'friends' Matilda and Joe and Daniel, right?"

Up came her chin. "How do you know I haven't told them about you?"

"Because I'm not an idiot, Zoe."

Her hands were on her thighs, rubbing up and down. Good. He wanted her to be nervous. He needed her to betray something.

"OK," she said, too levelly, "I didn't tell them because there's no point. This was a week, just one week. Why distress them for one—"

He banged a hand on the table. "Distress them? What about distressing *me*?"

"You're not distressed."

"You don't know that. You don't know the first thing about me, Zoe, because you haven't bothered to ask me how I feel or what I want or what I've been doing for the past ten years. Even when you thought you were interviewing me for an article you didn't look me up online, which would have told you whatever you wanted to know about my business, my marriage, my mother's death, everything that's happened to me since you threw me out of your hospital room. Is it that you don't care? Or is it that you do and you're scared?"

She fired up then. "Don't you dare try to tell me you've given me a second thought since that night! You didn't think about me until I showed up here, and you only cared then because you wanted to play games with me. *Come close, Zoe, keep your distance, Zoe.* Paying me back for that night."

"I wasn't playing games, and I don't care about that night, not anymore," he said, his voice rising. "I've stayed on Tiare for one reason: waiting for you to see me, to know me! I wanted to be good enough at last! I thought I *was*! I didn't want it to be like that summer, Zoe, two puzzle pieces that couldn't quite work out how to fit together, me wanting you like I've never wanted anyone or anything before or since, and that's a hard truth to confront, let me tell you, and you not having a clue about it. Do you know how it felt when you introduced me to Brad Ellersley that day in the Cove, dragging him over against his will to see me like I was some exotic wild animal in a cage?"

"That's not how it was. I wanted a…a relationship with you."

"Not the kind I wanted." He tore his shirt open. "Look, damn you, look! I'm proud of the marks you left on me. I want more, and more, and more."

"You never so much as asked me out on a date!" she said, scrabbling for ground.

"Considering you're twenty-eight today and still can't tell your parents about me—"

"That's not fair."

"That's so fair it's painful. Or are you telling me your parents would have welcomed me with open arms the way they did Brad?" He got to his feet, paced to the edge of the deck, tearing his hands through his hair. "Brad Ellersley," he said to the water, "Prince Perfect, who decided a girlfriend in a wheelchair was too much hard work and chose to tell her that while she was still in a hospital room."

"I didn't hold that against him, Finn, so why should you? I was the one who offered him the out. All he did was accept the offer."

Silence. A long, aghast moment of it. And then Finn faced her.

"You didn't hold that against him, but you're holding an ex-wife and six properties against me," he said. "Except that you're not, are you? They're excuses. You talk a good game, Zoe. You always did. Wanting to live your dreams without people rushing to protect you, pamper you, fuss over you, shield you.

That's what you said. But you never went all the way to get what you wanted. Even now you're playing the tragic damsel, living alone in a tower, but this time it's a tower you've built for yourself to keep you safe."

"Of course I want to be safe," she said. "*Everyone* wants to be *safe*. But…but there's a difference between being safe and being…being *saved*, which is what you want to do. Save me, just like everyone else wants to, save me because you couldn't save—" She broke off, sucked in a breath.

"My mother, Zoe?" He came back to the table, sat. "Did I want to save my mother? Of course I did, and of course I couldn't. She had cardiomyopathy. She was going to die, she knew it and I knew it, but that didn't stop me wanting to save her. Do I want to save you? Yes, I do. I'm not ashamed to say it. I want to save you in all sorts of ways. I wanted to save you from myself for those two years. I wanted to save you from the hurt of Brad Ellersley that horrible night. I wish I could have saved you from the accident, and you can believe I came close to ripping off Henry Hawkesbury's head for what he and Claudia did to you, but it was too late to save you from that and I knew you wouldn't want me to kill him for you the same way you wouldn't let me beat Brad to a pulp. I mean, you couldn't even bait a fish hook." He reined back the rage, compartmentalized the despair as he realized he was losing the fight, tried again. "What you choose not to see, Zoe, is that people want to save each other all the time. People want to help each other all the time. People want to look after each other. You let Malie look after you in Hawaii, why can't you let *me* look after you?"

"Because I… I'd be a *burden*! Not just for an afternoon or a night or a day, or a week or even a month or two, but for a *lifetime*. And I don't want to be a pity project, a…a barnacle on a stolen dinghy, along for the ride but not in the boat helping to navigate."

"That's not fair, Zoe! Not to me and not to you. It was never fair, what you said about pity projects, and you know it, Zoe, you *do*, it's there, the memory, waiting for you to find it, clear it out, to know I forgive you, the way I want you to forgive me for the things *I* said."

She shook her head, looking frantic. "I don't—I don't—" Stop. He could see her swallow hard. "I know what it's like, Finn, to be pitied! I know! People have always smothered me with it."

"But you never told them to *stop*, Zoe. You were the brave damsel in distress always. Stiff upper lip. Never shedding a tear, even though everyone around you did, even when you ended up in a wheelchair."

"When did I get the chance to shed a tear, Finn? Everyone was already crying over me. People had been crying over me for *eighteen years*. They're *still* crying over me."

"Zoe, you were in my arms last night, crying. Doesn't that tell you something? Doesn't that tell you that I get it? That you can stop being strong, brave, inspirational Zoe Tayler and just be Zoe Tayler with me?"

She shook her head, said nothing. She wasn't going to see it. Wasn't going to meet him even halfway.

"Don't you know, Zoe, that *you* saved *me*? I had no hopes and dreams until you gave me yours that summer."

Another shake of her head. She was a stone wall. She did not want him to breach it, she didn't want to know. And yet he had to keep trying.

"That time I told you to fight your big battles to the death but not to sweat the scrappy skirmishes if you wanted to win the long war," he said.

"That's what I've done. What I do."

"So when's the big battle?"

"I don't—huh?"

"The big battle? When is it? What are you waiting for?"

"But I've got everything I wanted."

"Where's your novel?"

"Fairy tales, Finn. Life isn't a fairy tale. I'm not Rapunzel or the Mermaid of Zennor. I'm just…me."

"Just you," he said. "Well, I'll tell you one thing you've been right about tonight, Zoe. I *didn't* think about you these past ten years. That's because while *I do* fight the big battles, and I have every day of my life, you were always too big a battle for me to win. People came out of the woodwork to tell me back then. The gang. Ewan. Everyone in the village. Your parents. Even my mother, who watched me turning myself inside out for you. After you left Hawke's Cove I wanted to forget you, to say goodbye, but I couldn't. And then when my mother died, and I left England, I actively, painstakingly, cut you out of my memories. I worked hard not to think about you when I got my first travel job. When I got married. When I got divorced. And I *resented* having to work at it. It takes a lot of energy to deliberately not think about someone. When I saw you again, here at Poerava, it was almost a relief to think about you again. So I'm going to let myself think about you, and wonder about you, and remember you. But twelve years…it's too long to want someone the way I want you, Zoe. That time machine we were talking about? The only reason I'd go back in time is to change how I acted and what I said to you that night ten years ago, because I was wrong, so wrong, and I hate myself for it. But other than that…"

He tore his hands through his hair. This wasn't working. He had to lay it on the line, make or break. "The truth is, Zoe, you were right when you said it's best to live in the present. I wanted you twelve years ago exactly as you were, but I probably would have messed things up. I wanted you ten years ago exactly as you were and I *definitely* would have messed that up. But now? *Now*, Zoe? I want you more than ever, exactly as you are, because of who you are, and I *know* I won't mess it up.

I'd steal a dinghy for you any day, but no way would you be a barnacle on the bottom, you'd be in the boat beside me, telling me where to go." He closed his eyes, laughed, though it cost him, took a deep breath, then opened his eyes. "But I'm done waiting for you to see yourself the way I see you, and I'm done waiting for you to see me any way at all. I'm not fighting the big battle anymore, not by myself. If you want me, come find me. If you don't, then I guess you don't."

It started to rain as Finn got to his feet.

He looked out at it for a moment, and then, without another word, he left.

A split second after the door closed behind Finn, Zoe's phone announced a text message.

For one wild, hopeful moment, she thought it was Finn telling her he was coming back, but when she opened the text she saw it was from Brad Ellersley.

Happy birthday, Zozer! Shayla sends her love—and hopes we got the time right this year. Did you hear Finn Doherty's bought that crumbling old manor and is going to turn it into a boutique hotel?

Automatically, numbly, she tapped out a return message, as bland as her emails to her parents used to be:

Thanks for the birthday greetings. You got the date and time spot-on. Yes, I heard about the manor. Give Shayla and little Robbie a kiss from me.

She hit send.

And then she burst into tears.

twenty-seven

FINN MIGHT HAVE DECIDED HE WAS GOING TO think about Zoe, and wonder about her, and remember her, but back in Sydney, Zoe—made of sterner stuff—resolutely blocked every memory of him.

She got on with her life for one full week, working out harder than ever at the gym, getting the physiotherapist in for an extra session, cleaning the house, sending the emails she owed and investigating her next travel destination with a vengeance. The only thing she didn't do was write her Poerava story, but she was certain she'd be mentally ready to make a start on that within two weeks. She had time. Plenty of time.

Her second week at home, the journals from under her old bedroom floorboards arrived by courier.

Zoe immediately emailed her parents to ask why they'd sent them; she hadn't asked for them. They responded with a question about when her Poerava story was being published. No mention of the journals.

Zoe thought about going back to them and pointing out that they hadn't actually answered her but she was so tired from her too-hard gym workouts she decided it wasn't worth the effort. She put the unopened journals in her storage cupboard and left them there.

The next day she received an email from Matilda asking about her Poerava story and mentioning that she and Daniel were scheduled on the same junket to Doherty & Berne's Langkawi resort. Zoe responded that she'd send a link when her story was up, then took to her bed for the day telling herself she was suffering from delayed jet lag.

A week after taking to her bed, she got a call from *Wanderlust Wheels* asking when they could expect the Poerava story. At that point, Zoe knew the universe was against her and she was going to have to write the bloody thing. It had been three weeks, and she hadn't thought about *him* once in all that time.

And so she wrote it.

Mistake.

Big mistake.

She cried for a solid hour.

Which made her think of Finn saying to her: *Zoe, you were in my arms last night, crying. Doesn't that tell you something?*

She cried for another hour.

And that night, the dream happened.

No, not a dream. A nightmare.

Scenes. Snatches. Memories. Reality.

The accident.

Coming to with something covering her mouth, someone pumping on her chest. Pain. Her head. Her *head*, oh God. One arm.

Lights, but also darkness. A siren.

Outside, she was outside.

Then she was inside. On her back. The feeling of rushing although she was still.

Eyes closing, then opening. Bright lights. Terse voices. Serious, looming faces. The knowledge that something was wrong without knowing what.

Panicking at hearing Victoria's name. *V. What's happened to V?*

Hospital. She was in hospital but how had she got there? And where was V? Malie? Lily?

Trying to speak, trying to ask, *What happened*, but the words wouldn't come out. Seeing Malie and Lily against a white background. Hugging each other. Crying. Why wasn't she with them? She needed to get to them. Ask about Victoria. But no. Not possible. Fury, agitation. Why couldn't she move? Disorientation. Being lifted. OK, she was hurt. Was Victoria hurt, too?

Mum. Dad. Crying. Trying to tell them she'd be OK. Wanting to ask if Victoria was all right? But the words still wouldn't emerge.

And then…knowing.

She woke with a start, her breaths heaving, tears falling.

Checked the clock on the bedside table.

Morning.

Time to get up.

But she didn't have the strength or the will to move, because the nightmare was over but she was reliving it, the memory intact at last.

Resuscitation. Twice they'd brought her back. The race into surgery. Her parents' faces when she'd come to in recovery.

This was no longer what people had told her. This was visceral. She knew, she saw, she heard, she felt. Harsh lights, antiseptic smells, whizzing walls, voices sometimes urgent and sharp, sometimes steady and soft and kind, beeping machines, weeping, pain, panic, confusion, the enveloping grief of her parents as they stared at her with swollen eyes.

She'd asked groggily about Victoria, remembered the head-spinning relief at the news that V was alive… The next time she dragged herself out of unconsciousness someone in her room was talking in hushed tones about Claudia being dead, and Zoe had been bewildered because Claudia hadn't been in the car with them.

And then—when? *When?* She didn't know, only felt the shock of trying to get out of bed. One moment she was simply in a hospital bed recovering from an operation, and the next she *knew,* and a dull heavy ache suffused her chest, like wet concrete being poured, and poured, and poured, unstoppable, filling the cavity until there was no room for anything else, and somehow still pouring even though there was no more room, and it *would not dry.*

She could feel the weight of it now. The stifling, overflow-ing, oozing squeeze.

It had stayed, that feeling, through her entire month in that hospital and two more months in the spinal cord center, the manic, ever-present, overly cheerful encouragement of her par-ents that slowly hardened the concrete until her chest felt like a solidified scream she couldn't let escape because she had to be brave for everyone else. And all the while the scream stayed trapped, her head was filling with a sluggish lassitude. Almost disinterest. How strange to want to scream with one part of her while the rest of her couldn't seem to care about anything.

It had been there, that apathy, the night Brad had come to break up with her. He'd come most evenings, each time a lit-tle more distraught, asking if he could fetch her this, get her that, do X, Y or Z for her, and she'd pasted on her smile but felt…nothing. She hadn't even noticed that he never got close enough to touch her.

It was the look on her mother's face that night that woke her up to what was happening. The sheen of tears as she'd said, in a voice that faltered, that she and Zoe's father were stepping out for a cup of coffee and would be just down the corridor in the visitors' lounge so if she called out, they'd hear.

They were giving them privacy, Zoe had realized with an odd sense of detachment, and it did not hurt and she did not care, she just wanted it done.

She'd waited for Brad to come to the point, but he hadn't been able to get the words out so she'd done it for him. He'd cried and left and then—before she'd had a chance to process what had happened—there was Finn.

And the strange lethargy had been wrenched right out of her head.

"I'll kill him, Zoe!" he'd raged.

Thoughts had tangled in her head, memories of that summer when she'd felt he belonged to her, the two years when she would have done anything to belong *to him* only to be spurned over and over, the fact he hadn't bothered to visit her, not once, since the accident. And yet he thought he could come in like a knight in shining armor and *save* her?

"*That's* what you've got to say to me?" she'd said, outraged. "He's done nothing wrong. If all you want to do is play the thug, just go. Go!"

She covered her face in her hands now, remembering that. A thug, she'd called him a thug.

And he'd started stammering out all those things, begging her to listen, insisting she could still be anything she wanted to be, do whatever she wanted to do, and he'd look after her. He'd promised to look after her with his dying breath. They could travel and she could write, if only she'd let him "make it happen" for her he'd *make* it happen, he promised, he did.

"Stop!" she'd yelled, actually *yelled* at him. "How are you planning on doing that, stuck in Hawke's Cove?"

And he'd held out his hands—no longer the cool, edgy bad boy of Hawke's Cove—and stammered out more things, about being strong enough, about finding a way, about how long he'd been waiting for her.

And it hurt to think about it now, it *hurt*, because she'd *meant* to hurt *him* when she'd laughed and said no thanks, no thank *you*, as *if*, and told him he should go back to his mother.

No! No, that wasn't what she'd said. She'd said: *If you need a pity project, go back to your mother.*

And he'd sucked in a breath; she could hear it right now, the sound he'd made. And there was a moment of absolute silence, like a storm was about to break. Airless, dreadful calm. He'd gone white.

Do you mean that, Zoe?

Yes, Finn, I do.

Only she hadn't meant it. She *hadn't*.

What she'd meant, in her deepest heart, was that she didn't want to be a burden. She wanted to be her whole self. She wanted, for that flashing moment—when Finn had told her she could be his whole world—to die, because if he hadn't wanted her during that magical summer when they'd been more than friends, they'd been soulmates, and he hadn't wanted her since, how could he want her now? He was only twenty! He'd been tied to his sick mother ever since she'd known him. How could she tie him to her, too?

No, she hadn't meant it, she'd lied, *lied*, then she'd called out to her parents, and when they'd come rushing in, she'd told them to get him out of there, to call security if they had to.

The look on his face! Shock. Pain. Fire in his eyes, and then ice.

And then the worst thing of all: acceptance.

That's what had hurt the most. It was as though by accepting everything she'd said, he was also accepting that he'd been wrong about her, that she wasn't the person he'd imagined her to be.

"You win, I'm leaving," he'd said, and he'd smiled but it

wasn't his real smile, his endearing, crooked, rueful smile. It was a bitter twist. "But if you think my mother's a pity project? My mother has lived her life to the hilt no matter what's been thrown at her. She might not live in a mansion but she's a queen, and a queen beats a pampered princess any day of the week. You lie there, like a wilted flower, but my mother never wilted in her life! Better get your parents to repot you, Zoe, because you clearly don't have the guts to repot yourself. You're worse than pathetic, you're lost, Zoe, and you don't even know it, do you? Poor lost Zoe."

And as Zoe had lain there, choking back tears because she was never going to cry in front of anyone, ever, the security guards arrived...but Finn was already gone.

She wasn't choking back tears now, she couldn't stop them. She was remembering his reaction, that night over dinner in his bungalow, when she'd said she knew he didn't care what people thought and he never had, and he'd said, *Proving that you didn't know me as well as you thought you did. Or any other teenage boy for that matter. We all care, Zoe.*

And at last, *at last*, she understood. He'd only been two years older than her for all that he'd seemed a thousand years beyond her reach. The grief in him was the same as the grief in her, the rage too. Things out of their control holding them back from the lives they were supposed to live. She'd been consumed by the knowledge that she'd never walk again, and she'd had no idea what to do, and she'd just been dumped, and her parents would not let up about taking her away to find a cure and "fix" her. And Finn? That scene had had nothing to do with the one summer they'd spent together and the ensuing two hideous years. He'd been exhausted—she could *see* him, crumpled, smelling of beer, desperate for a purpose. He'd been working so many jobs, caring for his mother and getting nowhere because his mother was dying, and he knew it. The anguish had been too much for him to play the bad boy. And so he'd tried to give her a piece of himself. And in return she'd given him…nothing.

Talk about life-defining moments!

Everything she'd done in the years since that night had been about proving she could make everything she wanted happen for herself.

She wiped her eyes with her hands and dragged herself out of bed thinking of what Finn had said about his mother. *You lie there, like a wilted flower, but my mother never wilted in her life! Better get your parents to repot you, Zoe, because you clearly don't have the guts to repot yourself.*

Well, she *had* repotted herself.

And now, at the very least, she could force herself to face the day.

But when she grabbed her phone to check her messages and saw an email waiting for her from her parents with FINN DOHERTY in the subject line, she thought for a moment she was imagining it as some kind of extra punishment for her soul and wondered if she should go back to bed.

But no. Once that subject line was seen it couldn't be unseen.

Besides, she was suddenly ravenous for news of him, even if it came from people who hated his guts.

She opened it with some trepidation, read it, and then sat there with her mouth hanging open staring at the words:

By now you'll know that your old friend Finn Doherty has bought the old manor house outside the village. Jocasta Whittaker spread that news like wildfire. Of course when she mentioned it to me I told her you'd spent a most agreeable week with Finn at his resort, Poerava, in French Polynesia. Couldn't let her have the last word.

We thought you'd like to know that we had coffee with Finn today and he told us he's also bought Sir Gaden Baxter's house here in Hawke's Cove. Top secret, mind! The only other person who knows is Marion Atwell. You know how close Marion and Margaret were, and Finn has recruited her to help with renovations. Not a word to Lily! Marion tells me Lily is still feeling the loss of Blake Hawkesbury quite deeply as well as driving herself into the ground over Victoria's wedding—when she hears that Finn is redesigning Sir Gaden's house she's going to want to help and she does not have the capacity to take on one more thing. Finn tells us he's renaming the house Merrow's Rest. Apparently "merrow" is Irish for mermaid. Which is possibly why he's named the beach there Mermaid's Kiss? Some mermaid theme, anyway. We thought that would appeal to you because you were always so interested in that mermaid legend. Our private opinion is that he bought the house for you, since he's brought that nice architect Jed Grierson over from Australia to fix it up.

Zoe, we so enjoyed your emails from Tiare Island. It was like our old Zoe, full of fun and stories. But one thing we really want to raise. It's all very well leaving us to google these things—yes, we saw the photos of you and Finn on that lovely girl Matilda's blog—but we do wish you'd have been more forthcoming about what—no, who—had made you so happy again.

Have you reread those journals we sent you? The one with the Z and the F in a heart on the front, perhaps?

And when is that Poerava article coming out? We want to make sure Jocasta Whittaker reads it.

Of course that sent Zoe tearing off to get the journals, and yep, there was one with a Z and F in a heart on the cover.

With a thumping heart she opened it and started reading:

Today, I met Finn Doherty, and when I smiled at him, he smiled back. Finn! Doherty!!!! I almost swooned. Wait until Malie hears about it! She thinks he's superhot!!!!!!

At six o'clock, when Zoe answered her phone, she still had a journal on her lap and had no idea who was calling or why she was answering.

"Yay we're all on! Happy birthday, V!" Malie.

"Happy, happy birthday, bride-to-be." Lily.

"Um... Zoe?" That was Malie.

Zoe gave her head a get-it-together shake. "Sorry. Happy birthday, Malie, no, Lily! Sorry! Happy birthday, Victoria. Whew. Did you get my measurements? For the dress, I mean."

"Hmm," Victoria said. "I got a set of measurements, but unless you've turned into eight hundred grams of tuna they're not yours."

"What?"

"You sent me a recipe for *poisson cru*."

"That was meant for Lily."

"Who got your measurements," Lily chimed in.

Zoe shook her head again, trying to clear the fog. "So did you forward my measurements to V?"

"Yes, I did."

"Good."

Silence.

And then Malie: "Zo?"

Zoe looked for her on the screen, found her face, and blinked at her. "Huh?"

"What happened to your hair?"

She raised an automatic hand, felt the tangled mess, but let her hand drop, impatient because her hair wasn't important. "Who cares?"

"Um...*you!*" Victoria said. "I haven't seen you without a hair clip or band or *something* in your hair since we were seven. And as for the state of it? We've spoken to you at midnight, at two in the morning, at five in the morning, and it's never looked like that at...what? Six o'clock in the evening?"

"Six o'clock," Zoe repeated. "Does that mean it's midnight in Hawke's Cove?"

"Nooo," Lily ventured. "You know international time zones better than anyone."

"So when is it midnight?"

"Why do you care?" Victoria asked.

But Zoe just shook her head. All she could think about was Finn on Sir Gaden's beach looking at the moon and waiting for a mermaid.

The mermaid.

His mermaid.

Her.

He was waiting for her to save him, and he wasn't worried about her drowning him while she did it because he wasn't drownable, he was too strong a swimmer. Except it had been twelve years—he'd been waiting for twelve years, and he wasn't going to wait anymore.

I'm done waiting for you to see yourself the way I see you, and I'm done waiting for you to see me any way at all. I'm not fighting the big battle anymore, not by myself. If you want me, come find me. If you don't...then I guess you don't.

The stories, *their* stories, were all in that journal with the Z and F in a heart on the cover. The legends. The fairy tales. The novels she was going to write. The adventures they wanted to have. Hopes and dreams and princes and princesses saving each other.

Only she wasn't a princess, she was a mermaid, and Finn wasn't a prince, he was her man, and she wasn't lost, she was found, and he was waiting for her to find *him*. He'd been waiting twelve years for her and she hadn't even looked him up online because she'd been playing it safe—and yet he was waiting for her still!

"I can't brush my hair or calculate time zones, I'm too busy staging an intervention."

Malie burst out laughing. "Again? Who's the lucky lady?"

"Me."

"Hang on." V, always the orderly one. "You're staging *your own* intervention?"

"I'm only kick-starting it. I need Lily to help me finish

it. Well, Lily and Mr. Michaels. He loves you, Lily. Can you call him and tell him I need him? And Gina, I need to set her straight. And I need sequins. I think I have those. Yes, that cerulean blue dress, the color of his eyes. I'm going to need my mum and dad to get my wheelchair there if I'm going by boat. I need Google because it's time to know everything. And I need to scream. All those things. Not necessarily in that order."

"What is going on?" Victoria asked.

"I had sex with Finn Doherty on Tiare Island. But that's not important. The important thing is I'm going to give him a mermaid at midnight on Sir Gaden's beach."

Malie whooped loud enough to raise the dead. "What did I tell you, girls? Lils, V, you each owe me five pounds. Suck it, sisters! Our girl's in love!"

twenty-eight

FINN DIDN'T KNOW HOW MANY MORE NIGHTS HE
could sit out here at midnight, waiting for Zoe.

OK, that was a lie. He knew. He'd do it for the next hundred years if there was a chance.

And he *knew* there was a chance because Lily had made some mysterious reference about Mr. Michaels's boat to her mother, and her mother...well, hello, Mrs. Whittaker, who could sniff out a story from the ether let alone a human being she was pumping for information.

So here he was, six weeks after he'd told Zoe he wasn't waiting for her, waiting for her.

He had the Australian South Seas pearl, in luminous white, on a platinum chain in his pocket, because Zoe didn't wear rings but he had to give her something. He'd already bought a wedding band for himself because he was going to wear one this time around; he loved the look of it on his finger and was looking forward to it being a permanent fixture. He'd wear a manacle around his ankle if he had to, to let everyone know he belonged to her.

He'd done all of his penances. He'd visited his mother's grave and cried like a baby and explained why he hadn't been back. He'd had a *just between us Zoe doesn't need to know* coffee with Noel and Selena Tayler in full view of Mrs. Whittaker. He'd said hello to Brad Ellersley, despite still wanting to beat the guy to a pulp. He'd even tried to see Henry Hawkesbury to apologize for almost bashing his head in, only to discover Henry hadn't been seen since Blake's funeral.

And that had spurred him to do the scariest thing on his list: going to see Lily Atwell. But he'd said he would become besties with Zoe's girlfriends and dammit he was making a start on the rest of his life so he was determined to do it.

No pressure, he'd thought, as he entered The Sea Rose.

No pressure, as he'd told the waitress what he wanted to eat.

No pressure, as thoughts of Zoe laughing over *poisson cru* in the Poerava kitchen tortured him so much he couldn't taste the meal.

No pressure as he'd asked to speak to the chef, even though he was experiencing a sensation he imagined was similar to rats gnawing at his insides.

And then Lily had emerged from the kitchen.

She'd checked at the kitchen threshold, her eyes widening, looked behind her as though about to flee whence she'd come.

And he'd thought, *OK this is pressure.* Was he going to have to chase her into the kitchen?

But no. One moment, that was all it took for her to contain whatever apprehension she was feeling and walk calmly, steadily to the table.

"Wine?" he'd asked as she sat.

"It's closing time so yes please," she'd said, cool as a cucumber.

He'd swallowed. "I hear Henry's back. Or he *was* back, anyway."

"How—"

"Mrs. Whittaker."

"Oh."

"Is he going to pose a problem? For the wedding? For…for anyone attending the wedding?"

"Anyone as in…"

"Zoe," he said, then shook his head. "No, not just Zoe, is he going to pose a problem for any of you. Because if you need me to sort him out I'll do it. I've wanted to tear his head off for ten years."

"Not necessary," Lily said, "I can handle him."

"Zoe would let me tear his h—" He stopped, laughed, "OK, that's a lie, I just *wish* she'd let me."

"You know Zoe very well, don't you?" Lily had probed gently.

"I know her like I know my own soul."

"Oh! Oh…my," Lily had said, and picked up her wine and sipped, sipped again.

"I'm not mucking around here, Lily."

"I can see that."

"She told me about *Gravity*."

"I'm sorry, I don't know what that is."

"The movie. The drifting thing. That she won't find a way back."

"Ah!" Lily had said, and looked at him, eyes searching. And then she smiled: she'd found what she was looking for, apparently. "I *do* know what that means. She might talk about the movie but it's real gravity, *actual* gravity, that's important to her. Drifting away from…from herself, from who she is. She needs something to anchor her to a world she's a little too fragile, a little too perfect, for. Something, someone…*imperfect*, perhaps?"

"Imperfect," he'd repeated, and then he'd smiled. "I think I love you, Lily Atwell."

She'd reached across the table and took his hand. "You'll do, Finn Doherty."

Had Lily told Zoe she'd talked to him? He couldn't know but somehow he didn't think so. She had depth, Lily. Hidden depth. But he wouldn't have minded if Lily had spilled the beans. He *wanted* Zoe to know he was waiting for her. He'd been pretty sure her parents would report back to her on the coffee meeting. He'd dropped enough information about the house all over the village expecting the gossip to get back to Zoe so she knew he hadn't meant it when he said he wouldn't wait. That he'd bought their house, that he'd called it Merrow's Rest, that the beach was going to be called Mermaid's Kiss. Surely she'd know those names were for her? She'd *have* to know he'd lied about not waiting. He'd outright told her he lied when the stakes were high enough and there was no stake, *none*, higher than her.

Time check: 11:55 p.m.

Finn sighed as he got to his feet, slapping the sand from the seat of his jeans. One more night gone.

He turned to go back to the house, then heard a slight swash. Different to the waves breaking on the sand. A paddle in the water.

He held his breath, listened intently, heard it again.

He faced the surf, peered out, saw the boat. A flash of something. Moonlight reflecting off something in the boat.

Dear God, it was a sequin!

She was here.

He went tearing down the sand, into the waves, up to his knees.

Calm down. Wait. You'll scare her.

And then he laughed, loud and long. Scare her? He didn't scare her. She was his kind.

The boat was close, he strode out, up to his hips, grabbed the stern, dragged it in to shore. And then he rested his forehead against Zoe's, waiting for the signal. It came, her arms twined around his neck, and he lifted her out of the boat and crushed her against his chest.

One long, intense, devouring kiss.

"About time," Finn said, when he came up for air.

"Finn! Mr. Michaels!" Zoe blushed but she was laughing too. "Have you no decorum?"

"No," Finn said. "I don't do decorum, I'm a thug, remember?" He spared a glance for Mr. Michaels. "Where's her wheelchair?"

"Her folks are bringing it. You'll find it at the front door."

"Thanks for bringing her, sir," Finn said.

"A fisherman doesn't say no to a mermaid, and that's what she told me she was," Mr. Michaels said. Finn saw that smile that everyone had been giving him lately and he decided he loved it.

As Mr. Michaels pushed his boat back into the water Finn looked down at Zoe. "No tiara?"

"No," she said. "I thought this glorious set of Tahitian black pearl combs was more appropriate. I mean, it's all very well being a mermaid on a beach at midnight, but I've decided a tiara is more about being a queen and I'm still working my way up to that. And I thought...well, to be perfectly honest, I'm intending to wear these combs—and *just* these combs—at breakfast tomorrow. I might not get away with a tiara when I'm dribbling whatever you're cooking for breakfast down my chin."

He kissed her again, long and slow and thorough, and when the shivers wracked her he groaned against her mouth. "How about you wear just those combs and nothing else tonight, and I'll buy you a tiara tomorrow?"

"That can be arranged. The 'just combs' thing. But I won't say no to a tiara for special occasions."

"Like, say, a wedding?"

"Yes, absolutely a wedding," she said. "I mean... I mean, what do you mean when you say that?"

"You know what I mean," he said, and kissed her once more. "Say yes, say it now."

"Yes!" she said. "But Finn, after what I said that night…" She laid her hand against his cheek. "I remembered it, I remembered it all, what happened. How can you want me?"

"I don't care about that night, not anymore. I was an idiot."

"And I was a coward."

"Subject officially exhausted. We need to write a new story, *our* story, Zoe. So who am I? The idiot prince in the tower or the mortal waiting for his mermaid? Don't get me wrong, I'll be anything you want because remember when we were talking about our dreams, and I didn't know what mine was?"

"Yes, I remember. I remember everything, *everything*."

"Well, I figured it out. My dream was you. Always, always you."

"Oh. Oh! Well, if we're going to get romantic—"

"We are!"

"Then I guess I'd better confess that you're every prince I ever imagined, but better. Every legend I ever loved, but more. You're my past, and my present and my future, and…mine. Just mine. And yes, I can write our story. A story where we do whatever we want and be whoever we want, as long as we're together forever."

And he was kissing her again, striding up the beach at speed with Zoe clasped tight in his arms.

"I thought we were staying here," she said.

"No, I've suddenly remembered sand's a bitch."

She started laughing helplessly. "OK but I have things to say about…well, other stuff. Like…like I read my old journals, and I figured out that I was googly-eyed over you that summer, and crazy jealous the two years following."

"Good to know."

"And I thought about what you said about letting me cry and I realized I want to cry all over you."

"I can handle that. I might cry all over you too, I've been waiting for you for so long."

"I'm up for it."

"I see we're going to get along very well."

"And I googled you, of course. And now I can recite every date you bought a property, and everything about each property. I know when you got married—I even saw your wedding photos—and when you got divorced."

Finn stopped, looked down at her. "I know what Gina said to you, Zoe."

Zoe tightened her arms around his neck. "I know. I talked to her before I came here, and I...I told her to butt out, and I'm sorry but I'm not sorry but I do understand. She was trying to save you, Finn, so *of course* I understand, because that's what I'm doing." She smiled. "The thing is, as soon as I saw those wedding photos, I knew she couldn't save you the way I could."

His crooked smile flashed across his face. "And how did you know that from a photo?"

"Because you weren't looking at her the way you look at me. And—not wanting to be mean about it—that woman could use a few sequins and a crystal embellishment or two, not that I'm brave enough to tell her that."

He started laughing. "And what else did you google?"

"I didn't need Google for the rest."

"The rest?"

"I didn't need Google to tell me that I love you."

The laughter stopped suddenly. "Say it again."

"I love you, Finlay."

Finlay. He didn't think his soul could take the joy of hearing her call him that right now, on this beach, after telling him she loved him.

"The thing is," she continued, "I've been feeling for a while now that when I left Hawke's Cove not all of me did. There was a piece of my heart still here. It just took me a while to figure out I didn't leave it in a geographic location, I left it in a person. I left it in you."

"Ah, Zoe, Zoe!" He could barely breathe; his chest was so tight. "Put your hand in my shirt pocket."

"Er...not the pocket I was thinking of but— Oh!" She stared at the pearl she'd liberated, dangling from its platinum chain, tears in her eyes.

"And now put your hand, that hand, on my heart, because we might as well make this engagement official."

She laid her hand there, and looked at him, smiling through those precious tears. "Is this where you tell me you love me?"

He shook his head. "More. This is where I tell you that every beat of my heart is for you. That my heart's been aching for you forever, and I knew it from the first time you smiled at me over those salt shakers. I've yearned for you for so long the yearning's become a part of me. This is where I tell you I don't just love you, I live for you. You are...everything, Zoe."

"Then there's just one thing I have to do, Finlay, and I'm doing it with you, because at last I can."

"And what's that, my princess, my mermaid, my queen, my dream, my love, my darling, *darling* heart?"

And Zoe—Zoe, his woman at last—threw back her head and screamed into the night sky.

★ ★ ★ ★ ★

Acknowledgments

Countless people scattered around the world have made this book what it is, and in my incredibly biased opinion I think it's a corker!

Avril Tremayne, thank you for being such a wonderful writing partner and for taking the care you did with every single aspect of this book. I am so tremendously proud of what we have accomplished and your passion is remarkable.

Enormous thank you to my editor Rebecca Slorach, you are thoughtful, special and incredibly kind. We've been on a spectacular journey together and I know we will be friends for life. Becky encouraged me to tell Zoe's story unapologetically—thank you for taking the risk of allowing me to have a complex and unconventional heroine. I really hope many of you find Zoe's story inspiring and refreshing.

Thank you to Lucy Truman for such a beautiful cover, it brings a smile to my face every time I see it. To the wonderful team at Mills & Boon and Harper Collins who have been pivotal from the start: Katie Barnes-Wallis, Kirsty Capes, Sophie Calder and Tom Keane. You give ceaseless enthusiasm to my books and it doesn't go unnoticed.

My darling Andrea, words fail me at the unwavering support, love and care you give to me and my work. You're a one-off and I hope we will keep rocking it together for decades to come. As I'm writing this, my naughty spaniel Monty just jumped on my laptop. It made me giggle and I wish you could read, alas, Montdog, thank you for being the better half of our little double act!

To my friends and family, I'm looking at you, Mummy Toff, Amy Hutch and PH! Thank you for keeping me cheerful and for the endless reassurance and laughter when I need it most, I am so lucky to have you all in my life.

Lastly, and very importantly, I am eternally grateful to everyone at Whizz-Kidz—especially Penny, Georgia, Sophie, Eddie, Freya, Ella, Hannah, Conor, Brandon and Lexi—without your experiences and support, this book would simply not be what it now is. Thank you for being such an inspiration to me.

Georgia